MERRY LITTLE LITTLE MIDLIFE MATCHMAKER

LILIAN MONROE

Print ISBN: 978-1-923187-45-0

Cover design by Qamber Designs
Editing by Shavonne Clarke at Motif Edits and Paige Kraft at PKEdits

ONE

LIZZIE

I'D JUST WRAPPED a microfiber towel around my hot-oil-treatment-infused hair and slipped into a lavender-scented bubble bath when my phone rang. A long, tired sigh slipped through my lips; I knew who was on the other side of the line. And I knew why he was calling.

Well, not *exactly* why. But if I closed my eyes and threw a dart at a board with a few options listed, I knew I'd get pretty close. Ex-husbands were like that. You got to know them pretty well in the years you spent hoping they'd turn into the man you pretended they were all along.

Between the first and second ring of my phone, I considered just...not answering. I could finish my bath, paint my nails, slather on a face mask, watch that episode of trash TV I'd saved for three weeks, and pretend I hadn't heard a thing.

Then the ringtone echoed through the bathroom once more, and a groan rattled up my throat.

I couldn't miss the call. I couldn't plead ignorance while I took this precious evening to myself because although it probably wasn't an emergency, there was always the off chance that this one time, it *was*. I wouldn't be able to live with myself if I was giving myself a mud mask instead of rushing to the ER when I was needed. From the moment my eldest had been born, that weight had pressed down on my shoulders. Responsibility. Duty. Motherhood.

There would be no luxurious bath for me tonight; I was almost sure of it.

Water ran down my body in rivulets as I stood, sluicing over the familiar scar just above my pelvis and down the legs that had once been my best feature and still weren't too shabby, if I did say so myself. The pink terry cloth robe on the back of the door was more than a little worn, but it had seen me through two pregnancies and a decade of motherhood, and I'd kept it around like a security blanket. I wrapped it around my body and wiped my hand on my thigh, then swiped to answer the phone still screaming at me from the bathroom counter.

"Yes?"

"Lizzie," my ex-husband, Isaac, panted. "Zach is puking."

I leaned against the vanity and rubbed my forehead. "Okay. How long has this been going on?"

A faucet turned on and off again. I heard my son's voice in the background, but he was too quiet for me to hear the words. Isaac said, "An hour or two, I guess. After dinner he just—oh God, Lizzie. The smell. There's vomit everywhere. I might throw up."

"Has he been able to keep any fluids down?"

"Fluids?" Isaac sounded lost; I could imagine his wide-eyed stare.

"Liquids, Isaac. Water. Juice. Electrolytes. Whatever. Something so he doesn't get dehydrated."

"Oh, right. Not much. Have you had any water, buddy?"

Zach mumbled something. A door opened and closed. "He's had a bit, he says. I'll get him some more."

"Does he have a fever?" I asked, glancing forlornly at my steaming bath.

"What?"

"A fever, Isaac. What's his temperature?"

"How do I find that out?"

I had actually been married to this man. For years. While in my right mind, I'd agreed to tie myself to him legally, emotionally, metaphysically—and it took me six years to figure out that it had been a mistake. Maybe I wasn't as clever as I thought.

"You should have a thermometer," I told him, forcing calm into my voice. "June would have stocked your medicine cabinet, I'm sure."

"June's visiting her mother in Wyoming. I told her not to go. She knew I couldn't handle the kids on my own. But she still went," he wailed, sounding close to panic. As if it were his wife's fault that his own son got sick. As if it were so outside the realm of possibility that a father would be able to care for his kids for two weekends a month on his own.

Never mind that I did it day in, day out the rest of the time. And there wasn't a single person that I could call in a panic because my kid decided to puke up his dinner.

Yes, I had been an idiot to marry him. Then again, this

useless man had given me two beautiful kids, so on the balance of it, I figured I'd come out ahead.

But I was still annoyed that I wouldn't get to enjoy my bath. Maybe if I picked the kids up and got Zach settled, I could top the water up when I got home and finish where I left off. As long as Zach wasn't worse off than it sounded, I'd probably be able to make it there and back before the water went fully cold. And even if it did, I could settle the kids and fill it up again.

I *would* have a bath tonight. It was going to happen. Tonight was relax-in-the-bath night, and I was *not* going to give that up. Not this time.

Plan made, I pushed myself off the vanity and shuffled to the bedroom. "I'll be there in fifteen minutes," I told him. "Is Hazel okay?"

"I think so. I don't know. She hasn't puked. At least, I don't think so. Hazel, have you puked? No. No, she hasn't."

"Fine. I'll see you soon."

I hung up and stared at the silent phone in my hand and let out a long sigh. It wasn't that I resented having to head over to my ex's house to help with the kids. It's that it happened *so often*. Ever since Zach, our eleven-year-old, had been born, I'd been thrown into the role called Mom and hadn't come up for air. Most of the time, I loved it. I was good at it. Actually, I was *great* at it. I spun plates and made macaroni necklaces and dealt with tantrums and moodiness, and then I got the smiles and the unexpected hugs and the *I-love-yous* that made it all worth it. Most of the time, I did it with a smile on my face and a positive attitude, because that's the face I liked to present to the world.

Once in a while, though, I wondered where the old me had

gone. The woman who threw dinner parties for her gaggle of friends, who was the group's designated photographer, who'd dreamed of shooting for NatGeo, who'd fantasized about sailing around the world for a year with a camera around her neck and a smile on her sun-bronzed face. Sometime over the last decade and a half, with two kids and a divorce on my record, that woman had faded away.

These days I couldn't even manage an uninterrupted bath.

But I was needed elsewhere, and this was a responsibility I had chosen. One I cherished. My kids needed me. The bath could wait.

I tossed my phone on the bed and grabbed a pair of sweatpants from where they'd been flung over the arm of a chair in the corner of my room. My ratty pink bathrobe took the sweatpants' place, and I grabbed an old sports bra and a T-shirt from one of the volunteer days at my kids' school—first one I picked up without any stains on it that passed the sniff test—and caught sight of myself in the mirrored closet doors.

With my hair still wrapped in the microfiber towel and my old clothes hanging off my body, I looked a decade older than my forty-one years. I blinked at myself, gaze snagging on the few spots of discoloration beginning to form on my skin, the ruddy texture of my cheeks the heat of the bath had brought out, and the shape of the body I'd once flaunted.

I was shorter than average, but I'd never been frumpy. The woman who'd thrown dinner parties and dreamed of a richer life had worn figure-hugging dresses that showed off her generous curves. She'd curled her hair and worn lipstick every day. She was a stranger, and I wasn't quite sure exactly when it had happened.

Shaking my head, I tore my gaze away from my reflection and pulled on some fuzzy pink socks. The hair towel would have to stay, because I didn't have time to wash out the oil. Besides, what was an extra half hour with oil on my scalp? Maybe I'd end up with luscious, shiny locks and this evening wouldn't end up being a wash, after all.

See? Positive attitude. Puking kids plus a hopeless ex-husband equaled nicer hair. That was Lizzie Math, and it was the way I liked to live.

I shoved my feet into Crocs and slung my purse over my shoulder, then paused with a hand on my front doorknob. I kicked off the rubber shoes and checked the bathroom medicine cabinet, clicking my tongue when I saw my stock of Pedialyte and ibuprofen was running low. I'd stop at the drugstore on the way to Isaac's house for supplies. When I texted him to let him know, all my ex responded was, "*Hurry.*"

Half of me wanted to wring his neck for being so useless. The other half was worried for my kid. So, dressed like a woman who'd stumbled into her dirty laundry basket and then stood up, looked down, shrugged, and said, *Eh, that'll do*, I rushed across town and ducked into the nearest drugstore.

That, as it turned out, was a mistake.

TWO

LIZZIE

IT'S an immutable rule of the universe that when you look your worst, you run into the one person you least want to see.

In my case, I was head down, ass up, grabbing the generic brand ibuprofen while I juggled a few bottles of Pedialyte in my other hand—in my hurry, I'd decided that not using a basket to shop would be faster, somehow—when I heard his voice.

"Liz? Lizzie Butler?"

I stood up so fast the edges of my vision went mottled and black, and the bottles of electrolyte drink made a last-ditch bid for freedom. I bobbled them—hands flailing, vision fading—while my brain worked on recognizing the vision of a man standing next to me.

My right hand forgot it was holding two boxes of ibuprofen, and it tried to catch a falling bottle of Pedialyte. The result was a crushed packet of pills that knocked the bottle clean out of my own grasp. The two other bottles I'd been holding to my chest took their chance to jump ship.

"Whoa!" Sean Hardy said with a laugh, reaching for one of the bottles. He caught it in mid-air, because of course he did, but he wasn't able to grab the other two.

I did my best to execute the same maneuver, but my balance was all wonky and I was a little stunned at how *good* my brother's best friend looked after all these years. The result was me reaching toward the bottles about two seconds too late, when they'd already hit the ground, and accidentally smacking Sean's beefy shoulder instead, a moment before I head-butted him in the chest.

His chest was solid. I think I hurt my forehead more than I hurt him.

His arms came around me while bottles rolled away from us, the towel turban on my head slipping to my neck to show off the mess of grease that was my soon-to-be gloriously shiny hair.

"Easy," he said, like he was talking to a skittish horse, and gently steadied me while he watched me with those green-blue eyes I'd mooned over as a kid. His thumbs swept over my biceps, under the gaping sleeves of my baggy tee, hot and strong and rough, and I felt some tension pull below my belly button.

That's literally all it took. His hands on my arms, holding me upright, combined with a slight brush of his thumbs over the distance of about an inch made my body say, *Hello!*

It would be embarrassing, if... Well, actually, the entire situation was embarrassing. In response to my growing mortification, I smiled at him and hoped I didn't look as deranged as I felt. "Sean!"

He was as tall as I remembered, just over six feet, and it looked like he'd kept up with his fitness habit. His shoulders stretched the fabric of the deep green knitted sweater he wore, his long legs clad in soft-looking jeans. His jaw was rough with stubble that shone with a few strands of gray, and those remarkable eyes were framed with a small network of crinkles that somehow brought out their color.

He was gorgeous. He'd been all floppy-haired and edgy when he'd been running around with my two older brothers, but now he was something entirely different. Not quite clean cut, but not too rough around the edges, either. Just the right amount of sharpness to be positively delicious.

There were shadows in his eyes that hadn't been there twenty-five or so years ago. He didn't look tired, exactly. He was closed off.

That didn't change the fact that my brother's oldest and best friend was the most attractive man I'd ever seen. And I was a greasy-haired, volunteer-T-shirt-wearing, ibuprofen-launching mess.

I gulped and forced my smile to brighten. "Sean, hi." I clawed at the towel and shoved it back onto my head. Judging by the hair sticking to my cheeks and neck, I wasn't doing a great job of containing it back in its microfiber prison.

"You okay?" His voice had a pleasant roughness to it, and when he dropped his hands from my arms, I missed them.

I needed to get a grip. Men who looked like him did not end up with women who looked like me.

Laurel, I thought. That's who would fit next to him. One of the architects at the firm where I worked as an administrator would be the perfect match for a man like this. She was sassy and had a wonderful laugh, and she'd get him out of his shell. Or maybe one of the moms from school. Cindy Reynolds. She was tall and built like a model, with that gorgeous long hair. She'd started dating again recently. They'd make sense standing next to Sean.

Fast on the heels of those thoughts was a wave of bitterness. Because one person who wouldn't fit next to him was a five-foot-three woman with curves that were a little too generous to be fashionable and a sense of style that had died when she'd pushed out her screaming babies.

But this was nonsense. I wasn't trying to set him up with anyone, and I definitely wasn't trying to date him myself. For all I knew, he was happily married to a modelesque doctor from a blue-blooded family who had twittering birds and puppies following her around all day like some kind of Disney princess.

Besides, I had more important things to worry about.

"I'm great," I lied. "Thanks for the save."

"Sure." He bent over to pick up one of the bottles of liquid electrolytes that was shoved under a metal shelf. I grabbed the other and eyed the third bottle still held in his other hand.

I nodded at him as he handed his two bottles over. Now to make a fast escape, because I needed to take care of my kids and not make an idiot of myself in front of the most beautiful man I'd seen in years. My mouth, evidently, had other ideas. It kept smiling as it said, "You in town for the holidays?"

Thanksgiving was coming up on Thursday, and the temperature outdoors was steadily dropping. Heart's Cove was a small town in Northern California full of artists and eclectics, with gray, drizzly winters that usually got a smattering of snow come December. A great place to raise kids, but not so many career opportunities for divorced women who had left the workforce to care for their brood.

"Mikey and I just moved here, actually," Sean responded. He cleared his throat, clearly not one to lean on false positivity to make it through awkward interactions. His gaze flicked from my hair to my shirt and down to my Crocs. "We, uh, somehow lost all of our toiletries on the trip over so we're stocking up."

My brows jumped. "Oh," I said, searching my memory. My brother Aaron had been to Sean's wedding over a decade ago, but as far as I knew, Sean wasn't on social media. I wasn't sure what else had happened in the interim. Something in my memory told me there'd been a divorce, but maybe that was wishful thinking, so all I said was, "Mikey is..."

"My son," Sean said, his gaze shifting over my shoulder. A boy of about ten or twelve shuffled past me and presented his father with toothpaste and two toothbrushes. "Thanks, bud. Mikey, this is Lizzie. She's my friend Aaron's sister. You remember Aaron?"

Mikey nodded at me. He had his father's eyes and the same shade of dark-brown hair. "Nice to meet you." He paused. "Your hair is really greasy."

"Mikey," Sean chided.

My smile stayed up through sheer force of will. "It's an oil treatment," I explained. "It'll make it shiny when I wash it out."

"Oh," the kid said, looking unconvinced. I didn't blame him.

"Sorry." Sean rubbed the back of his neck, then nudged his son. "Be polite, Mikey."

"I hope your hair looks nice after you wash it," the boy offered.

"Thanks," I told him. "And on that note, I need to scram. My own son has been vomiting." I lifted the bottles of Pedialyte.

"I won't keep you," Sean replied. "Nice to see you again. I'm sure we'll catch up at Aaron's sometime."

"Of course," I said. Then, because my embarrassment was mounting with every second, I forced some extra cheer into my voice as I said, "Looking forward to it!"

Sean gave me a faint frown, and I took that as my cue to cut this delightful catch-up short. My Crocs squeaked on the tile floors, and as soon as I was out of sight, I ripped the stupid hair turban off my head and shoved it in my sweatpants pocket. Greasy, oil-infused hair clung to my head and drew the cashier's gaze.

I scowled at her, which was rude, but I was feeling embarrassed and frumpy and dejected.

Sean's hands on my arms had turned me on. He was unbelievably attractive, and I was...me. There had been no electric spark between us that wasn't entirely contained within my own body. And there never would be. Men like him didn't end up with women like me. To be honest, I wasn't exactly sure what kind of man ended up with a woman like me. So far all my attempts had ended in failure.

But hey—at least I'd have shiny hair by the end of the night. I hoped.

Sighing, I paid for my supplies and headed for my car. When I pulled up outside my ex-husband's house, I squared my shoulders and put my brother's high school best friend out of my mind. I had at least one sick kid to deal with, along with a useless man-child. Gorgeous men who evidently married beautiful women and made beautiful babies were none of my concern.

The useless man-child in question flung open the door when I was halfway up the path heading toward it. It was probably uncharitable of me to think of him in those particular terms, but he'd ruined my bath and forced me to run into the handsomest man I'd seen in years looking like *this*.

"What took you so long?" Isaac demanded.

I lifted the bag. "I told you. I had to stop at the pharmacy."

"I gave Zach a glass of water and he threw it all up. It's all over the carpet, Lizzie." Isaac arched his brows at me like it was my fault.

"Did you make him drink the entire glass?"

"You said to give him fluids!"

"Small amounts, Isaac," I snapped, and shuffled past him into the beautiful home his new wife had decorated. I took a deep breath, smelling fresh flowers and the tinge of distant vomit, and I tried to calm myself. Isaac led me to the kids' bedrooms, and I found Zach curled up on his side on the bed with a bucket on the ground next to him. There was a towel in the middle of the floor which I suspected was covering the results of the water-induced vomiting spell.

"Mom," he croaked.

"Hey, honey," I soothed, and sat next to him. His hair was damp when I pushed it off his forehead, his skin clammy. He didn't feel hot, which was good. Poor baby. "I brought you some stuff to make you feel better. You think you can try to have some?"

"I threw up the water Dad gave me."

"Let's try just a little sip," I said, cracking the lid for him. "You'll feel better, and we need to keep you hydrated."

Zach, my brave boy, lifted himself up onto his pillows and let me help him with the drink bottle. He took a few small sips and nodded.

"Stomach's not too mad about that?"

He shook his head.

"I'll leave it right here," I told him, putting the bottle on his bedside table before smoothing his hair away from his forehead again.

He closed his eyes and leaned into my touch. "I want to go home," he told me in a small voice.

"Me too," Hazel said, creeping into the room. She burrowed against me, body between my knees as her hands went around my waist.

I kissed her temple. "I'll talk to your father. Are you feeling okay?"

My daughter nodded. "I just want to go home."

I stayed with them for a few more minutes and watched Zach have some small sips of the electrolyte drink, then went off in search of my ex-husband. All of a sudden, I realized how much my body ached. Tiredness seemed to slam into me like a croquet mallet to the side of the head, and my only option was to grin and bear it as I handled everything the evening flung at me.

Isaac wasn't in the bathroom, which was still covered in

vomit, and he wasn't in either of the bathrooms looking for a thermometer. I wandered down the stairs and found him sitting in front of the TV, watching sports replays.

I stood just behind him for a moment, the familiar noise of ESPN blaring on the television, and felt such a deep, unshakable revulsion that I had to cling to the wall for support. This, in a nutshell, had been my marriage. We lasted six years together, four of which had been consumed—for me—by childcare and housework. I'd watched Isaac do favors for his parents, for his siblings, for his neighbors, while he let me drown. He'd played the perfect, doting husband and father whenever he had an audience, and hadn't lifted a finger to help when it was just the two of us. I'd felt invisible and neglected, and every time I tried to bring it up, he'd brushed me off.

Then I found out about his coworker. About their text messages full of love hearts and inside jokes. About the business trip he'd told me was boring and routine. Still, I wanted to save my marriage. I'd been made so small and invisible that I was willing to fight for scraps like a mangy street dog.

It wasn't until Hazel, aged four, asked me why Daddy didn't ever want to play with her that I realized I needed to get out.

When I asked for a divorce, he said he was blindsided. All the social capital he'd built up doing favors for everyone but me paid off, and he waltzed out of our marriage with a thousand shoulders to cry on. I was the shrew who'd nagged him so much he had no choice but to pull away.

And still, I was here. Putting myself last.

But what choice did I have? It wasn't like Isaac was going to care for the kids the way they deserved.

"The kids want to come home tonight," I said, a little more curtly than I meant to. "We can make up the night on another weekend."

"Don't worry about it," Isaac said, not taking his eyes off the box. "I had them all day, and I've got Christmas this year. We can just stick to the custody schedule."

"Fine," I said. "I'll get their stuff and get out of your hair."

That got his attention. He spun around on the couch and frowned at me over the back of it. "What about the bathroom?"

I'd half turned around to head back to the kids, so I paused with one foot in the hallway outside the living room. I met my ex-husband's baffled gaze. "The bathroom?"

"It's covered in puke."

I blinked at him. He blinked at me.

"So...clean it up," I told him, speaking slowly because my patience for this evening was wearing thin, and I really just wanted to get my kids home and safe. And I wanted that bath, damn it.

He recoiled. "Me?"

"It's your house, ain't it?"

"June isn't back until tomorrow evening," he protested.

I pretended not to understand what he meant, even though I knew. I *knew*.

"I can't leave it like that all day," he explained, like it was the most natural thing in the world that he would wait for his wife to come home to clean up a mess.

And I should've left. I really should've. This wasn't my house, and it wasn't my husband. I'd divorced him because of things exactly like this, moments where he was so unbelievably inconsiderate and incompetent that it boggled the mind.

But I liked June. After things fizzled out with the coworker, he'd met June through an online dating site. She was a kind woman who'd been duped by him, just like I had all those years ago. I didn't want her to come home to crusty vomit after a weekend spent visiting her aging mother. And maybe I hadn't deprogrammed myself entirely from the grinding wheel my marriage had been, because I couldn't quite walk out and leave another woman to clean up a mess that Isaac refused to see.

So, sighing, I headed upstairs and I cleaned my ex-husband's bathroom, and then I scrubbed the carpet, and I packed the kids' things. By the time I got them all bundled into the car, Isaac had heaved himself off the sofa and come out to say goodbye, his relief at our leaving clear.

When everyone was in bed and the house was once again quiet, I trailed the tips of my fingers through my bath. Ice cold. I released yet another sigh, pulled the plug, and jumped in the shower to wash that silly oil treatment out of my hair. While I lathered, I thought of Sean, and my lips twisted into a bitter curve.

It didn't matter that he'd seen me at my worst. Even if he saw me at my best, it wouldn't change the fact that we weren't in the same league.

And when I poked my head into Zach's room to see him sleeping, my heart turned over. Yes, the old me had faded into nothingness, but hadn't I turned into something better? So what if occasionally I felt lost in motherhood, like what made me *me* was buried under the label? It didn't change the fact that I would always be my kids' mom, and I would always pick up the slack when it came to them.

That's what mattered. Not some passing attraction caused by some man's calloused hands brushing over my bare arms. Not a few extra clean-ups that really should have been done by someone else.

I loved being a mom. I loved being *their* mom.

Shouldn't that be enough for me?

THREE

SEAN

HEART'S COVE had changed in the years I'd been away. It'd been a little podunk town without much going on other than a bunch of hippies and artists that held no interest for a younger me, but now it was a vibrant municipality with many more restaurants and shops than I remembered. There was a buzz in the crisp late-autumn air, a vibrancy that filled me with a new kind of hope.

Then again, I'd changed since I graduated high school and got the hell out of here. Whether it was for better or worse, I wasn't sure.

One thing hadn't changed, though. The Heart's Cove Hotel still presided over Cove Boulevard like an aging queen. Against overcast skies and framed by bare trees, the patched-up parking lot and fading paint made the hotel look like it was in desperate need of some TLC.

I parked in the lot next to another pickup and made my way to the lobby—and stopped dead as soon as I made it inside.

My aunts—my elderly, *insane* aunts—were perched on the top of two matching ladders on either side of the room, a gigantic garland of fake pine strung up between them. Christmas baubles bounced on the garland while tinsel rained down like snow.

Dorothy wore a flowing tunic over a pair of black pants, her wild gray mane of hair curling down to mid-back as she flung the garland over and back to try to get it dislodged from one of the sconces on the wall between them. One of those red Christmas balls flew off and cracked against the wall. Dorothy swore, and her ladder wobbled with every vigorous movement of her hands. I took half a step toward her before stopping in case I startled her and caused her to crash to her death on the floor.

Margaret, the older twin, clung to the other end of the garland and shouted at Dorothy to try to get her to stop being so violent with it. Every yank of the garland made Margaret buck like she was holding on to some crazed animal with a fraying leash. Her own ladder was actually a stepladder, and it had been propped on top of the reception desk, which was crazy. Margaret was supposed to be the responsible one. She wore a navy pantsuit with a silk shirt, her hair in a classic French twist, her lips painted in a deep red. She played tug-o-war with Dorothy with a Christmas garland, looking nothing like the prim, responsible woman I'd known her to be.

"Stop—Dor—Stop it! You're going to rip it!"

"If I just"—Dorothy grunted as she tried to fling the garland off the sconce with a flick of her wrists—"just get it another inch..."

I cleared my throat. Margaret spotted me first and let out a cry of delight, which Dorothy must have interpreted as panic, because Dorothy whipped around toward me, holding the pine garland like she'd strangle me with it. Then her face cleared, and she recognized me. "Sean!"

Unfortunately, the rough whirling had set her A-frame ladder wobbling, and the delight on her face morphed to horror.

In three long strides, I was beside her. I grabbed the ladder to stop it from moving, but Dorothy had overshot her attempt to balance it. She let out a squeak, I held out my arms, and then my kookiest aunt landed on top of me. I staggered, caught my balance, and set her on her feet.

Without missing a beat, Dorothy flung her arms around my shoulders and planted a loud kiss on my cheek. "Sean! You made it! And you caught me! My hero!"

"Help me down, honey," Margaret called out, still perched on top of the stepladder on the reception desk. A minute later, she was on her feet, planting a kiss on my opposite cheek.

My twin aunts beamed at me, and I forced my lips into an answering smile. My face seemed to creak at the effort of unfamiliar muscles straining to make the shape.

"Where's Mikey?" Dorothy asked, glancing over my shoulder.

"Dropped him off at school before coming here," I explained.

"You have to come over for dinner. Both of you," Margaret commanded. "Hamish is a wonderful cook."

"You wouldn't know it to look at him, but it's true," Dorothy added, which made Margaret roll her eyes.

"Who's Hamish? And why wouldn't you know it to look at him?"

"Hamish is my lover," Margaret answered. "He rides a motorcycle."

"He rides a *hog*," Dorothy corrected.

Margaret nodded proudly. "So you'll come for dinner?"

"Sure," I answered, and my aunts smiled like I'd just given them the world. Despite my misgivings about moving back here, my shoulders relaxed. This was exactly the reason I'd made the move—family. Community.

Mikey and I had struggled in San Francisco in the three years since the divorce, and even with child support from my ex and as much work as I could manage, I hadn't been able to make the numbers work. Living was more affordable in Heart's Cove, and my aunts had made sure to put in a good word for me with a local carpenter. So not only was I walking into a full-time job, but I might also actually be able to finally gain some stability. My son might have a chance at a better life. I'd be able to watch him grow up instead of catching snippets with him while I shoveled dinner into him and sent him to bed.

That's when the door at the back of the lobby opened, and a man a few years older than me stepped out wearing a denim shirt and tan work pants. He nodded to me and turned to my aunts. "Easels are fixed. I put some extra bracing on a few of the wobblier ones, so you shouldn't have any more art class mishaps."

"Wonderful," Dorothy exclaimed, smiling. She pushed her

hair over her shoulder and gestured to me. "This is our nephew, Sean. Sean, this is Grant, the lovely young man we told you about."

Grant's lips curled slightly at that description, since he looked like he was pushing fifty, and he reached over to shake my hand. He had an easy, friendly look about him, but he studied me with incisive eyes. "Heard you were looking for work."

"I am," I told him. "Just moved back to town with my son."

"Things generally slow down in the winter, but I've been swamped with projects leading up to the holidays. If you're happy to start today, we can head over to a job after this. New kitchen, all custom joinery. We can talk about the particulars and see if the two of us are a good fit."

"Sounds good," I said. If things worked out with Grant, it'd be one less thing to worry about.

"Fantastic!" Margaret said. "I knew this was a good idea."

"Technically, it was my idea, but who's keeping track," Dorothy put in.

Margaret ignored her. "Now you boys go on and get to work. Dorothy and I will finish up here."

I glanced at the garland, then at the precarious stepladders, then at Grant. When I arched my brows, he grinned.

"We'll give you a hand," he said, and I figured I liked the guy for that alone. Ten minutes later, the holiday decorations were up and my aunts were still alive, so Grant and I headed out to a job across town.

I followed him in my truck and took a deep breath, my shoulders dropping another inch as I relaxed into the seat.

A job, a good school, my two remaining family members, and a smattering of people from my past. Things could be worse. I could be struggling through fourteen-hour days, keeping my son in San Fran on the off chance his mother decided to blow through town and see him between her business obligations.

Now I had *something*, at least. The beginnings of a support system. A chance. Maybe I'd be able to get my head above water after all this time.

I even had an invitation to Thanksgiving dinner at Aaron's house. I followed Grant's truck onto a winding road lined with huge houses, and I smiled at the run-in I'd had the day before with Aaron's younger sister. She hadn't changed either. Well, not as much as I felt like I had. She didn't look like life had chewed her up and spit her out the way it seemed to have done with me. Even when I startled her, she'd smiled through it. Being next to her had always felt like standing in a ray of sunshine. She attacked life like she could smile it into submission. It was completely foreign to me—had been when I was a kid, too—but I'd always liked being around her. She still had those cute red-apple cheeks and those dark, dark eyes. Still clumsy as all hell, too.

I shook my head. I'd hesitated about coming back here. I wasn't sure if I could ever be at home in this town with what had happened here growing up. But it was as good a place as any to try to start fresh, and Mikey had seemed cautiously optimistic about the school when we'd gone there together this morning. The robotics club had impressed him; his eyes had gotten that interested gleam I hadn't seen in a while.

Maybe I could take a leaf out of Lizzie's book and believe that everything would turn out okay. The thought made me slightly uncomfortable, so I decided to believe that things would turn out, if not okay, then at least not disastrous. And if disaster was in my future, I'd deal with that, too. Always did.

Familiar bitterness swept through me at the thought, and I forced it down. This was a fresh start. Stability for Mikey. Everything I needed to take care of my kid.

Grant's blinker came on as he slowed his truck, and then he turned into a long driveway leading to a beautiful home. I followed him, took a deep breath, and pushed all thoughts of old friends and dark eyes out of my mind.

What mattered now was making a good impression, getting this job, and making sure my son settled in as well as he could. Everything else was secondary, including how it felt to be driving these roads again and the effort it took to keep old memories at bay.

FOUR

LIZZIE

HOLIDAYS HAD ALWAYS BEEN chaotic in my family, and Thanksgiving was no exception. My elder brother Aaron and his wife Emily were hosting this year, but I'd been asked to make the turkey and two sides. I'd done my best to prep what I could during the week, but with Zach recovering from his illness, Hazel being cast in the school Christmas play, and my own work schedule, I was behind.

Thankfully, the kids were in a great mood. Hazel smiled at me as she pranced out of her room, giving me a twirl of her rust-red dress.

"Beautiful," I told her, leaning down to kiss her head.

"It floofs!" She twirled again, giggling at the way the skirt flew up and danced around her.

"Your aunt Emily chose well," I said, then turned to the hallway. "Zach! Are you almost ready?"

A muffled, "Yeah," was the only response I got, so I hurried to the kitchen to check on my stuffing prep. I'd perfected my stuffing recipe over the years, which had been passed down from my maternal grandmother, and it was one of my favorite things about Thanksgiving. Pork, turkey gizzards, sage, and apple came together with breadcrumbs and the bird's juices (and lots of butter) to create pure magic. There were never any leftovers. I couldn't wait to have some—but I needed to make it first.

While the stuffing got going, I worked on peeling potatoes. The turkey had been dry-brined overnight and was ready to start cooking. Oven space was limited at Aaron's house, so I had to be efficient.

I checked the time. Tight, but it should be okay as long as I could head over to Aaron's within the next half hour.

After cooking like my life depended on it, I checked on the kids. Hazel had her shoes on and a bow in her hair, and she was keeping herself busy with a princess coloring book in the living room. Zach was watching football on our TV while he held a ball.

"Zach, get dressed. We're leaving soon."

He looked down at himself, then dragged himself to his feet and shuffled to his bedroom. I decided to take my own advice. I jumped in the shower and scrubbed myself down in a record two minutes, slapped on some concealer, mascara, and lipstick, then pointed a blow dryer at my head for a few minutes. The children started bickering, so I sighed and wrapped my still-damp hair in a claw clip. It would have to do.

I would've loved to doll myself up, but another glance at the clock told me that I needed to get the food and the kids in the car so I could head to my brother's place and make sure everyone ate at a reasonable time. I threw on a wine-colored wrap sweater and the only pair of jeans that still fit and called it a day. I'd be running around all day, anyway, probably with all kinds of cooking splatter all over me, so there was no point in being too precious about it.

Ten minutes later, the car was loaded, the food was secure, and the kids had decided to make peace. I pulled up to my brother's house only fifteen minutes behind my self-imposed schedule and let myself inside. The house smelled like warm spices and vanilla, and the sound of conversation mingled with sportsball announcers talking about sportsball things on the television.

"Hello, hello!" I called out, and heaved the turkey in the direction of the kitchen.

I found Emily there, dumping chips into a bowl. My sister-in-law gave me a hug and waved at the oven. "Have at it. Do your thing!"

I smiled. "Of course. How're Jacob and Levi?"

"Jacob's excited for the game," she said. "Levi's Levi."

"Playing LEGO in his room?"

She gave me a side smile. "If you have a minute and you feel like coaxing him down to be with everyone, I'd appreciate it. You do seem to have a special way with him."

"Sure," I said, turning the knobs on the oven to start preheating it. I checked my watch for the thousandth time and allowed myself one deep breath, then headed back out to the car.

The potatoes and extra casserole dish of stuffing had been

secured in the footwell of the passenger seat, so I was once again face down, ass up when Sean Hardy pulled up behind me. I heard a door open, and expecting my middle brother Kyle, I spun around and thrust the gigantic pot of peeled potatoes at the body exiting the vehicle.

Sean blinked but, to his credit, grabbed the pot. "Happy Thanksgiving," he said.

"Oh," I replied. "Same to you. I thought you were my brother. I can bring that in."

"It's fine," he said. His son came around the car and stood next to him. I watched him study my hair and decided that we didn't need to address whether or not it looked shiny enough in his eleven-year-old opinion, so I grabbed the casserole dish and closed the car door with my hip.

"Everyone's in the den getting ready for the game to start. You want a drink?"

"Sure," he replied. "Mikey, grab the pies from the back seat."

"Pie!" I beamed at the two of them. "How wonderful!"

"Store-bought," Sean clarified. The sun's rays slanted against his face, gilding his skin and causing his eyes to look particularly striking. He wore a button-down and dark-wash jeans under an open wool jacket, and he looked both casual and put-together. And utterly edible.

I tore my gaze away. "If it's got a crust, and it's got a filling, it's called pie to me," I told him, then led the two of them inside to the kitchen. When Sean put the pot of potatoes down on top of the stove, his shoulder brushed against mine and I got a whiff of a delicious-smelling cologne. My lady bits went wild.

Forcing my expression to remain neutral, I thanked the two of them and checked the oven, then got to work.

"You need help?"

Surprised that Sean was still there, I spun around with oven mitts on my hands and gave him a smile. "It's all under control. Turkey's in, so we're on track. Beer's in the fridge, and I know Emily had some snacks out in the den. You just enjoy yourself."

He watched me for a moment, then knocked his knuckle on the countertop and grabbed himself a drink. I may have watched him walk away, but only because his jeans fit really nicely, and the sight of them made me feel a little woozy.

Which reminded me. I hadn't eaten anything yet.

I grazed while I cooked, and when things were under control, I finally poured myself half a glass of wine and followed the sounds of conversation to the den. People had moved in and out of the kitchen for the past hour and I'd gotten to say hello to everyone, so I snuck into the room and smiled at Emily, who nodded at me from her perch on the sofa.

I began to lower myself onto a chair and reached for a chip from the depleted chip bowl. My legs were already aching, and there was a lot more cooking and cleaning to do.

Emily glanced at the empty plate on the table. "Would you mind putting on some more of those pigs-in-a-blanket, Lizzie? And where's Levi? Have you had a chance to talk to him?"

My hand stopped halfway to the chip bowl. "Shoot," I said. "I'll go see him now."

"Anyone need a drink?" Emily asked, and made as if to get up. As she did so, she glanced at me, brows arched, and I waved her back down.

"I'll grab them," I said, and took everyone's order. When it came to Sean, I resisted the urge to avoid eye contact by staring at his chin the whole time and forced myself to meet those beautiful green-blue eyes. "Still working on that one?"

He checked the level in his bottle. "Nearly done. I'll help you." He began to stand.

"She's got it under control, believe me. Lizzie is everyone's mom. She loves it," Aaron told him, slapping a hand on Sean's shoulder and shoving him back down to his seat. "I haven't seen you in two years. We gotta catch up, man!"

I bristled, but...was Aaron wrong? I *did* like to play hostess, and I was already headed to the kitchen anyway. And Sean was a guest.

Sean nodded at my brother, and I noted the tightness of his smile. For a moment, I wondered what had happened in the years since he'd been in high school—and then duty called.

My brother shot me a grin and a thumbs-up, and I forced a smile onto my lips that dropped as soon as I stepped out of the room. It wasn't that he was wrong, exactly. I *was* the mom of the group. I'd been the mom of every group, and when I became an actual mom, that role seemed to cement itself in all aspects of my life.

It did cross my mind that I was doing a lot of work for an event that wasn't actually being held at my house. As I refreshed everyone's drinks and got the pastry-covered mini sausages warming, a traitorous, wriggling thought made its way to the forefront of my mind.

I would love to sit in the den with everyone and catch up. I'd love to be like Emily and have my head on my husband's shoulder while I sipped a glass of wine. I'd love to be seen as an actual adult who had interesting things to contribute to the conversation and not just the de facto cook and nanny for every family event.

But I *was* good at it. And I did enjoy seeing everyone loving my food. And it made me happy to care for my kids—and my nieces and nephews. So could I really complain? Lots of people didn't have what I had.

I wiped my hands on a dishtowel and headed for the stairs. Levi's room was at the end of the hallway upstairs, and his door was ajar when I got to it. I knocked lightly and poked my head in.

Levi glanced up, then went back to the LEGOs spread out on his desk.

"Whatcha working on?"

He pointed to the box propped against the wall. On it, Batman rode a LEGO Batmobile. I could see the beginnings of the project taking shape in front of Levi.

"Very cool," I said, leaning over his shoulder to watch him snap a tiny piece onto an array of other pieces that I thought would turn into the engine. "Do you ever try to do them without following the instructions?"

"Sometimes," he admitted. Levi was a year older than Zach, but the two boys had never really gotten along that well. Zach enjoyed action and sports, like Levi's brother Jacob. Jacob was nine years old, but he often dominated his brother.

I'd watched Aaron try to coax Levi into enjoying football and baseball and fishing, but the boy never really took to it the way Jacob did. And Aaron didn't really enjoy finicky things like

LEGOs, so there was a growing disconnect between them. Emily seemed content to let them figure it all out, but she also seemed to slightly favor Jacob. It was easier to get along with the kid who was gregarious and charming over the one who preferred quiet solitude.

I knew how that felt. I'd been the youngest and the only girl, and I often felt like the odd one out. Instead of retreating the way Levi did, I'd coped by making myself pleasant and accommodating. Days like today, I wasn't sure if that had been the right approach.

"What do you think about coming downstairs to say hi to everyone?" I asked.

My nephew shrugged a shoulder. "Maybe."

"I'll let you mash the potatoes."

Levi's lips curled into a tiny smile, and he shot me a quick glance. "Okay," he said, and slid off his chair and followed me out. We hung out in the kitchen for a while, and I made him a fancy mocktail with a maraschino cherry that put a big smile on his face. When Zach came stomping in from the backyard and invited Levi out to play catch with the rest of the kids, Levi slithered off his chair and ran out behind my son.

A pleasant warmth filled my chest as I watched the kids through the back window. Sure, sometimes I felt a little neglected and invisible, even with my own family, but wasn't it worth it for moments like this?

FIVE

SEAN

GROWING UP, Aaron's house had been my second home. My mom and I had been invited to every Thanksgiving and Christmas event at their place for three years before she died, and those were the happiest holiday memories I had. As I sat on the couch and listened to Kyle and Aaron talk about the game, along with the chatter of a couple of aunts, uncles, cousins, and the pleasant small talk Emily made, some of the tension that had crept back into my body over the course of the week dissolved.

"Grant's a good guy," Aaron told me when he heard who I was working with. "His wife co-owns the Four Cups Café with a few other women. Great pastries there."

"Jen, the baker, was on TV!" Emily cut in, beaming.

"I remember that," I said. "Couldn't believe Heart's Cove got put on the map."

The conversation shifted to football, and when a commercial break came on and I tipped my empty beer bottle to my lips for the third time, I heaved myself off the sofa.

"Oh, someone can get that for you," Aaron said, glancing around. "Where's... Babe, would you mind?"

"Sure," Emily replied, but I waved her away.

"I should check where Mikey's gone," I told her.

"Oh, he's probably fine," Aaron said.

"I'm sure Lizzie's keeping an eye on the kids," Emily added.

A frown tugged at my brows. Lizzie hadn't seemed bothered by the way her family treated her, but something didn't sit quite right with me. I'd been a single dad for a few years now, and I knew how much work it was to look after one kid, let alone half a dozen. Besides, Mikey was my responsibility. The kid was the best thing I'd done with my life, and I wanted to make sure he was doing all right on his own. The past couple of weeks had been full of change for both of us.

I brought my empty bottle to the kitchen and slowed when I saw Lizzie standing by the back window. The sunlight glistened over her lips and highlighted the generous curves of her body. She had a soft look on her face as she looked out the window, and it struck me for the first time that she was a truly beautiful woman.

I'd never seen it before. Or at least, I hadn't seen it like this.

Her features were soft and rounded. Her cheeks were full and her lips were plush. Her hair had been pulled back to reveal the small gold hoops dangling from her ears. Everything about her was ethereal and soft, like she'd been made for a different time—a different world—and transported here by mistake.

It stopped me in my tracks. Staggered me. She was soft as an unfurling flower, and I hadn't even bothered to notice until that exact moment. Seeing it now made me want to slow down and see what else I'd missed. It made me want to delve into this thumping in my chest and figure out exactly why that calm, peaceful look on her face filled me with such yearning. It made me want her to look at *me* like that—like I was everything she needed to be happy in life.

Hearing me, Lizzie blinked away from the window and turned to face me. Her usual smile returned to her lips, although I thought it looked a little strained.

"Here for a refill?" She moved to the fridge.

"Checking on my spawn," I said, and glanced out the window. The kids had set up a game and were running around and laughing. Mikey had a wide, beaming smile on his face that I hadn't seen in a long time.

"He's doing all right without you," she answered with a wry grin, exchanging my empty bottle for a full one. "It always stings when that happens."

I huffed a laugh, gaze catching on the darkness of her eyes. I wondered if she knew how pretty they were, those endless pools of brown. Wondered if she'd worn that lipstick because she knew it made her mouth look so kissable. "Smells good in here," I said, tearing my gaze away from her.

She was Aaron's sibling. There was no way I could lust after her, even though something about her had caught my attention. My oldest friend would murder me if I sniffed around his little sister. I'd come here to gain a community, not blow it up.

"Turkey's going well," she said, leaning over to peek through the oven window. Because I couldn't help myself, I watched the way her jeans revealed the lush curves of her ass. She stood up, and my gaze was dragged up her body to the curve of her neck. I wanted to taste her. "I'll pop the extra stuffing into the oven in..." She checked her watch. Her tongue poked out the corner of her lips as she tilted her head back and forth for a few moments, and I found myself caught up in the sight of her again. Cute. And pretty. And sensual in a way that seemed completely effortless. "Twenty-five minutes," she finally said, and I snapped out of my daze.

"Anything I can do to help?"

"Very kind of you to offer," she said, "but all you have to do is enjoy yourself. I know Aaron is thrilled to have you back in town."

I found myself not wanting to leave Lizzie on her own in the kitchen to do all the work. Hanging with Aaron and the rest of the family had made me feel at home for the first time in years, but being with Lizzie was like entering a calm, peaceful oasis. Besides, the light that came through the back window kept showing me new facets of her face that I wanted to study.

There was that slight dimple that appeared in her cheek when she tried to hold back a smile. Or the way her dark-brown hair curled around her nape, making my fingers itch to brush that patch of skin. Or how her sweater dipped down between her breasts, giving me the barest hint of what lay beneath.

I wasn't breaking any bro code. I wasn't chasing after my best friend's little sister. I was just keeping the host company while I made sure my son was doing okay. That was all. And if I enjoyed what I saw, what was the problem?

"It's been weird being back," I admitted.

"Oh?" Lizzie grabbed a neglected glass of wine from beside the stove. "How so?"

"Everything is different and also the same."

Lizzie lifted her glass. "I think that's called life." She took a sip and tilted her head. "So you're settling in with Mikey okay. And your wife...?"

A familiar pain pierced my breastbone. It frustrated me that even years later, the mere mention of Melody made my body tense. I wanted to move on. I'd gotten custody of our son and made a life with him. She'd chased the career she'd always wanted. We were both happier apart than we'd ever been together.

But still...

"Divorced," I told Lizzie. "Just over three years."

"Sorry," she said with an understanding smile. "For me, it's been five and a half...nearly six, actually. Still feels like I'm trying to pick up the pieces."

I huffed and took a sip of my beer. Not wanting to get caught up in those dark eyes of hers, I let my gaze drift out to watch my son chase after another boy as they both cackled. In the corner of the yard, a girl twirled in a red dress while another did the same in her jeans.

"Mine's the one your kid is chasing," Lizzie said, moving closer to point. "And that's my daughter. Zach and Hazel. Eleven and nine years old."

Her body pressed into mine as she gestured to the children,

all soft and giving. I wondered if her skin was as silky as it looked, if her body would feel as good to touch and hold as I imagined.

Clearing my throat, I pulled away a couple of inches. "Beautiful kids."

She stiffened for a moment, her smile losing its tenderness, then gave me a beaming smile. "They're the best thing I've ever done," she said, then turned at the sound of the front door opening. She didn't touch me again.

"Hello! Happy Thanksgiving!" a voice called from the foyer.

"In here!" Aaron's voice called out, and a moment later an older woman marched into the kitchen. When she saw me, her face brightened.

"Sean! Aaron told us you were in town." Sandra, Lizzie's mom, came to give me a tight hug. She was a short woman who'd always treated me like one of her own, and I didn't hesitate to hug her back.

"Hey, Mrs. B."

"So good to see you," she said, patting my cheek. Her face was more lined than I remembered, but she had the same vivacity as years ago.

The older woman turned to Liz and placed a peck on her daughter's cheek. "Smells good, honey."

"Thanks, Mom. You brought the green beans?"

"Of course. How long until we eat?"

"Probably just over an hour."

"Perfect." Sandra dropped the foil-covered green beans on the counter. "So, Sean, how are you settling in?"

MERRY LITTLE MIDLIFE MATCHMAKER

"Just fine, thanks," I answered, moving out of the way as the two women bustled around the kitchen. "Mikey seems to like the new school."

"Wonderful. Allan and I were so sad to hear that things didn't work out with you and Melody." She came over and squeezed my arms. "But don't you worry. We'll get Lizzie on it, and you'll find someone new in no time."

"Mom," Lizzie protested.

"'Get Lizzie on it?'" I repeated.

"Hey, Mom," Aaron said as he wandered into the kitchen. He kissed Sandra's cheek then went to the fridge to grab himself a fresh drink. "That's a good idea, actually," he said as he pulled a fresh bottle from the bottom shelf. He twisted off the top and turned to face me. "Lizzie can set you up."

"She's a born matchmaker," Sandra added.

I glanced at the woman in question, who seemed very interested in the state of the extra stuffing. "I don't know if I'd go that far," she said.

"Oh, don't be silly!" Sandra said.

"You set me and Emily up," Aaron cut in. He glanced at me. "And Lizzie found the perfect woman for Kyle, but she ended up moving overseas and it didn't work out. And then there was that mom at the school that you set up with your dentist."

"If only she had such good taste for herself," Sandra added with a laugh.

Lizzie's red cheeks had gone even redder. She didn't meet my eye.

I cleared my throat. "I'm not looking for someone to date," I said. "I'm just trying to settle in with Mikey."

"Sure," Sandra said, "but if there *was* someone..." She turned to Lizzie. "You must have someone in mind. You can always tell within minutes of meeting people who they'd pair up with." Sandra shot me a smile. "She's really good at it."

It seemed to take a lot of effort for Lizzie to meet my gaze. Her smile was bright as ever, but it didn't quite seem to reach her eyes. The dimple was nowhere in sight. "I can think of a couple of candidates," she said. "But only if you're interested."

"Of course he's interested!" Aaron slapped me on the back. "Sean has always been a ladies' man."

I snorted. "In high school, maybe."

"Everyone deserves to go out on a date once in a while," Sandra said, patting my cheek. Her face brightened. "And everyone deserves a New Year's kiss!"

"Haven't had one of those in a while," I admitted.

Lizzie snorted sympathetically, but no one else seemed to notice. Both Aaron's and Sandra's eyes were on me.

Sandra smiled. "You just let Lizzie work her magic. Now to New Year's is more than enough time. Isn't it, honey?"

"Sure," Lizzie said, inspecting the green beans. She squared her shoulders and turned to face us. Her smile was wide but almost brittle. "What do you say?"

I couldn't say what I really wanted to say, which was that the most attractive solution to this proposal was for Lizzie and me to be each other's New Year's kiss. Which obviously would be like taking a torpedo and firing it at the fresh foundations of my new home. Instead, I shrugged. "I'm intrigued by these matchmaking skills of yours."

"Game's back on," Aaron said. "How long until dinner?"

"Hour or so," Lizzie answered.

"Cool." Aaron towed me out of the room and Sandra followed with a fresh tray of snacks for the den. Before I turned the corner, I glanced over my shoulder and saw Lizzie standing in the kitchen, looking lost.

SIX

LIZZIE

MY MOM, Emily, an uncle, and a couple of cousins came to help set the table. The kids' table was in the living room, and while the others made sure the dining room was ready, I went outside to call the kids in for food. Then came a rush of serving plates and customizing them for every picky child, and I found myself darting between the kitchen and the living room while the adults made their way to the main table.

"Everyone good over there?" Emily asked, glancing toward the living room.

"Levi tried to scoop the gravy off his plate and accidentally flicked it at Hazel, but I'll clean it up," I answered.

"Thanks, Lizzie. You're a lifesaver," my sister-in-law said.

"Aaron, honey, are you carving the turkey?" Mom called out as she brought the bird to the table. Emily followed close behind with the huge platter of stuffing.

"Hey, can you guys make sure you save me some of that

stuffing?" I asked as I headed for the living room. "I'll deal with the kids and then be right over."

"No problem," my mom said. "Aaron, you do the honors! Kyle, do you need a refill? Don't give me that look, Allan. You've had enough until after dinner."

The sounds of pleasant chatter and clinking plates floated from the dining room, but I hurried to deal with the kids. A few cousins' kids looked happy with their food but needed new drinks, so I refreshed those and then dealt with Hazel's dress. Levi sat and pushed his food around the plate—he hated gravy, and his plate had been drenched by my mother—so I told him to sit tight and that I'd make him a new one.

Then Zach asked me for another roll, and my cousin's kid needed a napkin as a matter of emergency, otherwise every piece of furniture in the living room would end up covered in mashed potato and gravy. There were ten kids ranging from five to thirteen and only one of me, so I called out toward the dining room for some help. All I heard was laughter and the sounds of adults enjoying their meal.

"A little help! Emily?"

Utensils clinked on plates. One of my uncles told a joke and the room erupted in laughter. Then the kid with the mashed potato hands made a mad dash for Emily's prized velvet armchair and I had to catch him around the waist and bring him to the bathroom for a wash.

"There you go," I told him as I brought him back to the kids' table. My stomach grumbled. "Everyone good? I'm starving, so I'm going to go get some food."

"Mom," Zach said. "I need more gravy."

"Gravy's gross," Levi informed him.

"Gravy's the best part."

"Nuh-uh. Potatoes are."

"No way. Potatoes are nothing without gravy."

"You don't know anything."

"Neither do you!"

"Boys," I cut in. "Everyone has different tastes. I'll grab you some gravy, Zach. And then Mom needs food."

I ducked into the dining room and reached over my brother Kyle's shoulder for a gravy boat. "Just need a bit of this. Hey, save me some of that stuffing! Been looking forward to it all day."

One of my cousins nodded as she loaded a big serving spoon with a second serving of stuffing. "It's so good, Lizzie! You're amazing, as usual."

"Turkey's the juiciest it's been in years," my father said, lifting his glass toward me. The bird's decimated carcass sat like a centerpiece in the middle of the table. "We couldn't do it without you."

"The kids okay?" Emily asked.

"They're fine. A little low on gravy. I'll be right back." I darted back to top up Zach's plate, refilled two glasses of milk and three of water, cleaned up a minor spill near the five-year-old, then took a deep breath, washed my hands, and brought the gravy back to the adult table.

And my eyes landed on the empty stuffing dish.

I froze, standing in no man's land, staring at the plate that had been scraped clean. It was so silly that my eyes watered. After everything I'd been through, how could something like stuffing make me cry? I knew it was just food, and in the grand scheme of things, it didn't really matter.

But the feeling that came over me was exactly the same one I'd had at Isaac's place on the weekend. I felt so invisible, so trampled over, so *tired*.

I'd asked for one thing. *One* thing. I'd taken care of everyone's kids, cooked everyone's meals, and no one had the decency to save me even a tiny spoonful of stuffing.

But if I cried about it, it would be exactly like announcing that I was divorcing my husband of six years. I was the unreasonable one. I was overreacting. I was ruining everyone's holiday for the sake of a side dish, just like I'd ruined my marriage and my kids' lives for the sake of my own pride.

Blinking, I forced my lips into a smile and put the gravy back on the table, then sat between one of my aunts and cousins at the far corner of the table. The table leg was in my way, but at least I'd get to eat, finally. It didn't matter that I didn't get the stuffing I'd been salivating over all day. It really, really didn't matter. It was just food.

And not one single person at this table had thought of me.

I shook my head. Now was not the time to get weepy. Definitely not in front of the whole family, and not in front of—

I looked up and found Sean watching me. His brows were drawn as his gaze flicked to the stuffing dish, down to his almost-empty plate, over to the plates around him, and back to me. His lips parted slightly, and even with the chatter of conversation drowning out any noise he made, I knew he was pulling in a breath. He could tell I was upset about the stuffing, and that was just the most utterly humiliating thing I'd ever experienced. He probably thought I was ridiculous. Isaac sure did whenever I got upset about this kind of thing. My parents always told me to brush it off and not sweat the small stuff. They were probably right, and it was probably some character flaw that it hurt so damn much that not *one single person*—

I forced my lips into a smile as I shrugged. It was fine. It was really, truly fine. I probably didn't need the stuffing, anyway. A moment on the lips, as Mom so enjoyed reminding me. My own generous hips brushed against the chairs on either side as I shifted forward to grab a roll from the basket in front of me.

The turkey carcass had been picked over but there was enough for me, and I preferred the dark meat, anyway. The green beans were still going strong, and I'd made a truckload of potatoes, so between that and the rest of the sides that had been brought, there was more than enough food. Some of it was a little cold, and it wasn't exactly what I had wanted, but it was food. I was surrounded by family and friends, and this was a happy occasion.

This was Thanksgiving. I was thankful. I *was*. I wasn't some hysterical, unreasonable woman who threw tantrums over stuffing. I had a big, loving family. Friends. Food. Life was good. I just had to keep reminding myself of it, and this pit in my stomach would go away, just like it always did.

I tucked in, and when I heard screeching from the kids' table, I pretended not to. After a few long moments, Emily got up to go check on them, cracking jokes and acting like a martyr the whole time.

Never mind that I'd spent the *entire day*—

No. I was not a bitter woman. I would *not* let this day get to me. I was just hungry, that was all. Focusing on cutting my turkey into tiny, bite-sized pieces, then loading up my fork with the perfect bite, I let the anger drain away. I would *not* make a scene. I wouldn't ruin everyone's day.

"So, Sean," my dad said from his spot at the head of the table. "Are you in Heart's Cove to stay?"

"That's the plan," the man said.

"How wonderful," my mother added.

"We're glad to have you back," Dad agreed. "And Sandra told me that Lizzie was going to set you up with someone! A New Year's kiss!" Dad chuckled. "Not a bad idea. And we all know how scatterbrained Lizzie can be, so it's nice to give her a real deadline."

Scatterbrained? I blinked, probably more offended than I should be. If I sometimes forgot things, it was because I had so much to manage on a daily basis! It wasn't some innate character flaw. "Well—" I started.

"You have to put yourself out there, honey," my mom told Sean. "Lizzie, you've already thought of some options for Sean, haven't you?"

All eyes turned to me. My skin felt hot and tight, and I forced my aching cheeks into another giant smile. I would not cry. I didn't even know *why* I wanted to cry. Everything was *fine*. "I'll see what I can come up with," I said, adding extra cheer to my voice.

"If there's a woman out there who can cook half as well as you, I'm sold," Sean said to raucous laughter and agreement. He met my gaze until my brother thumped him on the back, then he smiled as someone refilled his glass of wine.

He probably meant it as a compliment, but his words stung. It was just another reminder that it would never be me who was chosen, who was seen. It was some other woman who could cook like me, who could clean like me, who could fit the role and the look that I had never quite managed to squeeze into.

The turkey turned dry in my mouth, and I gulped it down. By the time the day was over, my entire body ached. I brought my dishes home along with my small plate of leftovers, got the kids ready for bed, then sat on the couch feeling completely, utterly drained.

SEVEN

SEAN

THE DOORBELL CHIMED when I pushed the button, and I glanced down at the plastic container in my hand. This had been a stupid idea. I shouldn't have come here, or I should have at least called ahead—but then again, it's not like I had Lizzie's phone number, and I wasn't on social media so I couldn't message her...

Small feet came running toward the door, and Lizzie's daughter, Hazel, flung it open. Mariah Carey's "All I Want for Christmas" assaulted my ears, blasting from speakers somewhere deep inside the home. The scent of warm spices—cinnamon, nutmeg, cloves—floated through the doorway. It was like getting slapped in the face by one of Santa's elves.

I hated every second of it.

The little girl in the doorway blinked at me with her mother's dark-brown eyes and yelled, "Mom! There's a man at the door! He's here with Mikey."

"What? Who?" Lizzie's voice called out from the far end of the hallway.

"Mikey! From yesterday!"

A second later, Lizzie appeared, silhouetted against the patio doors at the other end of the house. She wiped her hands on a dishtowel, her brows jumping when she spotted me. "Sean?"

She was dressed in a cream sweater. In the middle of her chest was a felt appliqué of a reindeer featuring a flashing red light on the nose. On her head, a big red bow held her ponytail up. Her legs were clad in jeans, but on her feet, slippers designed to look like Santa's boots completed the look. It looked like Santa Claus had stopped by and thrown up all over her.

Ridiculous. And adorable.

I despised the holidays, but the sight of her dressed like that made me want to smile.

"Sorry to come over unannounced," I said, lifting the container in my hands. "I got your address from your mom. Figured you were owed from last night."

Her hips swayed as she came down the hall, her hand moving to caress Hazel's head as she reached us. "Owed? What do you mean?"

"Here." I extended my arm and gave her the container.

Lizzie frowned at it, then at me. She grabbed the plastic tub from my hand and cracked it open, and emotion flashed across her features almost too fast for me to read. Surprise, or maybe shock. A jolt of delight. Then her expression shuttered and something that looked like embarrassment. I had the horrible feeling I'd just made a terrible mistake.

"You...you brought me stuffing?"

"We had another Thanksgiving meal at my aunt's house today. Hamish's stuffing isn't as good as yours was, but I figured it might scratch the itch if you were still wanting some."

The look on Lizzie's face the day before had been like a punch in the solar plexus. I was so used to seeing her smiling that the raw emotion she'd shown when she saw that none of us had saved her the one thing she'd asked for...

I'd been ashamed. And just like the moment I'd seen her standing at the window with tenderness all over her features, it had made me sit up and take notice.

Lizzie had always been Aaron and Kyle's little sister. She tagged along whenever we let her as kids and mostly left us alone when we grew into teenagers. I hadn't paid much attention to her, other than to think she was a nice girl who wasn't really all that interesting.

But I was interested now. Not—not like *that*. Aaron was my oldest friend, and I couldn't date his little sister. But between her unabashed positivity in the pharmacy and what happened on Thanksgiving at her family's house, I was beginning to wonder if there was more to her than I'd previously thought.

She worked so hard for her family, and none of them seemed to notice it.

But I'd noticed.

Her throat bobbed. "This..." Her smile was shy, her red cheeks growing even redder. The dimple in her left cheek made an appearance. Had she always been this cute? "You didn't have to do this."

"We should have saved you some when you asked," I admitted.

"It wasn't your fault."

Hazel, evidently, was bored of our conversation. She looked at my son and asked, "Do you want to help us decorate our Christmas tree?"

Mikey, who'd been standing patiently beside me, glanced over with raised brows. I looked at Lizzie, whose face melted into one of those familiar sunny smiles. A real one. Both dimples on display.

"We put up our decorations the day after Thanksgiving," she explained. "Family tradition."

My instinctive refusal was on the tip of my lips. I wasn't a Christmas person. The next month and a half was something to be endured, not celebrated. Until life went back to normal in the first or second week of January, I'd have to wear a mask and pretend I didn't feel dead inside.

But Mikey had straightened beside me, and I could see him glancing curiously around Lizzie's hip.

"I just made my first batch of Christmas cookies," Lizzie added, grinning at Mikey. "I might need another taste tester."

My son's head whipped toward me, and there was nothing I could do but nod. How could I refuse the bald hope in his eyes? I wasn't a monster. He and Hazel were off like a shot down the hallway, and my gaze was once again drawn to Lizzie. She wore that soft smile again, the container of stuffing clasped in both her hands. She turned and caught me staring, blinked, and stepped aside.

She closed the door behind me and gestured down the hall-

MERRY LITTLE MIDLIFE MATCHMAKER

way, where Mariah had ceded to Frank Sinatra on the stereo. I shoved aside the discomfort at hearing the holiday tunes, choosing instead to glance around the room.

Lizzie's house was on the older side, with a kitchen that looked like an original from the nineties. The wood cabinets had that distinctive orange tinge, combined with brushed brass hardware and an off-white tile floor.

The kitchen opened onto a living room that was dominated by a brick fireplace. On the wall, pictures of her kids as babies were mixed in with beautiful photos of local landscapes. The mantel was strung with a green garland that twinkled with lights, and three stockings embroidered with Hazel, Zach, and Mom hung from hooks over the fireplace. The couch was dotted with holiday-themed throw pillows. Even the curtains screamed Christmas, with red fabric dotted with a snowflake pattern.

And in the corner of the room, an artificial Christmas tree had been put together and strung with glowing golden lights.

It was the exact opposite of my home, where Christmas didn't make it past the front door. Mikey went to his mother's house for that, and it was exactly the way I liked it.

My throat tightened as I watched Mikey accept a box of red Christmas ornaments from Zach. He plucked one of them from its plastic casing and considered the tree before choosing a branch on which to hang it. Zach gave him an approving nod, and Mikey grinned.

When Melody and I had divorced, the custody arrangement had been fairly easy to work out. She wanted time to pursue her career, and I wanted my son. When it came to holidays, she knew exactly how I felt about them, and I was more than happy to let her have Christmas with Mikey in perpetuity.

Now, as I watched his smile widen as he helped the other kids decorate the tree, I wondered if I'd made a mistake. I hated Christmas, but he didn't. Every time Melody came to pick him up for the holiday, it was a relief to have a week or two to myself. I didn't decorate our home, and I didn't cultivate traditions the way Lizzie seemed to. I'd get Mikey gifts, but that was the extent of it.

I'd never thought that I'd been missing out. Never considered that I might be depriving my son of something. Now, I wasn't so sure.

Lizzie dropped her dishtowel on the oven rail and pulled me out of my rumination by offering me a drink.

"Water'd be nice," I said, watching the way her jeans hugged the curve of her hips. She was short and curvy, and I found I liked watching the way she moved. There was something sensual about the way she shifted her weight, how she leaned over. Her dark hair caught the light, that big bow setting off the chestnut tones streaking through the darker brown, a few strands curling against her neck.

There was something innately feminine about her, in the curves of her body, the fullness of her cheeks, the plumpness of her lips. I wanted to feel all that softness pressed against me. I wanted to—

I blinked and looked away. She was completely off-limits. Aaron would kill me if I got involved with his baby sister, and then where would that leave the support system I was hoping to build? The whole reason I'd moved back to Heart's Cove with

Mikey was to be around people who knew and cared about us. I needed *help*. I needed to build a better life for myself and my son. Lusting after Lizzie would ruin all of that.

I watched her open up the container of stuffing and, with her face in profile, was able to glimpse the edge of a secret smile. My chest warmed as she glanced over at me, brows raised.

"Do you mind?"

"Brought it here for you to have," I told her.

She bit her bottom lip, scooped out a portion and placed it in a bowl, then warmed it in the microwave. Her first bite made her hips wiggle from side to side as her shoulders dropped and a soft groan escaped her throat. "That's good," she said.

"Yeah," I replied, caught up in the sight of her. In the small, pleasure-filled movement of her hips. The flush warming her cheeks. The sparkle in her deep brown eyes.

"Mom!" Zach called out. "I can't get the hook on the rocking horse ornament."

"Bring it over," she answered, and handed me my glass of water. Her smile was a little wry when she said, "I've been collecting Christmas ornaments since I moved out of my parents' house. Some of them require constant repairs."

When Zach deposited a small brown rocking horse into her hands, I watched her tease the metal hook into the tiny loop on the horse's back. She'd painted her fingernails a deep shade of red at some point, and they reflected the light as she worked. A few seconds later, a tiny toy rocking horse dangled from an ornament hook, and Lizzie beamed at her son.

His own face was alight with joy, and it felt like another

SEAN

punch in the chest. Maybe I shouldn't have given up Christmases with Mikey.

"Feel free to join in," Lizzie said, gesturing to the tree as the kids buzzed around it.

I shook my head. "They seem to be doing a good job on their own."

"I want to put my one on now!" Hazel called out, digging through a big brown box with the word "Christmas" written in Sharpie on the side. She pulled out a smaller box. With careful hands, she opened it up and pulled out a pearlescent ornament with pink embellishments all around it. Hazel walked toward us, holding the bauble like it was a baby bird. "Mom, look. Can I put it on the tree?"

"Of course, honey," Lizzie said.

Hazel looked at me and smiled proudly. "Mom bought this when I was born, and I'm the only one who gets to hang it on the tree every year. Zach has one too."

"That's pretty special," I told her through a tight throat.

Mikey watched avidly as Hazel showed off her glass globe, the three kids going quiet as Hazel hung it. She turned to her brother and gave him that same megawatt smile her mother had. "Your turn!"

"You must think this is all very silly," Lizzie said, eyes on her kids. Tearing her gaze away, she met my eyes. "I know I go overboard with the traditions this time of year."

"I don't think it's silly at all," I replied, and it surprised me to realize I was telling the truth. In fact, watching the reverence with which Zach and Hazel handled their birth-year ornaments made me feel like I'd failed as a father.

I had my excuses, of course. I had all those years of memories pressing down on me. All the drunken fights my dad picked with my mom. The anxiety of the weeks leading up to the holiday, wondering what mood he'd be in on the day. And then there was what happened after, when Dad was gone and Mom was sick. Every year, the anniversary of her death came around, and it never seemed to get much easier.

Then there was Melody. The years where things had seemed to heal me, only to have the rug ripped out from under my feet.

When Mikey was born, I'd vowed to be a better parent to him than my father had been to me. And I'd thought I'd succeeded. I couldn't give him Christmas traditions, but I could give him stability and a shoulder to lean on.

But now...

"Here," Lizzie said, placing a few star-shaped sugar cookies on a plate for me. Half of them had been sprinkled with red sugar crystals, the other half with green. "They're still warm."

They were delicious. I was on my second cookie when I turned to Lizzie and said, "I'm impressed you manage to do all this on your own. I haven't been able to think of holiday traditions, let alone put anything like this together for Mikey."

Lizzie waved a hand. "This stuff comes easily to me." She plucked a green sprinkle-covered cookie from the plate and bit off one of the star's points. I watched as her tongue darted out to pick up a sprinkle from the corner of her lip, tightness beginning to pull at my lower stomach. Had she always been this pretty? How had I never noticed?

Even in that ridiculous Christmas sweater featuring

Rudolph with a light-up LED nose, she managed to make my mouth water.

What would life be like with a woman like Lizzie by my side? Someone who cherished her children instead of seeing them as a roadblock to the life she wanted? Someone who put effort into the thousand little things that truly mattered. Someone who reminded me that life could be enjoyed in all the tiny little moments and traditions that I'd let lapse. Someone to lean on.

And, I thought, watching her lean a hip against the counter, someone I could unwrap like my very own Christmas present every single night from now until old age dragged me six feet under.

I cleared my throat. "I should probably get going."

"Oh." Lizzie put the cookie down and wiped her lips. "Sure. And in exchange for being so thoughtful, I think I really should set you up with a friend of mine. My mom was a little over-the-top about it yesterday, but I do have a bit of a knack for figuring out who will click. And everyone deserves a New Year's kiss."

At that moment, the only person I wanted to kiss was Lizzie, so maybe she didn't have as much of a knack as she thought.

But, I reminded myself for what felt like the millionth time, Lizzie was my oldest friend's little sister. If there was one person in this town I couldn't get involved with, it was her. So as much as I wanted to let her sprinkle some of that red and green sugar over her lips so I could lick it off myself, I knew that I needed to pull myself together and remember why I was here.

A support system. A community. A better life for my son.

So all I said was, "Maybe, but I'm out of practice with dating. Might be a harder match to make than you expect."

Her smile widened. "I'm not one to back down from a challenge," she told me. "Describe your perfect woman."

"I'll know her when I see her," I said, and it sounded like a vow.

She pursed her lips. "Not helpful, Mr. Hardy. Let's see." She tapped her chin. "You look like you still enjoy fitness. Is that true?"

She thought I looked fit? Through sheer force of will, I didn't let my chest puff out with pride. "I do," I told her.

"Outdoor activities?"

"I like the odd hike in the summertime. Haven't been snowboarding in years, though."

"Someone to make you enjoy the sweeter side of life."

"Yeah," I replied, gaze dropping to a sugar crystal on the corner of Lizzie's lips that her tongue had failed to lick up. "That sounds good."

"Leave it with me," Lizzie told me, eyes sparkling with mischief. "I'll see what I can do."

I left the warmth and light and comfort of Lizzie's presence and took my son back to the unpacked boxes and unfamiliar rooms of our new home, and I tried to stop myself from thinking of the one woman I wasn't allowed to have.

EIGHT

LIZZIE

MY JOB WASN'T ALL that exciting, but it paid the bills and allowed me to pick up and drop off my kids every day. I sat behind a glossy white reception desk at a local architecture firm and managed the thousand and one tasks that the higher-ups threw my way.

I stood next to the gigantic filing cabinet that held the architectural plans for the firm's projects, checking that the most up-to-date drawings were printed and filed correctly. My coworker Laurel sidled up to me. She was a beautiful brunette with the biggest blue eyes I'd ever seen, and a talented architect to boot, and I would definitely have been jealous of her if she weren't so lovable.

"How's the kid?" she asked.

"Zach's all better. Good Thanksgiving weekend?"

"Ate way too much, drank more, and moved as little as possible. It was amazing." When I laughed, she tipped her head toward the exit. "Coffee break? I need to get away from my computer for twenty minutes or I'll go crazy."

"Sure," I said. "Just let me finish this up and I'll meet you at the front desk."

A few minutes later, we were bundled up in our jackets and walking the couple of blocks that would take us to the Four Cups Café. It was a cute little coffee shop on Heart's Cove's main drag that boasted the best baked goods in the county. I was unsurprised to find it bustling with people, the three employees behind the desk clad in their usual pink T-shirts with glittery writing that proclaimed them *Heart's Cove Hotties*.

We got our drinks to go but ended up at one of the tables near the wall, where my eyes were drawn to a landscape painting of one of the cliffs on the coast. I'd been out there to take photos eons ago and they'd turned out pretty good. That had been a long time ago, though, before life and kids got in the way. My camera hadn't made it out of its case in years.

Laurel regaled me with details of the proposal she was working on for the refurbishment of the Heart's Cove Hotel. "I think it could turn out really good, but I don't know how serious the twins are about fixing the place up."

"Is it true they're getting a new manager in?"

"Those are the rumors," Laurel said with a shrug. She glanced over when a man called out toward the kitchen, and one of the owners—the redhead, Simone—came out with a giant smile on her face. She wrapped her arms around the man and gave him a kiss, then towed him toward the entrance with a glint in her eye. I watched the two of them disappear through a door just beside the plate-glass windows at the front of the café.

Laurel shook her head. "What I wouldn't give for a man who looks like that to look at me like *that*," she said.

Sean's handsome face popped into my head. Quiet, handsome Sean who went out of his way to bring me a portion of Thanksgiving stuffing. What I wouldn't give for *him* to look at me with one-tenth of the love and desire that Simone's husband had just shown her.

But Sean wasn't for me. I knew that. He might, however, be the perfect man for Laurel.

He was a single dad, which might be a dealbreaker for Laurel, who had no kids. But she was sassy and opinionated, and I thought she'd be a good foil for him. Besides, she loved fitness; she was always telling me about the gym and her weekend hikes and her winter ski trips.

They fit together in my head, and I had a feeling they'd get along. She'd tease him out of his shell in a way that I didn't think I could. He'd probably treat her like a queen.

I ran my finger along the lid of my coffee cup, and for a brief moment, considered saying nothing. We were coworkers, after all. It wasn't my place to set her up with anyone.

And, okay, there was a part of me that didn't want to set *him* up with anyone, either. It was ridiculous, really, because he'd pretty much asked me to follow through on the whole matchmaking thing before he left my place on Friday.

Yes, I was attracted to him. Who wouldn't be?

It wasn't like he would ever be interested in me. And he'd made that comment about my cooking—if he found someone half as good as me, he'd be happy.

But not *actually* me. Never me.

Laurel and Sean fit together because they were beautiful and outdoorsy and fit. I was a little too curvy to be fashionable, and, well, I was a mom. Everything I did, every choice I made was done with my kids in mind. There simply wasn't enough room in my life for romance, even if there were a man who saw me and saw what he liked. Which, I'd learned, wasn't likely.

I'd learned my lesson with Isaac. It was better to be on my own than to be dragged down by a man who didn't care.

So, even though I wanted to hoard Sean for myself like some kind of deranged dragon, I knew that he and I could never, ever, not in a million years, *ever* be together.

And that wasn't even considering that he was my brother's best friend.

It really was a never, ever, ever.

So I met Laurel's gaze and said, "Actually, an old friend just arrived in town, and as soon as I saw him, I thought about how the two of you would get along."

Laurel's brows lifted, and interest sparked in her gaze. "Go on."

"He's my brother's friend, and he has a son. Is that a deal breaker?"

"Not unless the son is a terror or there's serious baby mama drama."

I huffed out a laugh. "The son is wonderful, and I can try to find out about the mom."

"What does he do?"

"Carpenter. Just got a job with Grant Greene."

Laurel hummed. "Works with his hands."

"And they are nice hands," I informed her.

Laurel's lips curled into a smile as her sharp gaze read me like a book. "Are you sure you want to set us up, Lizzie? Sounds like you might have a thing for him."

I took a sip of my coffee and gave her a flat look. "I do not have a thing for him. He's my brother's best friend, and he's not interested in me in the slightest."

"But are you interested in him?"

"No," I lied and, seeing Laurel's eyebrow lift in a skeptical arch, I added, "but he is very handsome. I'm not blind."

She laughed and leaned back in her chair, shrugging. "Maybe. I haven't been on a date in a while. Couldn't hurt."

A gentle kind of grief swept through me, and I mercilessly beat it back. Sean was not for me. He never would be. The sooner I realized that, the better. "Great," I said, forcing a smile on my lips. "That's settled."

"I'm not making any promises," Laurel warned.

"Neither am I. And neither is he."

She nodded. "Good. Let's head back. I think I can face my computer again. Oh! And send me a picture. I want to see if he's as hot as you seem to think."

I grinned. "I'll work on getting one," I said, then gathered my things and followed her out the door.

THE OPPORTUNITY TO get that picture presented itself just a few hours later, when I waited outside the school gates for my kids to come out. A black pickup truck pulled up on the other side of the road, and I spotted Sean's chiseled profile through the driver's window. My mouth went dry.

Shaking myself, I lifted my arm in a wave when he met my gaze, then smiled when he made his way across the street toward me.

"I have news," I announced cheerfully.

His gaze was suspicious. "Oh?"

"My friend is interested."

"Interested in what?" His brow furrowed, and he watched me with green-blue eyes in a way that made me dizzy. There was something about being the focus of his attention, of being seen.

I knew I was torturing myself by indulging in this attraction. Still, it was hard to shake the giddiness of being so near to him.

"Interested in you," I answered, laughing.

His brows jumped. "That was quick."

"There's a dearth of devastatingly handsome men in this town," I said, which wasn't exactly true, but it fell out of my mouth regardless. "Not hard to get a woman interested."

"Devastatingly handsome, huh?" he said, leaning against my car as he crossed his arms. He wore a tan quilted workman's jacket that was open at the throat. When he tilted his head to pierce me with his eyes again, my knees went a little wobbly. "Is that your opinion, or hers?"

"Neither. It's just a fact."

Amusement seemed to glimmer in his gaze. "I'm not sure that's how it works, Lizzie."

"Are you trying to get me to admit that I think you're handsome?" I leaned a hip against my car to stop myself from keeling over. My heart thumped a little too hard.

"Maybe," he admitted. "Do you?"

"Fishing for compliments, Hardy?"

"Just trying to get a read on you." His lips tilted. Oh boy.

I tore my gaze away from him and stared at the front of the school. "Let me ask you this. When you look in the mirror, what do you see?"

Despite my best efforts, my gaze was drawn back to him as he rubbed the side of his jaw with a broad palm. "Depends on the day. Few more wrinkles than I'm used to. More silver in my beard these days."

I rolled my eyes. "Give me a break."

"What's that supposed to mean?"

I turned to face him and swept my hand up and down in his direction. My eyes bulged. He was a perfect male specimen, and those wrinkles and grays only made him hotter. "Do I really need to spell it out for you?"

"Maybe I want you to." That tilt returned to his lips.

My breath left me in a huff. "You're hot, Sean. Okay? Happy?"

His smile spread, and I felt a little woozy. "You sure know how to make a compliment sound like an insult, Lizzie."

"Stop calling me that." I scowled at him and turned back to the school so I didn't have to look at his stupid, handsome face. A face that looked real nice with a big smile on it. So nice it made my heart bang against my ribs, even though I knew he would never think of me that way. When he said my name, it made me feel things that I wasn't used to feeling. The roughness in his voice made my name sound positively sinful on his tongue, and I absolutely would not indulge how good it felt. No way.

"You want me to stop calling you by your name?"

"Yes."

"Why?"

"I just do." I crossed my arms and frowned, staring at the school's entrance like I could will it to open. I knew I was being ridiculous. I knew I probably sounded like a maniac. But I felt all out of sorts from being so close to him, and all he'd done was call me by my own name and do it with those lips and that mouth and those eyes.

Silence stretched between us for a few moments, until Sean said, quietly, "Have I done something to upset you?"

All the fight left me in a rush. I shook my head. "No. Long day. Sorry."

"If it makes you feel any better, I know I'm hot shit. I just wanted to hear you say it."

My lips twitched. "That does make me feel better. Thank you." I could feel his gaze on the side of my face, that focused attention that made me feel somehow prettier and more aware and more womanly and just *more*, but I kept my gaze facing forward and pretended not to.

More cars had arrived, and parents hung around the gates in clumps. A lot of the moms were sending curious gazes our way, and all the attention was beginning to get to me. So, when Cindy Reynolds detached herself from the clump of gorgeous moms standing not far away, I was both relieved for the distraction and annoyed at her for interrupting.

"Hi Liz," she greeted, then immediately turned to Sean. "I'm Cindy. My girl is in the fourth grade. Saw you here last week but didn't have time to say hello. You and your son just moved to town, right?"

When she stuck her hand out, Sean took it. I pretended that it didn't bother me, even though it did, which was another sign that I was going insane. I had no claim on this man. Actually, I had less than no claim. I *knew* he wasn't into me—he'd basically said so himself—and he was my brother's best and oldest friend. And on top of that, I was trying to set him up with someone else, and one of the options that had popped into my head when I'd first run into him at the pharmacy was the woman I currently wanted to decapitate for daring to shake his hand.

I was not having a good day.

They exchanged pleasantries, and the petty, awful part of me loved that Cindy didn't get any of those glittering looks or half-tilted smiles that I'd gotten from him. Which was a problem, because it wasn't like he'd meant anything by them in the first place. I knew he was quieter and more withdrawn than the average man. He was probably just more comfortable with me because he'd known me longer.

When the school doors opened and finally let out the tide of running students, I let out a relieved breath. Hazel found me first, her backpack hanging off her arms as she sprinted toward me with a smile on her face. She gave me a quick hug, said hi to Sean, and dove into the car. Zach wasn't far behind, and Cindy's daughter, thankfully, came out in the same rush.

When Mikey emerged and made his way to Sean, he dipped his chin at me in goodbye.

"Wait!" I said, and dug my phone out of my pocket. "For my

friend." I pointed it at him and clicked a photo, then spun it around so he could see.

He blinked at the screen, then at me.

"I'll send you a picture of my friend Laurel," I promised. "It's only fair."

He nodded, and I thought I saw a tiny spark of amusement in his gaze when we exchanged numbers, and we parted ways.

NINE

SEAN

I WAS SITTING in front of the TV on my own—Mikey had decided he wanted to play video games in his room—when my phone buzzed. I picked it up off the coffee table and saw an unfamiliar number, then unlocked the device to see a picture message. Lizzie texted like she talked, bubbly and sweet and without advance warning. First was a photo, then a slew of follow-up messages.

> **LIZZIE**
>
> As promised.

> **LIZZIE**
>
> Fair's fair.

> **LIZZIE**
>
> Laurel is the one on the left, in case it wasn't clear.

LIZZIE

It's Lizzie, by the way.

I clicked on the photo and huffed a laugh. There were only two people in the photo: Lizzie on the right, and another brunette on the left. I probably could have figured out who was who—and when I answered Lizzie to tell her as much, she sent me a string of emojis that only made partial sense.

I wasn't sure when I started smiling, but at that point I definitely was. I opened the photo again and zoomed in. The other brunette, Laurel, was pretty and slim, with her head tilted toward Lizzie's. Lizzie was wearing a figure-hugging black dress that hit just below the knee, her legs covered in sheer black tights that ended at shiny black ankle boots. Her hair fell in shiny brown waves around her shoulders. I'd never seen it down before, and I liked how dark and glossy it looked. I bet it was as soft as the rest of her, and my fingers flexed with the desire to feel it running through my fingers. The two of them were standing in a bar or restaurant, and the light was low, but Lizzie's smile still shone through the picture.

A notification popped up at the top of my screen.

LIZZIE

Thoughts????????

LIZZIE

That's the only photo I have of her, but
I could probably get another one.

I blinked. Right. I'd zoomed the photo in far enough that the other woman had been partially cropped out while I studied

Lizzie, so I panned over and had another look. Laurel was a good-looking woman. Her smile didn't have the same kind of brightness as Lizzie's, but she looked nice. Not sure she would've turned my head if I walked past her on the street, but that wasn't saying much. I hadn't been looking to date anyone recently; I'd been too focused on providing for Mikey.

> **LIZZIE**
>
> She likes going to the gym, does yoga, and hikes a lot in the summertime. No kids. She's an architect, super smart, very funny. You'll love her.

> **SEAN**
>
> You work fast. You sure your skills as a matchmaker haven't just been bullying people into dating and not taking no for an answer?

> **LIZZIE**
>
> Rude. She's interested, btw. I'll send you her number. I like her a lot, so don't make me look bad. Kids are screaming, gotta go.

Another message came through with Laurel's phone number. I stared at it for a while, then set my phone aside and rubbed my face with both hands. Being set up on a date wasn't an awful thing. It'd been years since I'd been out with a woman, and I wasn't opposed to meeting someone. This Laurel woman seemed to tick a lot of boxes.

So why did I not care about contacting her at all?

I let my eyes glaze over as I watched the TV for a while,

pretending I didn't know the answer to that question. Then I picked my phone up and probably made the wrong decision.

> SEAN
>
> How should I save your number in my phone?

It took Lizzie nearly thirty minutes to answer, but when she did, all she sent was a string of question marks.

> SEAN
>
> If I'm not supposed to use your name.

LIZZIE

Har har.

> SEAN
>
> Is that a childhood nickname?

LIZZIE

This better be your way of telling me that you and Laurel have hit it off already.

> SEAN
>
> You're relentless.

LIZZIE

One of my many talents.

My mind took about three milliseconds to go straight to the gutter, and my fingers moved before I could stop myself.

SEAN

What other talents have you been keeping hidden all these years?

I hit send, then I froze. Three dots appeared on the screen to show that Lizzie was typing a response. Then they disappeared. Then reappeared and kept flashing for an excruciating two full minutes. Then they disappeared again.

I swore quietly and tossed my phone aside before scrubbing my face with my hands. The light from the TV flickered over the room as I slumped down on the couch, and a gust of wind blew against the house. My phone remained still and silent.

What was I thinking? I couldn't flirt with Lizzie. And I *had* been flirting. I'd been thinking about those sparkling eyes and the curves I hadn't noticed when I'd first run into her. Or the cute way she glared at me outside the school, and how it made fizzy bubbles explode in my chest.

I was thinking about untying that red sweater she'd worn to Thanksgiving and letting my fingers drift over the edges of her bra. I'd been thinking about laying her down on my bed and watching her back arch while I tasted her. I'd been thinking about how my cock ached to feel the heated clasp of her.

But I couldn't have her.

She was my best friend's little sister. Worse, I'd just moved back to Heart's Cove, and the whole point of coming here was to try to build a more robust support system.

How would Aaron react if he found out I was texting his sister? He'd probably punch me in the face; he'd been protective of her when we were younger. He didn't seem to appreciate her now, but that didn't mean he'd want her dating the likes of me.

Indulging this attraction would only get me in trouble. Maybe contacting Laurel was a good idea. That way, I could get Lizzie out of my mind and get this tension out of my system. But instead of grabbing my phone and making contact with the other woman, I flicked off the television and made my way upstairs.

I'd rented this three-bedroom house for a year's lease and hired movers to get all our stuff up here in one truck. The kitchen was half-unpacked and most of the furniture was in place, but boxes still gathered in the corners of every room. Mikey had unpacked his clothing and made his bed, and a few of his favorite toys were lined up along the wall, as if waiting for the appropriate shelf on which they could be displayed.

He'd been excited about the move, but it had been hard to pull him out of school and away from his friends. Now that we were here, I wondered if I'd made the right decision. All this upheaval, all these boxes, the packing and unpacking...for what?

I couldn't mess it up. He only had me. I couldn't afford to make big mistakes when my son was involved.

He pulled his headphones off when he saw me in the doorway. His game froze on the screen when he paused it, and he arched his brows at me.

"Almost bedtime, buddy."

Mikey's shoulders slumped, but he nodded and got up. He brushed past me on his way to the bathroom, then paused at the doorway. "Hey, Dad?"

"Yeah?"

"Can we get a Christmas tree this year?"

My lungs collapsed on themselves and cut off my breath.

The discomfort stopped the immediate refusal from leaving my lips. Instead, I swallowed hard, inhaled, and forced myself to sound as calm as possible when I said, "Your mom does Christmas, Mikey. You know that."

The look he gave me was a punch to the gut. He nodded, lips turned down. "Okay. I just... It was fun decorating the tree with Zach and Hazel. I thought..." He trailed off and shook his head. "Never mind."

When he'd disappeared into the bathroom, I leaned against the wall and closed my eyes. The coming month would be excruciating. It always was. Memories pressed on me from every direction, each and every one of them like a razor blade across my chest. I wanted to be the best father I could be, and I wanted to give Mikey the world.

But could I give him this?

Could I pretend to put on a happy face? Put decorations up with him and celebrate a holiday that had only brought me misery?

TEN

LIZZIE

HAZEL HAD BEEN CAST as one of the candy canes in the school's holiday play, and I'd volunteered to help with the production. The director had asked me to help with set design and costumes, so after work, I headed to the school to do my time. I was neck-deep in red glitter and cardboard when Hazel came running over to me, a bright smile on her face.

"Mom! We learned the candy cane dance!"

Kneeling on the hard linoleum floor with the beginnings of a piece of decor in front of me, I leaned back on my heels and smiled. "What's the candy cane dance?"

"This." Hazel demonstrated with a series of wiggles and hops, and I couldn't help but grin.

"Very nice," I said, then nodded to the director. Astrid, the art teacher, had volunteered to direct the play while the regular theater teacher was on maternity leave. Astrid was an exuberant woman who always had a smile on her face. She came over to compliment Hazel on her hard work, which I appreciated.

"Should be a good production this year," Astrid said with a bright smile. Her dark-blond hair curled in ringlets, and her blue eyes sparkled under the auditorium lights. "And I so appreciate you helping out with the set."

"I do what I can," I told her, stretching out my back as I heaved myself to my feet.

"Hazel is a hoot."

"You can say that again."

"She's whipped the candy canes into shape without me having to say a word," Astrid admitted. "And the candy cane dance?"

"What about it?"

"She came up with it," Astrid said, laughing. "Choreographed the whole thing, taught the other kids, and then pitched it to me today."

I couldn't help the smile that bloomed over my lips. "Sounds like my daughter. She doesn't take no for an answer."

We exchanged a few pleasantries as Hazel chatted with her friends, and I let my shoulders relax. Astrid was exuberant and funny. She talked with her hands and wasn't shy to give me a quick hug and a squeeze on my upper arms as she told me goodbye.

I liked her, and she was kind to Hazel. Ever since Thanksgiving, it felt like I had to keep reminding myself of all the good things in my life. The people that made my life better, the teachers that cared, the family that stuck around when things got tough.

But I still felt tired.

I gathered my things, trailing red glitter everywhere. My entire body ached. I couldn't wait to get home, get dinner done, and collapse on the couch. It had been a long day, as most days seemed to be.

Laurel had told me that Sean finally texted her this morning. Pretending to be excited for her had sapped my energy, and it hadn't even been ten o'clock in the morning when she'd told me about it.

Hazel hummed and hopped beside me as we made our way out of the theater room. Zach had joined a computer club, so Hazel and I picked him up from the classroom where the club was held and headed out. The end was nigh. It was only Tuesday, but every minute I spent on my feet felt like an eternity. I was digging through my purse for my car keys when my phone rang. My brother's name flashed on the screen.

"Hey," I said, pinning the phone between my shoulder and my ear while I hunted for my keys.

"Hey, Lizzie. Are you busy tonight?"

The movement of my hands stilled. I blinked at my distorted reflection in the car windows and bit back a groan. "Why?"

"Emily has a work thing, and I've got an appointment. You mind watching the kids for an hour or two?"

Visions of a quick dinner and a leisurely hour spent zoning out on the couch disintegrated. For a brief moment, I considered saying no. Aaron did this kind of thing all the time. He'd call me in an emergency and expect me to drop everything to head over and babysit for him. Most days, I barely got a thank you from him, never mind reciprocity.

Up until that exact moment, I hadn't realized how much that bothered me.

My fingers finally wrapped around the hard plastic of my car fob. "Your babysitter can't make it?"

"It's not enough notice," he said, which wasn't exactly an answer, and didn't address the fact that he was calling *me* on short notice too. I'd probably been his first call. "Please, Lizzie? I'm supposed to head out and Emily said she won't be home until eight. You can bring Zach and Hazel."

I rolled my eyes. That was generous of him. "Fine," I said. "Be there in a few."

Pressing the button to unlock the car, I called the kids back over from where they'd wandered to the playground and loaded them into the car. My lower back ached something awful, and my head had begun to pound. But the kids were in good spirits and when I told them we'd be seeing their cousins for the evening, their smiles eased some of the mounting bitterness that had crept into my mood.

When I got to my brother's house, there was a familiar truck parked in the street. I slid in behind it and quickly glanced at myself in the visor mirror, sighing. I had glitter all over my face, and my attempts to wipe it off only smeared it further. Once again, I'd be seeing Sean looking like a mess.

I didn't know why I cared. My own vanity had left me years ago, but I seemed to be increasingly aware of just how frumpy I looked all the time. Maybe the fact that Sean was a single parent and he managed to be fit and dashing had something to do with it.

Besides, Laurel told me they'd set up a time to get dinner and drinks together on the weekend. So if there had been any doubt in my mind about whether or not he'd been flirting with me through his messages last night, those doubts had been thoroughly extinguished.

But I squared my shoulders and painted a smile on my face, then herded the kids up to the front door. I knocked and let myself in, then followed the noise to the open kitchen/living area. Sean leaned against the kitchen island, looking lithe and muscular. He lifted a bottle of beer to his lips as my brother did the same, and I planted my hands on my hips and glared at my brother.

"An appointment?" I demanded.

Aaron glanced over. "Hey, Lizzie. Did I say appointment? I meant I was supposed to go out and see some old buddies of ours play at the Cedar Grove. Sean hasn't seen any of those guys in almost a decade."

"Uh-huh," I told him, and the ache in my lower back pulsed.

"The kids haven't eaten yet, but I've left some money for pizza. Don't tell Emily."

"I think she'll figure it out when she walks in and smells it."

My brother grinned. "I meant don't tell her it was my idea."

"I'm not taking that fall for you," I told him, and dropped my bag on a nearby chair. "Hi, Sean."

"Hey. Thanks for watching Mikey. If I'd known you were doing it under false pretenses, I wouldn't have agreed."

At least he sounded sincere.

"Lizzie doesn't mind," my brother said. "Do you?"

"What's one more?" I said, forcing lightness into my voice. All the reasons that I shouldn't be resentful flooded my brain in a familiar rhythm. I *did* love the kids, and Sean had just gotten back to town. A couple more hours on duty wasn't the end of the world. Hazel and Zach would be happy. Aaron was family. I didn't mind being here, even though I had been looking forward to my hot date with my couch.

The tiny part of me that had gotten upset about the stuffing at Thanksgiving made herself known, pointing out that the number of favors I did for Aaron seemed to eclipse the number of favors he did for me. When did *I* get a break? When did *I* get to have an evening at a local bar with a few friends?

I squashed the thought and gave Sean a tired smile. "Heard you and Laurel are meeting up on the weekend."

"Figured it was better than feeling your wrath for leaving her hanging."

I snorted. "And don't you forget it." I grinned, then felt it fade. "She's great. You'll love her."

His eyes held mine for a moment, and I felt...

I don't know what I felt. A little zing that went down my spine and settled somewhere in my gut. I felt like he was trying to tell me something, like there was a layer to his look that I hadn't seen in a man's eyes in a long, long time. That he might be seeing me. Really *seeing* me.

I wasn't just the default babysitter. I wasn't just Zach and Laurel's mom, or Aaron's little sister. I was *me*, and I was worth looking at just for the sake of it.

Then he cleared his throat and straightened, blinking those

beautiful eyes away from mine and toward my brother. The two of them said goodbye to their kids and made their way toward the front door, and I stood there like a piece of furniture.

A few hours later, with the kids (and me) full of pizza and plonked in front of a Christmas movie, I was relieved to hear the front door open. Emily needed a few minutes to get herself settled after work, so I leaned an elbow against the couch arm and watched the end of the movie with the kids, then gathered Zach and Hazel and finally took them home.

When I got in bed, exhaustion dragged at me, but I stared at the darkened shape of the ceiling fan above my bed for a long time. In the quiet of the house, with just me in my big bed, I felt very sad and very alone.

But that was ridiculous. My life was rich, and full, and *good*.

Gritting my teeth, I tried to distract myself. I thought about my to-do list for tomorrow. I thought about the fact that I was almost out of laundry detergent. I thought about the Christmas cookies I was planning on making on the weekend.

And I thought about Sean.

My thoughts ran toward him like a dog who'd just slipped the leash. The look he'd given me in my brother's kitchen had made me remember what it was like to feel like a woman. That, combined with the borderline flirtatious text he'd sent me about my "skills," had my pulse picking up. I thought about his rough, working-man's hands on my arms, and then—yeah, then I was distracted.

I don't know when my hand dipped below the waistband of my pajamas, but by the time I started touching myself, there was no going back. Besides, it was just me, myself, and I, wasn't it? Couldn't I think about a big, broad, strong man draping his body over mine? Couldn't I wonder how it would feel to have him press my thighs open and look at me like he had earlier today?

I wasn't hurting anyone. Maybe I needed this—a quick release. I could get it out of my system and go back to the way things had been just a couple weeks ago.

The wetness between my legs surprised me. A sigh slipped through my lips as I touched myself, imagining rougher hands in place of mine. I wanted to feel the stretch of him at my entrance. Wanted to feel his skin against mine, all that hard, naked flesh pressing me into the mattress while I panted his name.

My free hand slid up to cup my own breast. I closed my eyes and flushed at the thought of kneeling before him and taking him in my mouth. I wanted him to say my name again. I wanted him to be desperate when he did, to feel the tug of his fingers on my hair.

I came in a rush, thinking about the sound of his voice and the look in his eyes if I pushed him down to his back and sank down on top of him. I could almost feel the touch of his hands on my hips, rocking me to orgasm, and release went through me in a flash. It felt so good. *So* good. Nearly as good as the real thing.

Panting, I curled onto my side and waited for my heartbeat to slow. When my thoughts knitted themselves back together enough that I could think in full sentences again, only one thing became clear: I should not have done that.

Mostly because I wanted to do it again.

And I wanted the real thing.

I jumped when my phone rang. Scrambling to grab it from the nightstand, I gasped at the name on the screen—and swore.

ELEVEN

SEAN

LIZZIE ANSWERED on the third ring. "Sean? Is everything okay?" She was breathless, her voice strained.

I frowned. "Everything's fine. Bad time?"

Her voice was rough around the edges when she replied, "No, you're fine. I just got into bed."

I hummed, liking the thought of Lizzie in bed. I liked the intimate sound of her voice right now. I wondered how she'd sound after being thoroughly fucked, if her voice would get drowsy and sated, or raspy, or thin. I wanted to know exactly how my name would sound at the peak of her orgasm, and how—

I squeezed my eyes shut and pushed the thoughts aside. She wasn't for me. I had a date with another woman lined up. Thinking carnal thoughts about my best friend's little sister had to be some kind of punishable offense.

"What's up?" she asked after a breath, sounding more like herself.

I marshaled my thoughts into order and slapped the horny part of my brain back with a stick. "I just wanted to say thanks for tonight. Aaron invited me out to the bar, and he said he had a babysitter lined up. I didn't know it was you."

"He has a babysitter built in, more like," Lizzie answered dryly. "I'm always only one call away."

"You could've said no."

Lizzie made a noncommittal noise. "Well, it was no problem. Mikey and Zach seem to be getting along, and I got to have a night off cooking."

Somehow, babysitting five kids didn't seem like a night off to me, but I didn't mention it out loud. Instead, I took a deep breath and broached the second reason I'd called. "I was also calling because..."

She shifted, and I imagined rucked sheets and plush pillows. I wondered what she wore to sleep. Something silky and soft and pink, that I'd enjoy peeling off to reveal one inch of her skin at a time—

I cleared my throat. "I have a favor to ask. But you can say no. I don't want you to feel like you have to agree."

"Okay." Suspicion laced the word. "What is it?"

I took a deep breath and sat up on the couch, glancing down the hall to peek at the bottom of the stairs. Mikey was in bed, and I hadn't heard any creaks or footsteps that would tell me he'd snuck out of his room. "Mikey asked me if we could get a Christmas tree this year," I finally said.

"Right," Lizzie said. "Do you... Is that not something you normally do?"

"His mom does Christmas," I explained.

"Every year?" Shock vibrated in Lizzie's voice.

I cleared my throat. "Just the way the custody agreement shook out. But after seeing how happy it made him to decorate your tree, I was thinking that maybe it would be good to have our own holiday. You know, the two of us. Even if it isn't on the actual day."

"Oh, Sean," Lizzie said, and I could just picture her smile. "Of course. You need help? What do you need me to do?"

"I, well..." I laughed self-consciously and scrubbed the short hair on my scalp. "I'll be honest, I don't know the first thing about shopping for a Christmas tree. If you could help me out with a list, or tell me where I should get one..."

"Real or fake?"

"Excuse me?"

"The tree. Do you want a real one or a fake one?"

"Oh. Um. Real?"

"Great! There's a man who sells them just outside of town in a big grocery store parking lot. Zach and Hazel are actually hanging out with my parents tomorrow evening, so I could drive out there with you uh! But you probably want to do this just you and Mikey, right? I can just send you the location. And you probably need ornaments. You think Mikey will want to choose them?"

"I was kind of thinking it could be a surprise. Have the tree and the ornaments at our place, and then Mikey can decorate it."

"Perfect. I can call my parents and ask if they mind watching him tomorrow night, and then we can dart over, get the tree, choose some ornaments, and have everything ready for him when he comes home."

My heart squeezed. She made it sound so easy. The hot coal burning in my chest told me that this would be uncomfortable, with a tide of memories already trying to flood my brain, but it would be worth it to see my son smile. "Your parents wouldn't mind? I've been relying on you guys so much since I got back."

"That's what family's for," Lizzie answered brightly. "Let me call my mom and I'll text you. This is going to be so much fun!"

I couldn't have stopped the smile from spreading on my face if I tried. "Thanks, Lizzie."

"Talk to you soon!"

We hung up, and I slumped down on the sofa, exhausted. It was the right thing to do, to put myself second in order to make my kid happy. But it still made my body feel stretched with tension. Leaning into the Christmas spirit wasn't something I'd done in a long, long time.

Still, when Lizzie sent a text a few minutes later saying her parents would be happy to watch Mikey, I let out a long breath.

I was getting a Christmas tree for the first time since my divorce. And I was doing it with Lizzie Butler by my side.

I would *not* mess this up. There was more at stake than just my lust for a woman it'd taken me forty-odd years to notice. There was her family's support, my place in this community, and my son's happiness.

Still, a part of me mourned what couldn't be. Those sunlit

smiles, soft curves, and dark eyes. The lightness in my chest whenever she met my gaze. The way my heart seemed to have started beating again for the first time since my marriage fell apart.

But if there was one thing I had to remember, it was that Lizzie wasn't for me.

TWELVE

SEAN

LIZZIE WAS BUNDLED up in a puffy jacket, a thick scarf, and a hat with a gigantic pompom. Her cheeks were red with the cold, and she smiled at me as I pulled up in front of her house. Then she wiggled the end of a power cord at me and made a big show of plugging it into the outdoor outlet on the side of her house.

Lights blazed on her eaves and around her windows, with lit-up icicles hanging from the gutters. She ran down the path toward me, practically skipping, and I couldn't help but laugh in response. My window whirred as I rolled it down, leaning an arm against the frame.

"What do you think?" she asked, spinning around to take in her work. "It took me four hours." She gazed at the lights. They reflected into her eyes, and I watched the glow of them against her skin. For a second—just a moment—all the negative memories associated with the holidays faded, and I just watched the way Lizzie's smile lit up her face. My chest felt like a warm, crackling fire, like the coziness of a fuzzy blanket and a soft woman snuggled in the crook of my shoulder.

Then her words sank in. "You did this by yourself?"

She nodded. "Uh-huh. I work half days on Thursdays, so I figured it was the perfect time, especially with the kids hanging out with Grandma and Grandpa after school. They're going to be so excited when they drive up." She beamed at me. "You inspired me with your talk of surprises and happy kids."

My heart gave a lurch. "You could have called me."

"Weren't you at work?"

"Well, yeah, but..." I looked at the eaves. Putting those lights up was a two-person job. "What if you'd fallen off your ladder?"

She grinned. "Don't worry. I've learned to live without a big strong man in my life for this long. I can manage a few Christmas lights. Speaking of which, you ready to head out?"

I nodded. She walked around to the other side of the truck and got in, then directed me down the road and through town.

"Thanks again," I told her. "I feel like I owe you about a dozen favors by now."

She smiled and shook her head. "It's my pleasure. I love Christmas tree shopping. I ended up getting the artificial one because I just couldn't manage hauling the kids and the tree around on my own every year, then dealing with getting rid of it and cleaning up, but I miss doing this. It used to be one of my favorite holiday activities. Mikey's going to be thrilled. You sure you didn't want to take him along?"

I massaged the steering wheel and took the turn that Lizzie pointed out while I mulled over my answer. The truth was, I hadn't told Mikey that I'd be going Christmas tree shopping. I hadn't wanted to get his hopes up in case I chickened out. But all I said was, "I wanted to make sure I could still get one before making any promises."

"Oh, there'll be lots," Lizzie said with a wave of her hand. "They won't run out for weeks. We might have to make a few stops for ornaments, but we'll manage. You really have *no* holiday decorations?"

I could feel her gaze on the side of my face, and for reasons beyond my reckoning, my mouth began to move. "Christmas was never a good time for me growing up. I put on a happy face when Mikey was young, but...yeah. Not really my thing. My dad... Well, before he left, he made sure the holidays were full of stress. And then my mom—you know."

"I remember," she said softly. "I'm sorry."

"Thanks," I said. My mom's death had rocked me, and it had happened right before Christmas after a short, brutal fight with ovarian cancer. That year was a blur. Every year since then was marked by it. "Anyway, when my ex and I divorced, I agreed to give her every Christmas in our custody schedule."

Lizzie was quiet for a beat. "I'm sorry," she finally said.

"Don't be. It worked out fine. I get him most of the time anyway, so it seemed like a fair trade."

"So this is a big deal, huh?" She pointed to the parking lot where a fenced-in area had been set up with dozens of Christmas trees displayed on wooden trestles for sale.

I pulled in and found a spot, then stared at the forest of pine. "It's a pretty big deal."

When I met Lizzie's gaze, her eyes were shining. "You're a

good father, Sean. I can tell by the way Mikey behaves and the way you two interact. And this? Putting your kid ahead of your own pain?" Her smile was a little sad. "I get that. Big time."

My throat was tight. "Thanks," I croaked with a nod. "That means a lot."

And it did. I'd been a father for a decade, but sometimes it still felt like I was barely keeping the two of us alive. Lizzie seemed to spin a dozen plates for fun while managing her life and kids. She never broke a sweat. To have her notice and compliment my parenting...it made me want to know more about her. It made me want to let her in, so she could know more about me.

"Shall we?" she asked, smiling.

"Lead the way."

Her jeans hugged the generous curve of her ass as she marched toward the Christmas trees, and my gaze was drawn to the movement of it. I had to stop. Even asking her for this favor had been questionable, when I was supposed to be Aaron's oldest friend and he wouldn't want me anywhere near his little sister.

Then again, Aaron didn't seem to see his sister at all. In fact, he seemed to use her without really appreciating her for who she was.

The thought felt like a betrayal of my friendship with him, so I shoved it aside and followed Lizzie. She waved at the man sawing off the bottom of a tree next to a trailer, then stared at the rows of evergreen trees and took a deep breath. When she met my gaze, her smile made my chest feel lighter. It was impossible not to feel good around this woman, not to get caught up in the magic that seemed to cling to her.

"Love that smell," she said, then clapped her glove-clad hands. "Okay. Douglas fir." She pointed to the sign at the start of a row and tilted her head from side to side. "Hit and miss, honestly. They can be nice, but sometimes when the branches fall they have these massive gaps that you don't expect. Real *Charlie Brown* kind of trees, which can be fun, but I'm guessing you're not going for an ironic tree this year. What's your budget?"

"Whatever it takes."

"Dangerous words," she said, eyes glinting, then waved me onward. She was like a tiny, curvy, holiday-fueled military general, and I felt like I'd follow her anywhere. "Fraser fir, gorgeous. Canaan, beautiful. Balsam, another option," she announced. "Anything catch your eye?"

It all looked like a sea of green needles to me, but I took a deep breath and lifted a tree off the nearest trestle, shaking it out a little so we could get a look at its shape.

"Big gap between the branches on this side." Lizzie made a buzzer sound then formed an X with her arms. "Next!"

I laughed and put the tree back where I'd taken it. We did the same routine half a dozen times, me displaying the trees and Lizzie proclaiming them inadequate, until I reached for a particularly tall tree that had been leaning against the fence.

I realized I was grinning when Lizzie stopped considering the tree like our lives depended on the decision and finally met my gaze. Those dark eyes of hers sparkled, and her lips curled into a witchy smile.

I was desperate to kiss her. I wasn't even sure it was a lust-fueled urge at this point. It was just a pull in my gut that made me want to wrap my arms around her and taste her lips. I wanted to hold all that happiness and cheer and sunshine in my arms just to feel what it would be like to call her mine.

I wanted to do a whole lot more than that, and it killed me that I couldn't. I'd never be able to. Not when the only true friend I had would kill me if I did.

My father left when I was a young teen, my mother had passed when I turned nineteen, and then I'd left Heart's Cove and all its memories behind. I'd gotten used to being on my own —until Melody. Until I thought I'd found companionship and stability.

And look how that turned out.

So I couldn't lose sight of the real reason I was here. I was here to reconnect with my aunts and with the one family that had been there for me through thick and thin: the Butlers. Aaron, and to a smaller extent, Kyle, Lizzie, and their parents, had made those tumultuous teenage years bearable. Indulging in some ill-conceived lust with Aaron's little sister would put my entire support system in jeopardy. Where would I go if I torched the last stable relationship I had? How would I explain it to Mikey? How could I call myself a good father if I put my own needs ahead of the stability and community I wanted to nurture for him?

And even if it wasn't for Aaron, Lizzie had set me up on a date with another woman. Even today, with the lights glowing on her house, she'd just reminded me that she didn't need a man in her life. She was busy with kids and work and everything else. Who was I to bulldoze my way into her schedule? Who was I to think she even wanted me the way I wanted her?

"It's big," she finally said as she studied the tree I held, and I pulled my thoughts back to the task at hand.

Well. I tried. What actually came out of my mouth was, "I get that a lot."

Her cheeks grew redder, and Lizzie let out a snort and a giggle as she shook her head. She tried to give me a stern look. "Save it for your date this weekend," she chided.

But I didn't want to. I wanted to hear that laugh again and again and again until the scent of evergreen trees reminded me of Lizzie instead of death and drunkenness and broken relationships.

"Here," Lizzie said. "Let me hold it, and you take a look."

Dutifully, I waited until she'd grabbed the trunk, and I took a few steps back to admire the choice. It was tall, but its branches were lush and had that perfect conical shape. Lizzie stood there, a hopeful expression on her face, as I walked over to the other side and inspected the back of the tree.

And the back of Lizzie. She glanced over her shoulder and arched her brows.

Dragging my gaze back to the tree, I cleared my throat. "I think that's the one."

"Yay!"

"You folks ready?" The man by the trailer ambled up to us and made the easiest sale of his life. He trimmed the bottom of the trunk with a few neat swipes of his hand saw, and then I hauled the tree to my truck and placed it in the bed.

Lizzie leaned against the sides of the bed and helped me tie the load down, her smile irrepressible. "Excellent choice. For a rookie, you did good."

I grinned. "Let's go get some ornaments."

We went to Target, and I let Lizzie have her way with my credit card. She asked me about color schemes and decor styles, took one look at my face, and told me she'd handle it. By the time we hauled the gigantic bags full of Christmas paraphernalia to the truck, I'd almost forgotten that I hated the holiday.

As we drove back toward Heart's Cove, I relaxed into my seat and let out a long breath. That hadn't been so bad. And I couldn't wait to see the look on Mikey's face. I should've done this years ago, even if Melody got to spend the actual day with him. Put my son ahead of my pain, as Lizzie had said. I glanced over at her, wondering what pain she was smothering for the sake of her kids.

"I'll set up the tree stand while you bring it inside," Lizzie said when I pulled up to my house.

"Done." I tossed her the keys and went to work on the ropes. A few minutes later, I was dragging a tree through the front door and raining Canaan fir needles all over my stoop and entryway. I hauled it into the living room and found Lizzie kneeling by a tree stand, her jacket stripped off to reveal a tight-fitting top that wrapped around her body and tied at the side.

My mouth watered.

From where I stood, I could see an expanse of chest that I had no business seeing. She was *lush*. All soft and round and bitable. All thoughts of being loyal to my best friend and giving

Lizzie space fled from my mind, because there was a beautiful woman kneeling in my living room like an offering from a carnal god.

Her bra was cream and had a lace trim. I could see the way it shaped her breasts when she bent over and struggled with the tree stand, her movements making all that flesh jiggle and bounce.

I was hard. Harder than I'd been in a long, long time. Hard enough that if she glanced at my crotch, she'd probably be able to tell.

And I didn't care, because I wanted her.

"Nearly there," she told me, and I blinked back to myself.

Shifting the tree into the living room, I cleared my throat and averted my gaze.

Lizzie sat back as she looked up, pushing a strand of hair from her forehead. "That thing looks a lot bigger when we're indoors." She paused and stuck her finger up at me. "And don't you dare make a dirty joke about that, mister."

I was so far beyond dirty jokes, it wasn't even funny. I managed a smile, then levered the tree to a vertical position, wincing when it scraped against the ceiling.

"Didn't you say you had ten-foot ceilings?"

I looked up at the tree, its top branch bent against the ceiling. "I might have been wrong about that."

Lizzie snorted. "Well, that branch is probably long and skinny enough that we can trim it and hide the evidence with the tree topper instead of sawing the base off. Let's just get it in the stand and deal with it later."

I nodded, unable to contribute meaningfully to the conver-

sation because a lot of my blood was keeping my erection throbbing behind my zipper. Every time Lizzie moved, I saw a new
angle of her that I wanted to touch and lick and caress. When
she got closer, the scent of fir mingled with the scent of her, and
blood rushed south once more.

But I managed to lift the tree into the stand.

"Okay, try to hold it straight," she told me, directing me with
her hands to angle the trunk this way and that. When she was
satisfied, Lizzie slithered onto the floor on her stomach and
reached for the tree stand to secure the trunk.

And I must've turned into some kind of degenerate piece
of shit, because all I could do was stare at the way her hips
moved when she shimmied her way closer to the tree. I stared
at her lower back when she arched it, mesmerized by the strip
of skin that became exposed when she moved. Her jeans dug
into the flesh at her sides, and my throat got tight. There was a
little bulge of flesh above the waistband, and all I wanted to do
was put my lips to it. I wanted to grip it with my hands so I
could feel that softness fill my palm while I pulled her on top
of me.

Everything about her was pure sex. The way she moved.
The way she was shaped. The way her clothes clung to the
curves of her body.

The tree stand had three screws that needed to be tightened
against the trunk to hold the tree in place. Her thighs spread
slightly as she tried to reach around the trunk to get at the back
of the stand for the third screw, and she propped herself up on
her knees to arch her back even more. Her shirt slid down to
expose another inch of back.

I wanted to take her just like this. Notch myself between those thick thighs and drive my cock inside her—

My heart beat so hard I felt lightheaded. All I could see was that soft, round shape of her body positioned in a way that I had no business seeing.

And I should've looked away. I really, really should've.

But I couldn't.

Her thighs were thick, and my fingers tingled with the need to trace the crease between them and the generous curve of her ass. I wanted to see just how far my hands could span across all that flesh. I wanted to feel how soft and warm she was. I wanted to spread those thighs even wider so I could run my thumbs—

"Are you sure you're still holding it straight? The trunk is moving."

I squeezed my eyes shut. "Sorry."

"Almost done with the last screw. Just hold tight."

"Yep," I forced out through pinched lips, my eyes slicing open and immediately dropping to the shape of her. I could bend her over, just like this, and lick her until she screamed. Then when she was wet and ready and begging, I'd—

"All done!" Lizzie called out, and I tore my gaze away from her to stare at a spot on the wall. She emerged from under the tree red-faced and smiling, her clothes and hair in disarray, looking rumpled and delicious. A quick glance told me the neckline of her sweater had dipped, revealing the lacy trim of her bra.

I was a complete depraved asshole for thinking these things when she was just trying to do a good deed. But why did she have to look so damn good while she did it?

"Let go of it and we'll see if I did a good job."

I did as she said because I was unable to form a coherent thought or sentence by myself, and following her instructions seemed like as good a plan as any. Stepping away from the tree, I let my gaze trace the shape of her body one last time before turning toward the tree. It was upright, though it was nowhere near straight.

"Maybe once we trim the top it'll stop leaning so much," Lizzie suggested, ever the optimist.

I nodded. "Yeah," I managed, which had to be some kind of miracle performed by the synapses of my brain. Actual speech was beyond me. Most of my attention was still focused on the woman to my left. Her shoulder brushed against my arm, and a waft of her scent hit me. Functioning would be difficult for the next little while unless I got a grip on myself.

"Okay. Have you got any shears? Otherw—" A gasp tore out of Lizzie's mouth as she threw her arms out toward the tree.

The tree was no longer just crooked—it was leaning. In fact, it was full-on falling.

And it was going to hit Lizzie in the face unless I did something about it. Acting on instinct, I knocked her arms out of the way and shoved at the tree, but those nice, full branches I'd admired in the Christmas tree yard got in my way, and the tree stand provided the perfect pivot point for the tree to slip from my grasp and continue on its mission to land on top of Lizzie.

So I changed tack. I let go of the tree and wrapped my arms around Lizzie. I cradled her head and tackled her to the ground, grunting as ten feet of Canaan fir landed across my spine.

Lizzie wheezed, spitting green needles out of her mouth.

"You okay?" I rasped.

She opened her eyes and met my gaze. My hand was still cradling the back of her head, and our faces were only two inches apart. "I'm okay. Kind of trapped."

I grunted. "Stop wiggling." Because her wiggling was making the tree scratch against my back, and it was also reminding me that the blood flow in my body was still undergoing some significant irregularities. She was as soft as I'd imagined, and the feel of her body beneath mine was the stuff of fantasies. My free hand was propped on the ground just above her shoulder and I had put as much distance between our bodies as possible, but we were still touching from chest to hip.

Her knees fell open and came up along my thighs as she planted her feet on the ground. "Just trying to—"

Her hips cradled mine like they were made to hold me. The gasp that slipped from her lips was soft, and I knew she'd felt what I'd been trying to hide.

My cheeks flamed as I lifted my hips as far as they'd go, the evergreen tree brushing against my ass. "Sorry," I rasped as I stared at her ear.

"It's not... I'm..." She stopped talking and ceased that incessant wiggling.

I cleared my throat. "I'm, um. Yeah. Sorry." I forced myself to look at her face.

She blinked at me once. Twice. Three times. Those soft lips parted on an inhale, and she dipped her chin. "It happens," she said, but her voice trembled the tiniest bit.

I huffed a laugh. "Twenty-five years ago, maybe."

"Right," came her whisper.

We lay like that without moving for a few long moments. She didn't move toward me—but she didn't tell me to get off. Her eyes were wide and dark, and I lost myself in them. After a second, I lowered my hips back down and was rewarded with the feel of her trembling breath skating across my cheek.

She made the smallest movement with her hips. It was barely a twitch, could hardly qualify as a movement at all, but it sent fire racing up my spine as if she'd reached between us and grabbed my cock with her dainty, red-painted fingers.

I pressed myself into her and reveled in her trembling gasp. Her hips made another twitch, this one longer, slower. She rubbed herself against me, slowly, almost tentatively, and all I could do was respond in kind. We moved in millimeters. We breathed in silent exhalations. The heat of her blazed against me through our clothing, and all I wanted to know was how it would feel to plunge myself inside her.

Unable to resist, I ground myself against her fully. Her thighs pressed against the outside of my hips, pinning me there, and it was nearly enough to send me over the edge. I wanted her so much my vision was fuzzy around the edges. I didn't care about the tree, or the decorations, or the fact that we were on my living room floor.

If she gave me the slightest sign, I'd have her naked and spread beneath me in an instant.

"Lizzie..." I grated—then froze when I heard a car engine outside.

Lizzie jerked under me, inhaled sharply, then shoved at my

shoulders to get me off. The tree went tumbling beside us as I rolled off her, and she shimmied her way across the floor so she could stand, her chest heaving with every breath, her eyes wide as she met my gaze.

Then the front door opened, and Mikey called out, "Da-ad! I'm home!"

THIRTEEN

LIZZIE

TEN SECONDS AGO, there'd been a boner pressed up against my crotch. Ten seconds ago, I'd been imagining how good it would feel to have said boner all up inside me. My mind had conjured up all the images I'd told myself were a bad idea, the ones that had made me shiver with pleasure with my hand between my thighs.

Now there was an eleven-year-old kid stomping his way into the living room, sheer joy painted on his features, and I was trying to come to grips with whatever the hell was going on in my body.

I knew I was attracted to Sean; after all, I had a pulse.

But I hadn't known that *Sean* was attracted to *me*.

I took a deep, gasping breath and painted a smile on my face. My mother poked her head into the living room, saw me, and smiled. "Oh! You're here."

"We just got back." I gestured to the tree and avoided

looking at the man currently ruffling his son's hair. "Sean picked a tree."

Simple, obvious sentences were good when most of my body was busy frantically trying to slow down my pulse.

"How wonderful," Mom said. "Why is it on the ground?"

I cleared my throat and dragged my gaze to the tree, then to Sean. He reached down, picked it up, and straightened it as much as he could, but the whole trunk listed dangerously to the side.

"I'll hold it," I told him. "You do the tree stand."

There was a tiny twitch of his eyebrow, but Sean nodded and got on his knees. I glanced down at him and away.

"It's *amazing*," Mikey exclaimed, fingers stroking the evergreen needles with awed reverence. He looked at me with wide eyes. "Can Zach and Hazel help us decorate it?"

"They're in the car," my mother explained. "We stopped by here on the way to your place."

I nodded, then dragged my gaze down to Sean. Sprawled on the floor at my feet, he looked completely unruffled. No hint of blush on his cheeks. No pulse thudding in his neck. He shrugged at me and said, "Sounds fun to me."

"Sure," I said.

"I'll grab the kids," Mom said.

Sean's head disappeared beneath the pine needles, and I forced another deep breath into my lungs. Of course he was unruffled. His erection had probably been some physiological reaction he had no control over, like a rogue wave on the ocean. Maybe he got erections every time he ended up on top of a woman, which meant it wasn't *me*, specifically, that made him get hard. It was just the fact that I was there.

As much as the thought made my throat clench, it made sense. Why would a tall, handsome, muscular man like Sean Hardy want a short, frumpy woman like me?

I wasn't the kind of woman that turned heads on the street. I hadn't been that woman in a long, long time. I was a mom. People saw me walking down the street and thought, *yeah, she's got kids*. I was the one that people handed the camera to and asked to take photos instead of waving at me to enter the frame. The one who got relegated to babysitting duty, who made sure everything happened without a hitch in the background and didn't expect to be noticed or thanked for it.

It just didn't make sense that a hunk like Sean would be attracted to me, so I stopped trying to make sense of it. I just held the trunk and avoided gazing down at the long legs stretched out on the hardwood floors, holding the rough fir trunk until it was secure.

"Ooh," Mikey said, pulling a box of ornaments out of one of the Target bags. "Whoa! Look at these, Dad. Red with sparkles."

"They're pretty," Sean replied, crawling out from under the tree, but his eyes were on me. I watched his gaze narrow slightly and found myself patting my pockets as if I were looking for something, just to give myself an excuse to look away.

"I'll play photographer," I said, and dove for my purse. "I don't have my camera, but the phone'll do just fine."

Zach came skidding into the living room on sock-clad feet, then let out a whoop of excitement. Hazel's eyes were bright. I smiled at the three kids as they tore through the bags and judged my decorative choices.

"We have to put the lights on first," Hazel proclaimed, bossy as ever. "That's how it works." She pulled out the box of lights and thrust it at Sean.

I fumbled with my phone until I had the camera app open, then used it to distract myself from spinning out about what had just happened. Which was nothing. Nothing had just happened. A rogue wave had hit Sean's bloodstream, landed in his penis, and then he'd landed on top of me.

Yeah. That made sense. It made more sense than my brother's best friend actually being attracted to the little sister who'd let herself go after two kids and a divorce.

I snapped pictures while my mom rustled up some drinks and snacks for everyone. Sean untangled the lights and got them working, then strung them up on the now secure tree. Most of the pictures I took were of Mikey. His face beamed with such pure joy that it was easy to take shots of him. I snapped a great one of him holding up two ornaments to a laughing Sean, the two of them wearing the exact same smile on their faces. That one was a keeper.

When it came time to put the tree topper on, Mikey took the star out of its box with careful fingers, a deep sigh making his chest rise and fall. He glanced up at the tree—which was still bent across the ceiling—then at Sean.

"Let me get some shears," Sean said, then ruffled his son's head while he brushed past. His eyes flicked to me, then he ducked out of the living room.

"Your tree looks really good," Hazel told Mikey. "And it smells nice."

Mikey puffed up with pride. "Thanks. You did a good job decorating it."

Hazel nodded as if the compliment was her due. "Thank you. You too."

I smiled at the kids, then at my mother, who sat on the couch and rested her head on her hand. We waited until Sean came back, got on a step stool, and trimmed the top scraggly branches so there were a few inches of space between the tree and the ceiling.

Mikey lifted the tree topper—a golden star that was already twinkling in the lights of the living room—to hand it to his father.

Sean looked at it, smiled, and got down off the stepladder. "I think you should do the honors, buddy," he told Mikey.

My heart clenched. It was such a small gesture, but it made Mikey's whole face light up. And I saw, in that moment, just how much Sean cared about his son. It was like opening a door to a room I hadn't realized existed. I saw another facet of Sean's personality that had previously been invisible. The caring, thoughtful man who knew exactly what his kid needed.

And it wasn't a surprise, really. He'd brought me stuffing. He'd enlisted my help to get the tree in the first place, which I could tell he'd done for Mikey's benefit. I knew he was caring, but seeing it written so plainly on his face was something special.

It made my heart grow in my chest, but it also made my eyes

drift to my own children, and I felt a pang of sadness. Their father bulldozed his way through everyone else's preferences to make sure he got what he wanted. As long as Isaac was happy, there was peace. But any inconvenience was treated as a calamity.

I wished my kids had a man like Sean in their lives. Someone who put them first.

Well. Someone other than me.

I got another great picture of Sean lifting Mikey up and Mikey fitting the topper onto the tree. Sean's face was soft as he watched his son reach for the branch, and Mikey's eyes were alight with the glow from the twinkling Christmas lights on the tree.

When Mikey was on the ground again, I looked at the picture and smiled. That one was worthy of a frame.

"Okay," I called out when all the boxes and bags were cleaned up. "It's time for us to get ready for bed."

"Mo-om," Zach complained.

"Shoes," I replied.

Zach's shoulders dropped, but he headed for the foyer. My mother followed, and I brought up the rear.

"Thanks for watching them tonight," I told my mother.

"No problem at all. I'm glad we got to help Sean out with his decorations. I'll wait for you in the car." She kissed my cheek, then kissed Sean's, and hustled the kids out to her vehicle.

I pulled my shoes on and ignored the press of Sean's presence. He leaned on the wall opposite me, his long legs dominating my peripheral vision.

Finally, I stood and zipped my jacket. I gave him a bright smile. "Well. Goodnight!"

"Lizzie—" His voice was quiet, but it stopped me in my tracks. He glanced around the edge of the wall to check on Mikey, then turned to me. "About earlier..."

Nope. We were *not* doing this. It was humiliating enough to know that the erection hadn't been caused by me, but by a random reaction of his body. I didn't want to have to fumble my way through this conversation and possibly reveal the fact that I was desperately, hopelessly attracted to him.

The fact that I'd basically humped him from underneath him was mortifying enough as it was.

He'd made me remember far too many things that were better left buried. Like the touch of a man's hand against my bare skin. Or the press of his cock against my opening. Or the tight, hot release of a strong orgasm.

He wasn't for me. I couldn't have him, and I wouldn't torture myself by indulging thoughts about the impossible.

"Oh, don't worry about it," I said, waving a hand and affecting a casual laugh. "It happens. Night!"

If my cheeks were red when I got in my mother's car, it was probably because of the cold.

FOURTEEN

SEAN

IT HAPPENS. Those were her exact words. I stared at the ceiling in my bedroom and frowned, sheets twisted around my restless legs.

Did it happen, though? How often did it happen that men got hard and pressed themselves against her the way I had? And why did that thought make me want to tear my own skin off?

She'd waved me off like it had meant nothing to her, and I'd nearly lost my mind.

Maybe it was all this talk of matchmaking. I hadn't been on a date in a long time, so the prospect of spending time with a woman was making my body go haywire. Maybe the Butlers had been right, and it was time for me to put myself out there. I could date someone; it didn't have to be anything serious. I didn't have to introduce her to Mikey or think about marriage and commitment.

So maybe my agitation was generalized; I needed to blow off some steam.

Or maybe it was just the fact that Lizzie was soft and plush and kind and perfect. I didn't want to blow off some steam. I wanted *her*. I wanted to tug the knot of her sweater and let it fall open so I could admire her body. Touch her. Taste her. Watch her face while I made her come on my hand. I wanted her writhing and desperate and begging for me.

But—*it happens*.

Sighing, I scrubbed my palms over my face. It was all well and good to find her irresistible, but she was my best friend's little sister. I couldn't mess things up. Not when Mikey was smiling and laughing so soon after the move. Not when he seemed to have found a friend in Zach, when he'd integrated into his school so well and so quickly.

"Dad?"

I turned to see my son in my doorway, his hand gripping the jamb while one foot scratched at the back of his opposite calf.

"Yeah?"

He took a step into my room. "I just wanted to say thanks. For the tree and everything."

All the fight and tension went out of me. I pushed myself up to a seated position and leaned my head against the headboard. "You were right about the tree, buddy. It looks really good, and it was fun to decorate it together. I should have gotten one every year."

"Do you think..." He bunched his lips to the side, then wandered into the room and climbed onto my bed.

"Do I think what?"

Mikey brought his knees up and rested his cheek on them, eyes shining in the dark as he looked at me. "Do you think we could spend Christmas together next year?"

Guilt churned my stomach to a froth. I swallowed thickly and put my arm around Mikey's shoulders, pulling him in for a hug. "Your mom gets Christmases, kiddo."

"I know." He sounded sad. "I just thought it would be nice. Maybe we could visit Aaron and Lizzie and everyone. When I'm with Mom, there's no one else around."

Kids had a special kind of skill for finding weakness and stabbing you there, then casually twisting the knife. I kissed the top of his head. "We'll see," I said, cursing myself for promising Melody every Christmas.

Then again, the closer we got to the holiday, the more vivid my memories would become. I knew from experience that things only got worse from here. Setting up a tree in my living room was one thing, especially when I got to distract myself with my son's smiles and Lizzie's presence. Actually putting on a happy face for longer than an hour or two was another story.

Soon, when holiday music played everywhere and red, green, and gold tinsel decorated the whole town, it would be harder to ignore memories of my father's angry drinking. My mother's body wasting away. And the final, horrible Christmas when I found out about Melody's betrayal.

I'd need to retreat somewhere safe and isolated. I knew it, because it happened every year.

I asked Mikey about school and listened as he told me about

his classmates, his teacher, and the new friends he'd made. When he got drowsy, I carried him to his room like I used to do when he was half the size he was now. He curled into his pillow and was asleep before I straightened up.

Watching the rise and fall of his chest for a few moments, I wondered how many of my decisions had been mistakes. Should I have forgiven Melody? Should I have fought harder to make things work between us? Should I have moved here earlier? Should I have found someone else to act as a mother figure to Mikey? Should I have worked shorter hours to spend more time with him years ago, and dealt with the financial pressure that would follow?

Just like every other time doubts swarmed me as a parent, I had no answers. I brushed my hand over my son's shoulder and left his room on soft feet.

THE NEXT DAY, when I asked Aaron about finding a babysitter for my date on Saturday, his response should have been predictable.

"Just ask Lizzie," he said, the sound of the TV blaring in the background of the call. "She'll be happy to help."

"She's done so much for me already," I said, "I don't want to bother her."

"She loves it," Aaron said. "Really. It's no problem. She basically lives and breathes kids twenty-four-seven. You want me to ask her?"

"No, it's fine," I said.

"Who's this chick she set you up with?"

"Coworker of hers, I think."

"She hot?"

I sipped the coffee I'd just picked up from Four Cups on my way to work and shrugged, even though Aaron wouldn't be able to see the movement. "Sure," I replied.

"You don't sound convinced."

"Haven't been on a date in a while."

Aaron laughed. "Me neither. You'll be fine."

I got in my truck and set my coffee in the cupholder, huffing. "We'll see."

"I'll talk to Lizzie for you, tell her you need her to watch Mikey."

I opened my mouth to protest, then sighed. "It's fine. I'll call her."

"Suit yourself."

We hung up, and I made my way to work. If I didn't call Lizzie right away, it was because I was focused on the job—and on making a good impression with Grant. It wasn't because I was avoiding her or because there was something weird about lusting after her last night, then asking her to watch my kid while I went on a date a few days later.

Maybe I could cancel the date altogether. It was already turning out to be more hassle than it was worth.

So, by the time school pick-up rolled around, I still hadn't made the call. I pulled up outside the school and found Lizzie standing in a clump of other mothers, their breaths puffing white in a cloud above them. As soon as I got out of the car, half of them turned to look.

When Lizzie finally followed their gazes and saw me, her smile bloomed as it always did, showing off the dimples in her full cheeks. She walked toward me. "My brother just asked me if you'd talked to me," she said by way of greeting. "Any idea what it's about?"

I rubbed the back of my neck and glanced toward the school doors, which remained closed. "I asked him about a babysitter for Saturday night, and he said you might know someone," I lied.

Lizzie's eyebrow arched. "He said I might know someone, or he told you to ask me?"

I huffed, tilting my head. "Told me to ask you. But you've done enough favors for me. I hate to ask you for another one."

"That's very thoughtful of you," Lizzie said, reaching over to squeeze my forearm. Her eyes were kind and a little sad. She took a deep breath, like she was bracing herself. "Tell you what, how about we organize a sleepover? Zach would love it. That way you don't need to worry about being home by a certain time in case things with Laurel go well."

"Lizzie..."

"It's no problem," she insisted, her smile brightening, but not quite shaking the shadows from her eyes. "Mikey is so well-behaved, and it would make Zach happy. I really think you and Laurel are a good match. I'd hate for you to have to cut your date short if you're getting along. Trust me! It's a win-win."

It didn't feel like a win-win. It felt like Lizzie was taking a giant step away from me, but I knew how to take a hint. I'd made her uncomfortable with what happened with the tree, and she was drawing a thick line in the sand between us. So despite the pinch in my chest, I dipped my chin. "Thank you," I told her. "That sounds great."

She gave me a nod, then turned to look at the school doors. We didn't speak until they opened and released the horde of children to their waiting parents' arms.

FIFTEEN

LIZZIE

SATURDAYS WERE ALWAYS BUSY, with swimming lessons for both kids in the morning followed by dance for Hazel and sports for Zach in the afternoons. The baseball season was over, but Zach had signed up for indoor soccer at the insistence of one of his friends this year, which he was enjoying. I played taxi, my favorite game of all.

On this particular Saturday, I tried not to think about what was to come this evening. I dropped my kids off then ducked home to do errands and chores, including the usual seventeen metric tons of laundry, picked Hazel up, fed her, and dropped her off just in time to do the same with Zach. It was hectic up until about five o'clock, when the kids arrived home with appetites that belied their ages. I could only imagine what kind of bottomless pits their stomachs would become in a few years' time.

An hour later, when the dishes were done and I was doing

my best not to watch the clock, the doorbell rang. I took a deep, calming breath. I did not think about the Boner Incident. And if a hint of it drifted through my consciousness, I chose not to acknowledge it.

A bright, happy smile stretched my lips as I looked at myself in the hallway mirror. It came out a bit deranged, so I dropped it and tried again, turning down the wattage by about thirty percent. There. Better.

The front door hinge squeaked as I pulled it open, my just-right smile still plastered on my face. "Mikey!" I exclaimed. "Come in. The kids are in the living room."

"Go on," Sean said, squeezing his son's shoulder.

Mikey didn't hesitate. His shoes were off in a flash, and then he was hurrying down the hallway toward the sound of my children playing.

I brushed my cheek to make sure my smile was still intact, then turned to the man on my stoop. "Hi," I said, impressed by the way my voice sounded nice and casual. That was good. I'd need to sound nice and casual when he and Laurel hit it off and started dating in earnest. But maybe it would be easier then, when these silly possibilities about me and Sean were proven to be just that: silly. The sooner he found a new girlfriend, the sooner I could put my attraction to rest. "You look nice," I added.

Sean looked down at himself like he was surprised to find clothes on his body and he wasn't a grown man who'd dressed and groomed himself presumably only an hour or so earlier. "Thanks," he said. "Haven't worn a shirt in a while." He rubbed his jaw and gave me a half smile.

It would be a lot easier to do this if he wasn't so dang attractive. Every time his lips tilted this way or that, my hormones went on a wild roller coaster ride.

"It suits you," I declared, nodding. "And black is a classic color. Serious but not brooding. Very good balance to strike. The Spiderman backpack is particularly good."

"Oh, shit." Sean jerked and slipped the backpack off his shoulder. "Mikey's things."

"I figured." My smile felt a little easier as I curled my fingers around the strap. The tips of them brushed against his warm palm, and I ignored the pitter-patter of my heart. The man was going on a date with another woman. A date I had set up. He'd probably pop a boner with her too.

"You okay?"

I glanced up to see Sean frowning at me and discovered my smile had fallen off my face and clattered to the floor. I nodded and forced myself to brighten as I picked it back up and slapped it on my mouth again. "Long day," I explained.

He dipped his chin. "Thanks for... Thanks."

"Of course."

"If I'm done before Mikey goes to bed, I can stop by and pick him up."

"And deny him the sleepover he's so excited about?" I shook my head, my resolve firming. This man was not for me, but his son was a darling and I would do my best to be a good friend and great hostess. Sean was my brother's best and oldest friend, and he'd be part of my life for the foreseeable future. I had to get used to being near him. I waved him off. "Just go and enjoy yourself. You'll love Laurel. I just know the two of you will hit it off."

"Okay."

"Here, let me fix your collar." Before I could stop myself, I reached up and pulled his collar out where it had folded under itself. He lifted his chin slightly as he watched me, his Adam's apple bobbing with a swallow. The black fabric of his shirt needed smoothing on his shoulders, so my fingers went on a journey, feeling the hard, warm flesh beneath the weave of the shirt. When I finally pulled my hands away, I had a sneaking suspicion my cheeks had gone red.

"Thanks," Sean said, and his voice sounded rough around the edges.

"Well. I've done all I can do." I was getting sick of forcing smiles, but I gave him one last good one. "Have fun."

"Call me anytime, Lizzie. If you need anything, or if Mikey—"

"Go." I put my hands on his shoulders and gently pushed. "We'll be fine."

He nodded. "Good. Good. Okay. I'll, uh, see you later."

"Uh-huh," I said, and closed the door slowly but firmly. When I heard his engine roar to life, I let out a very long sigh.

Then I squared my shoulders and ignored the pang in my chest. This was for the best. Maybe if I repeated it to myself a million or so times, I'd start to believe it.

SIXTEEN

SEAN

LAUREL HAD OPTED to drive herself to the restaurant, but she wasn't there by the time I arrived. The hostess led me to an intimate table tucked into a little alcove in the corner, a tea light burning in a glass holder atop a crisp white tablecloth. She handed me the wine list and nodded when I placed an order for the house red. Melody had been the wine connoisseur. I didn't mind the stuff, but I wasn't able to tell plum notes from leather from the vinegar of a bottle that had gone off.

I ran my fingers over the edge of the tablecloth as I waited, eyes drifting from the door to the other patrons. The restaurant was called Dolce Vita, an Italian joint that handmade all their pastas and apparently had great cannoli. Nodding my thanks to the waitress as she dropped my wine off, I found myself glancing toward the door again.

My knee was bouncing, so I forced it to still. There was no need to be nervous. It was just a date.

But when my thoughts turned to the look on Lizzie's face when she'd stood in her doorway, my leg began to jiggle again. I'd hated feeling that distance widen between us. But she was right to take a step back, to set boundaries. We couldn't get involved. I couldn't afford to mess up the only support system I had left. And she had her hands full with her own life.

Pushing thoughts of my best friend's sister to the side, I studied the restaurant's decor.

The walls were exposed brick, and a few Christmas garlands had been strung up around the alcoves and the hostess's stand. Delicate music mingled with the chatter of patrons and the clink of cutlery and plates, giving the dining room an intimate, warm feeling.

They weren't playing Christmas music, which I appreciated. My nerves were stretched thin enough as it was.

It had been years since I'd been on a date. After the divorce, I'd gone out a grand total of two times before I decided that my time was better spent taking care of Mikey and making sure ends met every month. Now, somehow, I'd been coerced into going on a date with a woman I'd never met while my thoughts kept drifting to the one woman I could never have.

The entrance opened, and the brunette from the photo stepped in. Her hair shone under the low lights of the restaurant, red lips curling into a friendly smile as she greeted the hostess. When the hostess nodded and began to head my way, I stood up from my seat.

She wore heels and walked like she was used to them. Her dress was fitted and a dark shade of purple, with a collar that skimmed the tops of her breasts. She was prettier than I'd thought when I first saw her photo, especially when she smiled at me and extended her hand.

"You're the famous Sean Hardy," she said. "Lizzie has been singing your praises for two weeks. And first impression: she wasn't exaggerating." Her eyes were blue and they twinkled with mirth. Her hand was soft in mine. It felt nice, but it didn't give me that rush of adrenaline that touching Lizzie's skin did.

But I wasn't on a date with Lizzie. Thinking about her was counterproductive.

I huffed a laugh and took my seat again. "Hope you don't mind I went ahead and ordered myself a wine while I waited."

"If I minded that, I would be the definition of a wet blanket." She smiled at the waiter who approached. "I'll have a glass of whatever he's having."

"It's only the house red," I said. "Nothing fancy."

"Good thing I'm not a fancy woman." She shot me another smile as she settled into her seat, then placed her elbows on the table and rested her chin on her braided fingers. "So. I've never been on a blind date before."

"Neither have I, but I've been assured that Lizzie's a professional at this."

"Set up half her family with their partners, or so I hear."

A smile worked its way onto my lips. "She's pretty determined when she sets her mind to something, so it doesn't surprise me that everyone falls in line."

"Tell me about it. The office wouldn't run without her at the helm. Even the days she works from home, it feels like things are just on the edge of falling apart."

"How long have you worked with her?"

Laurel tilted her head. "Oh...four, five years? No, longer. She got divorced, what, six years ago? So it'd be six and a half. She started right before that all happened." She gave me a significant look.

"Was it bad?"

"Not as bad as it can be, I guess. But divorce is never easy."

A frown pulled at my brows. I'd never spoken to Lizzie about her divorce, and I found myself wanting to know what had happened between her and her ex.

"What about you?"

I blinked and brought my attention back to Laurel. "Oh, I've known Lizzie since we were kids. Her older brother, Aaron, was my best friend growing up. Best man at my wedding. We've kept in touch. Lizzie was always hanging around when we were little, but we lost touch as we got older. I knew she was married, and I remembered Aaron telling me she and her ex had separated, but it wasn't until I moved back here that we really reconnected. She hasn't changed at all, you know? Same smile, same laugh. She's great. So good with her kids—and with mine." I huffed a laugh and realized I was babbling, so I stopped and reached for my wine.

Laurel gave me a strange look, and when she smiled, it was softer than before. Like she'd just seen something in me, or understood something, but I had no idea what it was. "Yeah, she is great. I was actually asking about you, though. Lizzie mentioned you have a son. Have you been separated from your ex for a while?"

Ah. I licked my lips to catch a drop of red wine and forced a laugh. "Oh. Right."

"By all means, though, sing Lizzie's praises." Laurel grinned. "I don't mind. I happen to agree with you."

Rubbing my jaw, I laughed at myself. "I'm sorry. I haven't been on a date in a couple of years. I'm...out of practice."

"You're doing great."

"I've been divorced about three years. My kid's ten. He's awesome. We put up our Christmas tree this week, and you should've seen his face. Can I be a lame dad for a second?" I said, pulling out my phone. "I want to show you a picture."

Laurel leaned forward. "Sure."

I pulled one of the shots Lizzie had sent—the one where Mikey looked thrilled and I was laughing beside him. "Here. That's him."

Lips curling as she looked at the photo, Laurel nodded. "That's a fantastic shot."

"Lizzie took it, actually." The words slipped out before I could stop myself. I knew I shouldn't keep talking about another woman while I was on a date with the one across from me. But all roads seemed to lead back to Lizzie.

Besides, Laurel didn't seem to mind. "She's a really talented photographer. Has she shown you any of her landscapes?"

I put my phone away and shook my head. "No. I had no idea she did it professionally."

"Oh, she doesn't. But she could. She has a few hanging in her living room, shots from the bluff overlooking the ocean just on the edge of town."

I thought of the pictures I'd seen in her home, and my brows jumped. I'd thought they were professional prints.

The waiter came by to take our orders. I found myself

relaxing as the date progressed. I could see why Lizzie thought Laurel and I would get along. Laurel was gregarious and funny and charismatic. We shared a lot of interests, and she promised to send me a list of good hikes to check out in the spring.

But there was no spark. No pit-of-my-gut thrill every time she looked at me. When the candlelight flickered over her skin, I found myself thinking about Lizzie's full cheeks, and how they showed every shade of red depending on her emotions.

We decided to skip dessert. I paid the bill and walked Laurel to her car. With her keys in her hand, she glanced up at me, the light from a nearby streetlight illuminating her face. When she stepped into me and tilted her head to press a kiss to my lips, I kissed her back. It was a short, almost chaste kiss, and the only thing I felt when she pulled away was relief.

Laurel smiled at me, that same soft, strange smile as before. "Just had to check," she said.

"Check what?"

She shook her head. "Never mind. Thank you for dinner."

"I had a good time."

Her smile turned a little wry. "I did too, but—and you can tell me if it's just me—I think you're not feeling a spark."

I straightened. "I... I mean, I'm... It's not..."

A laugh trilled out of her and she shook her head. "Don't worry about it, Sean. Thank you for a nice evening. Say hi to Lizzie for me."

"Will do," I said, and waved at her as she drove away.

My shoulders dropped with an exhale when I stood alone in the parking lot. There would be no sleepover. No awkward morning after. No need to ring Lizzie's doorbell knowing I'd been with another woman the night before.

And I was glad.

SEVENTEEN

LIZZIE

I ALMOST DIDN'T HEAR the knock. Frowning, I glanced toward the hallway as if I'd suddenly developed X-ray vision and could see through walls and doors to figure out who had just rapped on my door. Then my phone buzzed, and a name popped up on my screen.

SEAN

It's me.

My heart gave a lurch. I stepped down the hallway and pulled the door open, half-expecting to see someone else on the other side.

"What are you doing here?"

"Kids still awake?"

"Just went down," I said, then checked my watch. A few minutes past ten. "Did the date not go well?"

"It went fine," Sean said, brushing past me as he walked in.

I frowned as he kicked his shoes off and ambled down the hallway like he owned the damn place. Closing and locking the door with a quick flick of my fingers, I hurried after him. "So what are you doing here? Did you not like her?"

"I liked her just fine. You want a drink?" He grabbed an opened bottle of white from my fridge door and lifted it toward me.

"Did I just hit my head and forget that this is actually your house and not mine?" I planted my hands on my hips and glared at him. "What are you doing here?"

He dangled the bottle so the wine sloshed, brows raised.

I relented. "I use that for cooking. It's old. Open one of those." I waved my hand at the wine rack in the corner where I kept my stash. If he wanted to treat this place as his own, he could open the bottle and pour the drinks.

Long fingers curled around the bottle in the bottom slot of the rack, and Sean pulled it out and tilted it toward the light to read the label. His jaw was sharp, the shadow of his cheekbone stark. He was all angles, and he made no sense.

"You still haven't told me why you're here."

"Figured I'd check in on you and the kids."

"The kids and I are fine."

He twisted the top of the bottle off—I wasn't some sort of cork-only purist—and poured two glasses. "Did Mikey behave himself?"

"Mikey is a dream," I said as I accepted the glass he pushed across the island toward me. "We made gingerbread. I hope you don't mind, I told Mikey he could help us decorate them tomorrow if you agreed." I walked to the corner of the kitchen, where the slabs of gingerbread were cooling on wire racks.

Sean wandered over, close enough that I could feel the heat of his body next to my shoulder. "I don't mind," he said quietly. "I really appreciate how generous you are with your time. How easily you include Mikey. It means a lot, Lizzie. Really."

The compliment made me want to squirm, but not in a bad way. It was rare for someone to see all the work I did and actually appreciate it. I was the designated babysitter in the family, and most of the time I enjoyed spending time with the kids. But there were times—like this year's Thanksgiving—when I wished people saw me as more than just the built-in, default childcare. Times that my family's treatment felt uncomfortably close to Isaac's. I'd been invisible to my ex-husband for years, and I sometimes wondered if I was invisible to everyone else too.

But not to Sean. He stood in my kitchen, looking at me like a few batches of gingerbread meant the world to him.

"It's nothing," I said, and waved a hand. "Tell me about your date. Are you going to see Laurel again?"

"No."

"No?"

He swallowed a sip of wine and set his glass down on the counter. "No."

There was a strange mix of relief and disappointment in my gut. The relief, I knew, was ridiculous. That came from the fact that I was attracted to him, and I needed to get over it pronto. The disappointment made more sense. I was proud of my knack for matchmaking, and I didn't like misjudging the people I set up. "What happened? You didn't like her?"

"She was great. We just didn't click."

"Didn't click."

"That's what I said."

I frowned at him. "In what way?"

He spread his arms in a slow shrug. "I didn't get butterflies when she smiled at me."

Snorting, I lifted my glass to my lips. "And does that happen to you often?"

He eyed me for a long second. "Sometimes."

In another life, I might have thought he was trying to tell me something. But in another life, I wouldn't be a woman who'd never shed her baby weight, who'd been left by her husband, who'd been relegated to default babysitter because that's all anyone saw in her.

All the evidence for the past decade told me that a man like Sean Hardy would never be interested in me. Believing otherwise was just setting myself up for disappointment. Even after my divorce, when I'd most needed the support of my family, they'd poked holes in my self-confidence and asked me if I was sure I could handle life and the kids on my own.

Their questions were valid. Being a single mom was hard. But what I'd needed then was unwavering belief. For that, I'd had to dig deep inside myself.

So thinking about opening myself up to a man like Sean— no. Not a man *like* Sean. Thinking about opening myself up to *Sean* was a terrifying prospect. It was like digging up the foundations I'd spent so long building on my own. It was opening the gates and letting a gigantic Trojan horse enter right into the heart of my inner fortress.

I couldn't afford to be vulnerable when I knew that the only person who'd be there to pick up the pieces was me.

I took a gulp of wine and set my glass down. "Fine. First date was a bust. But you gotta give me something to work with. Be specific. What are you looking for in a woman?"

"Up until I got strong-armed into going on this date, I wasn't looking for a woman at all."

I ran my fingers up the stem of my glass and studied him. "I'm sorry if you felt pressured into it. Truth be told, I felt pressured into setting you up too." I gave him a small smile. "We can just drop the whole thing. If you're not ready to date, you're not ready to date. I get that."

The relief sweeping through me became harder to ignore. I'd spent the evening distracting myself with the noises of the children playing, with taking on an ambitious gingerbread house project on a whim, with cleaning up the disaster that was made of the kitchen afterward.

But the truth was, I'd been thinking about Sean and Laurel together. A beautiful, attractive couple who made sense together. I'd imagined them hitting it off and ending up at his house—or hers. I'd imagined opening the door in the morning and seeing Sean's hair freshly washed, knowing why he had to take a shower.

And I'd felt sick.

Maybe it was simply because it had been so long since I'd been attracted to a man. But I couldn't have chosen a more appropriate man to remind me that I was a woman with needs beyond eating and sleeping? It had to be my brother's best friend? It had to be the kid who practically grew up at our house, who ruffled my hair and teased me, who would never in a million years betray Aaron by dating me, even if he wanted to?

Sean let out a long sigh and leaned against the sink. He ran a broad hand over his short hair and shrugged. "It's not that I'm not ready to date," he finally admitted. "I think I am ready. Laurel just wasn't the one. She wasn't New Year's kiss material for me."

My gulp of wine turned sour in my mouth, but I hid it by swallowing hard and nodding. "Right."

"What about you?"

I frowned. "What about me?"

"Have you dated since your divorce?"

A harsh laugh fell from my lips. "Me? No."

"Why is that funny?"

I wanted to say, *Look at me. Do I look like dating material to you?* But I knew that would sound pathetic, like I was fishing for compliments. So I just shrugged and said, "I wanted to put my kids first."

"I know how that feels."

The bitterness in my heart faded, and I met Sean's gaze. I smiled sadly. "No matter how well you co-parent with an ex, there's still a lot of juggling to do."

"I was lucky," he said. "Melody has always been career-focused, so she was happy to give me primary custody."

"Oh?"

Sean smiled. "Don't look so horrified. She wasn't a bad mother. I think... I think she felt pressured into having a kid."

"By you?"

"Partly. We'd always talked about having kids, but it was always later. In a few years. The time was never right. She was always on the verge of a big promotion, in the middle of a big project, on the cusp of her next big jump. I felt the years slipping away. Her parents badgered her about it with nearly every conversation they had with her. I think that's what got to her in the end."

"They wanted grandkids."

"Mm-hmm."

"Is that why things didn't work out between you?"

Sean ran his fingers along the base of his glass and took a sip before answering. He walked back to the other side of the island and topped up his glass before passing the bottle over to me to do the same. "She cheated on me at a company event." He cleared his throat. "At the company Christmas party, actually. We tried counseling, but I just couldn't forgive her, and I think she resented me too much."

"Oh. I'm so sorry."

His eyes landed on me. "What about you? What happened with your kids' dad?"

"He had an affair with a coworker as well," I said, then shook my head. "I mean, it was never physical, or at least he swore up and down they never slept together. But they got close. She was his 'work wife.' They started working late together, calling and texting daily." I gulped and stared at the liquid in my glass, trying not to let my thoughts spiral back to those dark years, to the moment of discovery that had sent me sprinting for the toilet so I could get sick. "Our marriage just—deteriorated.

He stopped caring, and I guess I was in denial. In the aftermath, when they finally got together, I felt like the emotional affair hurt worse than a one-night stand would've done. I would've preferred for him to sleep with her, for it to just be about sex. But he told me he fell out of love with me and into love with her."

When I realized what I'd said, I clamped my lips shut and jerked my head up to meet Sean's gaze. "I didn't mean—I'm sorry. I wasn't trying to minimize what you went through. I—forget I said anything."

"Lizzie, stop." He shook his head. A few feet of distance separated us, but it felt like if there hadn't been a piece of marble between us, he would've crossed the distance and wrapped me in his arms. More evidence of my endless delusions. Sean smiled sadly. "For what it's worth, I think they're as bad as each other. I drove myself crazy imagining her with another man. But if she'd fallen in love with someone else right in front of me..." A harsh breath blew out of his nostrils. "I don't know how I would've reacted. It would've been worse. It would've made me question everything about myself, about our relationship. I'm sorry he did that to you."

Silence settled around us, but it wasn't the uncomfortable, tense silence that I would normally rush to fill. It was like a still summer day, where silence felt like the sun's rays on bare skin.

When my marriage had shattered, the fact that Isaac hadn't had sex with his coworker was something he threw in my face at every opportunity. How could I be so upset about the betrayal, when he hadn't even done anything with her? What was I even upset about? It wasn't like he'd *cheated* on me. I was unreasonable, emotional, and ridiculous.

Over time, as our fights became more frequent and divorce reared its ugly head, I began to believe his words. And I heard the same thing from my family and friends. They said it like it was a good thing: at least he hadn't slept with her. At least he'd remained faithful.

But it wasn't until that moment—with my fingers clasping the stem of my cheap wine glass and a kind, thoughtful, generous man standing in front of me telling me he would've felt the same way—that I realized my feelings were valid.

It *was* a betrayal. It was deep, cutting duplicity from the man who'd vowed to stand by my side forever. He let me take care of the home and children, let me struggle to contribute to the finances while I took on the lion's share of the housework, and he went elsewhere to get his ego stroked.

The life I'd worked so hard to build with him had been a lie. And then I'd had to rebuild my idea of a future all by myself, with two young kids to take care of, with lawyers' bills and a new job and all the disappointed clucking of everyone who told me I'd overreacted.

But I *hadn't*. I'd been right to be mad. I'd been right to be hurt.

"Thank you," I croaked, and dragged my gaze up to his.

"For what?"

"For saying that. For making me feel like it was okay for me to be upset."

His lips curled slightly, but his eyes were sad. "We definitely sound like two people who are ready to get back on the dating horse."

I laughed, and a snort came out, which made me laugh harder. The sound of Sean's chuckle wrapped around me like a warm hug, and when we finally quieted down, he grabbed the bottle and topped up our glasses again. It was going down way too easy, so I forced myself to slow down.

"So," he said. "Why do you get to have all the fun match-making? How about you tell me about your ideal man."

Oh no. Definitely not. We were *not* going there. That way lay dragons, and my sword and armor were unfortunately rusty as all hell. The wine in my bloodstream wasn't helping. I deliberately pushed my glass away and gave him a flat look. "That's not how this works. You tell me why you think Laurel wasn't a fit, and we'll go from there."

"A truth for a truth," he hedged, eyes sparkling.

This way lay dragons too. Oh boy. Apparently I was in a mood for danger, because I said, "He's got to like kids. Not just tolerate them. He's got to know that my kids mean everything. If the kids don't like him, he's out."

Sean inclined his head. "She has to know how to laugh at herself."

I reared back. "And Laurel doesn't? Her middle name is self-deprecation!"

"I wasn't talking about Laurel," Sean answered, grinning. "I told you. There was no spark."

"She's hot. How could there be no spark?"

He shrugged, his gaze holding mine. "There just wasn't, Lizzie."

There were a whole lot of sparks in the pit of my stomach when he said my name in that low, rumbly voice. I wrestled myself back under control and went through my mental list of potential matches. Cindy had been my second choice for him. "Okay. How do you feel about dating a single mom?"

His eyes never left mine when he said, "I'm open to it."

The sparks turned into a full-on inferno and moved between my legs. Uh-oh.

I forced myself to nod in a businesslike manner. "Good. Give me something else."

"You first."

"This isn't how this works, Sean."

His smile widened as he swirled his wine in his glass. "What if I like it when your cheeks get all red and flushed?"

He *had* to stop saying things like that to me. I was getting all kinds of ideas that would only lead me to a sad, broken heart later on. I tried to glare at him. "I hate my cheeks."

He jerked. "What? Why? I love your cheeks."

I blinked rapidly and felt the prickling of even more blood flowing into my face. "Stop it, Sean. You're being very difficult." I needed to get this conversation back on track. "Okay. How about you tell me about the last woman you were attracted to?"

He opened his mouth and closed it again. Then he took a sip of his wine and stared at the glass for a while before finally meeting my gaze. "She was kind. Thoughtful. Really funny without even trying. Sometimes I felt like I was the only one who noticed her, which made me feel like I was carrying this illicit secret around with me all the time."

My heart thumped. Part of me felt like he was describing

me. But most of me just felt sad that I was so hopelessly attracted to a man who obviously would never date me. Why else would he be asking me to set him up with other women?

Kind and funny without trying. I focused on his words, and an idea sparked. "You should meet Astrid," I forced myself to say.

He was quiet for a second, then seemed a bit resigned when he inclined his head and said, "Tell me about her."

EIGHTEEN

SEAN

I POKED my head into the boys' bedroom to find them both sleeping soundly, then left Lizzie's house about an hour later. She walked me to the front door and gave me one of her soft, irresistible smiles, and I realized I didn't want to leave at all.

But leave I did, and I went back to my cold bed in my empty house. The date had been a bust, and I hadn't been able to stop myself from going over to Lizzie's afterward.

I knew I was playing with fire, and I didn't care.

So, the next morning, my feet carried me back to Lizzie's doorstep with a bag full of gingerbread house decorations and a tray with two coffees balanced in one hand.

Hazel flung the door open. "Mo-om! Sean's here!"

She took off at a sprint before I could say anything, and I took the open door as an invitation. Lizzie's head appeared at the end of the hall, her hair in wild disarray, her cheeks red with laughter or exertion or both. Her smile drew me like a magnet, and I found myself in the kitchen without ever really remembering walking there.

"I brought stuff," I said, presenting her with the candy and the coffee.

"You're so thoughtful," she replied, and beamed at me. Her hand came up to squeeze my bicep before helping me with the tray of coffee and bag. I felt her touch through my sweater, remembered how soft she was when I had her pinned beneath me.

"Dad! Look! We made these last night. First we got templates off the internet, and then we made the gingerbread mix. We burned the first batch so we had to make more but now we're ready to assemble. Me and Zach are gonna make one together."

"And I'm making my own," Hazel announced.

I wandered over to where the kids were set up on the dining table, the pieces of their gingerbread houses laid out before them like a puzzle.

"Who's making this one?" I pointed to the third station and lifted my head in time to see Lizzie blush.

"Can't let the kids have all the fun, can we?" she quipped. "If you're nice, I'll let you help me decorate it."

"I can be nice," I answered with a grin.

Her eyes were dark over the rim of her coffee cup, glowing like hot coals. She looked a little bit wicked like that, like there was a drop of fae blood coursing through her veins, and I wondered just how many sides of herself she kept hidden behind the Suzy Homemaker exterior.

"Okay. Let's assemble." I watched her spoon icing into

piping bags and hand them to the kids, who went to work gluing the pieces of the house together. Hazel looked determined and a little uncoordinated, leaving globs of icing all over her house as she huffed in frustration at herself. The boys were serious and focused within seconds of starting. I liked watching Mikey's head bend toward Zach and the way Lizzie's son turned to mine for advice and help without hesitation.

"Here," Lizzie said. "Hold these together and I'll glue."

She propped a wall against the front of the house, and I put my fingers where she motioned. Her shoulder brushed my arm as she navigated the piping bag in place, and a neat line of white icing secured the two pieces together.

When she pulled away and smiled at me, I was a little dazed. "That wasn't too hard," I noted, then jerked when Lizzie cried out in dismay.

The two pieces of gingerbread fell flat on the cake board.

"I'll hold them until they stick," I said, and we tried again.

"Mom, can you help me?" Hazel asked, frowning.

"Of course, honey."

With my hands holding the two pieces of gingerbread together, I watched Lizzie circle the table and go to her daughter. She was patient and warm, and Hazel beamed when they got four walls up in no time. I managed to get another wall on by myself, but my eyes kept being drawn to Lizzie and then over to the boys.

My heart was calm. Here I was, engaging in a Christmas-themed activity, surrounded by a truckload of decorations in every corner of Lizzie's house, and I felt none of the discomfort that usually came with reminders of Christmas. There were no old memories of parents—or newer memories of exes and betrayals. There were just sticky fingers and happy children, the smell of gingerbread, and the soft laughter that seemed to come from Lizzie at every turn.

"Not bad," Lizzie said with a nod, coming to stand beside me. "Let's do the roof."

She reached across me to grab the appropriate piece of gingerbread, and her breast pressed into my shoulder. She smelled sweet and spiced, just like the structures we were building. I sat very, very still and tried not to think about the feel of her body against mine.

"Sean," she chided, and I jumped.

"What?"

"What the heck is this?"

I followed her gesture to the back wall of our gingerbread house, which had unfortunately suffered some structural damage that required extensive repairs. Icing was globbed along the walls and bottom, with another smear covering the big crack that went from the window to the ground. Truthfully, the kids were doing a better job than I was.

"I did my best," I said, and was rewarded with a laugh. Her hand squeezed my shoulder, and a wash of warmth went through me. We put the roof on, fingers brushing each other, smiles stretching wide.

I felt a quiet kind of happiness, one that came from peace and contentment. When we finally opened up all the bags of candy to start decorating, I stole glances at Lizzie every time she snuck a treat between her lips. Her eyes glimmered in challenge until I reached over and popped a Fuzzy Peach of my own into my mouth. Then she grinned, and it was sweeter than the sugar melting on my tongue.

Later, when it was time to go, Lizzie slipped a piece of paper into my hand. "Astrid's phone number," she said. "I got in touch with her this morning, and she'd be happy to go out with you."

"Oh," I said, glancing down at the paper, all the sweetness of the day melting away. "Sure. Thanks."

Mikey came trotting down the hallway holding his gingerbread house. He and Zach had negotiated an agreement where Mikey got to take it home as long as Zach was invited over to admire it after school. Seemed fair to me. My son smiled at me, then at Lizzie. "I had fun," he announced.

Lizzie's smile was soft. "Good. That makes me happy."

"Maybe next time Zach can come have a sleepover at our place. Right, Dad?"

"Right," I said, nodded to Lizzie, and followed my son out the door.

When he was buckled in and his gingerbread house was held firmly on his lap, Mikey looked over at me and said, "Dad?"

"Mm?"

"Lizzie's nice."

I nodded and turned the key in the engine. "Yeah," I replied. "She is."

"And she's really pretty."

The steering wheel was smooth beneath my fingers as I gripped it. "Yeah," I repeated. "She is."

NINETEEN

LIZZIE

ON MONDAY MORNING, Laurel leaned on the reception desk and placed a takeout coffee cup from the Four Cups Café in front of me. "Good morning." The look on her face was all-knowing and amused.

"Good morning to you too," I said. "What's this for?"

"For setting that date up on Saturday. I had a good time."

A frown tugged my brows as I spun the cup around so I could take a sip. "I see," I replied. Hadn't Sean said it was a bust?

When I glanced up at Laurel, her smile had widened. "So do I. A lot of things became clear to me over the course of that dinner."

"What's that supposed to mean?"

"It means you set me up on a date with a man who waxed poetic about *you* half the time."

I didn't quite know what to say to that, so I said nothing and took a sip. The coffee was silky and delicious, and my shoulders eased. "Sean and I have known each other a long time," I finally said.

"Did you ever date?"

I jerked. "Me and him?"

"Yeah."

"No."

"Why not?"

"He was—is—my brother's best friend."

Laurel sipped her own coffee then said, "So?"

"So it's not like we knew each other that way. I was the annoying little sister. Then he graduated and moved on."

"And now he's back."

"And now he's back," I repeated, wrapping both hands around the paper cup to warm them. "Are you trying to tell me something? Because I'm not following."

"Lizzie, you are too cute."

Okay, this conversation was beginning to annoy me. I gave her a flat look. "What the hell is that supposed to mean?"

"I'm going to spell it out for you."

I rolled my wrist to motion that she should.

Laurel spoke slowly and deliberately. "Sean is totally into you."

I leaned back in my chair and frowned at her. The leap in my heart was bad news. "No. No, he's just an old friend. My brother's old friend."

Laurel shrugged a shoulder. "If you say so."

"I've already set him up on a date with the art teacher at my kids' school."

She straightened. "And he agreed?"

"Of course. I'm trying to set him up with someone. We have this whole plan to get him a kiss for New Year's."

"But...why?"

We stared at each other for a beat. I blinked a few times and shook my head. "Because he asked me to."

"Did he?"

"Well, not precisely. He was kind of strong-armed into it by my family. But he was willing."

"Hmm."

This conversation was going nowhere, and I didn't like the little bud of hope that had sprouted in my chest when Laurel had said Sean was interested in me. It was impossible. He was a six-foot-something Adonis, and I was the designated mom of every group. We didn't fit. I just couldn't see *him* being into *me*. Sure, he seemed to notice me a bit more than my family, and he was appreciative of all the time and effort I put in with Mikey, but that was different. I might as well have been the house-keeper who went above and beyond to scrub the range hood filters once in a while. Him noticing and appreciating it didn't mean he wanted to date me.

Then again, there was the boner. His hard cock had been pressed up against me, and he'd shifted his hips to make sure I felt it. Repeatedly.

But maybe that was just an involuntary reaction thing, like a teenage boy would have. Lord knew most men were like teenage boys in all other respects. Why not this one?

I met Laurel's eyes and dropped my voice. "Did he get aroused when he was with you?"

She choked on a sip of coffee. "Excuse me?"

"Well, you know—" I gestured to my lap. "Did he?"

"How the hell would I know?"

"Maybe you felt it."

"What?"

"I'm just asking!"

Laurel burst out laughing. "No. I mean, I can't be sure, but I would bet my life savings on no."

"Oh." I frowned. That didn't make sense. That would mean that he was turned on when we were putting the tree up in the living room. But...why? I looked up at her again. "You're sure?"

"Let me put it this way. After dinner, I kissed him, and there was nothing. No spark. No reciprocity. Nada."

I knew my expression had turned a little frozen at the thought of Laurel kissing Sean, and I also knew getting upset about it was ridiculous. I was the one who'd set them up on the date!

"Don't look at me like that," she reproached.

"Like what?" I picked up my coffee and took a bracing swallow.

"Like I just punched you in the gut."

"Oh, stop it."

"Lizzie, if you're into him, you have to stop setting him up with other women. I'm telling you, he would be receptive to your advances."

I waved a hand. "Easy for you to say."

"Oh yeah? Why's that?"

I waved both hands in her direction, gave her a significant look, then waved both hands at myself. "Need I say more?"

"If you're insinuating that you're less desirable than I am, you need to get your head checked."

"I'm a single mom of two kids who can barely keep up with the laundry, let alone the thousand and one other tasks I need to do. I'm not exactly the type of lady men are beating down the door to date."

"You don't need men in general to beat down your door," Laurel responded sagely. "You need *one* man to beat down your door."

And he had, two days in a row.

"You're wrong." My voice was emphatic. "I don't need a man. Been there, done that, got the T-shirt."

"When was the last time you went out with a guy?"

"Like, on a date?"

Laurel huffed and gave me an exasperated smile. "Yes! On a date."

I gulped. "Isaac, probably. And we stopped doing date nights when Hazel was born. So..."

"Over eight years."

"Right." That was nothing to be embarrassed about, and I didn't know why my cheeks had begun to burn. I had a rich, full life and I hadn't missed dragging a man around like an anchor on a chain behind me. After the divorce, I discovered that my house was easier to keep clean when I didn't have a third person to pick up after. I could manage the kids' activities and appointments by myself, because I wasn't constantly worried that Isaac would forget or be late or drop the ball. I did it. I managed everything, and my life got easier. My kids thrived. Everything worked out.

"I don't need a man," I repeated.

"Sure," Laurel conceded. "No one *needs* a man. But aren't they fun sometimes?"

"Not the ones I've met."

Laurel threw her hands up and dipped her chin, relenting. "Fine. Forget I said anything. Sean's a great guy and I had a good dinner. Let's leave it at that."

"Thank you for the coffee," I said, relieved. She gave me one last smile, then wandered to her desk. I drank my coffee and told myself she was delusional.

If Sean Hardy were interested in me, I would know. Besides, he wouldn't have agreed to go out with Astrid; he would've made a move on me.

Right?

TWENTY

SEAN

I SCHEDULED my date with Astrid at the Four Cups Café on Saturday around noon. Mikey was at Aaron's house, and I liked the idea of having an out in case the date went sideways. I trusted Lizzie's taste, but my heart wasn't exactly in it. I figured I could go on this date and go through the motions, and if nothing came of it, drop the whole endeavor.

Astrid blew through the door wearing a bright orange pea coat over a low-cut brown dress, with her hair bouncing in ringlets around her face. Her gaze cut to mine immediately, and an interested sparkle lit her eyes. She'd told me she'd be wearing orange when we'd set up the date, so I knew it was her.

"Hello, stranger," she said.

I wasn't sure if she was trying to be funny or seductive, so I settled on an easy smile and thanked my past self for scheduling this date at a coffee shop. Easy to escape. "You must be Astrid." I stood and shook her hand. Her grip was a little limp, and she batted her eyelashes at me like she had a piece of dust stuck under her eyelid.

"Lizzie was telling the truth. You. Are. *Delicious*."

"Um." I cleared my throat. "Can I get you a coffee?"

"Only if I get to drink *you* later."

We stared at each other. Maybe I could leave now, before things got worse.

Then she smiled. "I'll have a strong cappuccino. I have a feeling I need to get my energy up." She wiggled her eyebrows.

I pushed my chair back to stand, then paused. Bad innuendo was one thing. Could I handle it for the length of time it would take to finish a coffee? "Listen, I feel like I need to say something."

Astrid leaned forward, her arms pressing her breasts together to show off the valley of her cleavage. "You can tell me anything." She winked. "Made you look."

"I'm, ah—" I jerked my gaze up at her face. "I'm not sure we're really on the same page here."

She tilted her head. Dirty-blond curls fell off her shoulder as she blinked big blue eyes at me. "What do you mean?"

"I'm more of a take-it-slow kind of guy," I admitted, which I wasn't entirely sure was the truth but definitely seemed like something I needed to say.

"Yummy." She leaned back and brushed her finger across her collarbones. "Don't mind a man who knows how to take things slow." Then she arched her brows at me. "So? Cappuccino?"

"Right." I stood. "Give me a sec."

In the few minutes it took me to order and pay, I tried to

shake the fuzz out of my head. Lizzie thought *this* woman was a good fit for me? I glanced over my shoulder and caught Astrid glancing at me. She gave me a coy smile and blew me a kiss.

Lord. I waited by the counter for the barista to finish up, just to give myself a few more minutes before I had to sit down again. I should've gotten my coffee in a to-go cup.

By the time I dropped Astrid's cappuccino on the table, I'd braced myself—and come up with a plan of attack.

"So you teach at the school?"

"Sure do, big guy." She smiled. "Art—because I like to get messy."

I blinked and cleared my throat. "Right. That's nice. You like kids?"

"I'd much rather talk about you." She took a sip of her cappuccino and licked the foam off her top lip, holding my gaze the whole time.

My stomach churned, and I frowned. "What exactly did Lizzie tell you about me?"

"Tall, gorgeous, single. She said you liked to work with your hands."

I did my best to ignore the suggestive tone of her voice and nodded. "I work as a carpenter with Grant Greene. You know him? His wife co-owns this coffee shop, actually."

"Sure." She did the foam licking thing again. "What about me? Hope Lizzie didn't tell you any crazy stories from my younger years."

"Um," I started, "no. She said you were her daughter's director for the school play. I wasn't aware you knew each other from before."

"Oh, we don't," she said. "But sometimes these stories make the rounds, you know?"

There was absolutely no way I was asking for any details whatsoever about Astrid's stories of her misspent youth. I needed to get out of here, because my interest in the woman across the table from me was so low it was subterranean. But I was aware that she was a teacher at Mikey's school, so I had to tread carefully. I'd learned how easily teachers and administrators judged single fathers, how the PTA moms were quick to spread rumors. Extricating myself from this situation would require some delicacy.

"Do you enjoy teaching?"

Astrid nodded. Her face was all angles; it had none of the softness that Lizzie had. She wasn't a bad-looking woman, but I was so put off by her first impression that it was hard for me to see anything attractive about her. "I love my job," she said, "but I don't really want to talk about that right now."

"Oh?"

She leaned forward. "I'd much rather talk about what you and I should do once we finish our coffees."

"I, uh, have to pick up my son, actually. So I'm not...free."

A pout tugged at her bottom lip. "Shame."

"I know," I replied, then spread my palms. "Life of a dad, huh."

"Well, there's always next time."

I cleared my throat and racked my brain for something to say, then glanced up at the eclectic artwork for sale on the café walls and asked Astrid for detailed opinions on all the pieces we could see. When my coffee was empty, I checked my watch and made my excuses.

Fifteen minutes later, I pulled up outside Aaron's house to see Lizzie climbing out of her car in the driveway. She turned toward me and waved, a broad smile on her lips. Her kids were already sprinting toward their uncle's front door, and I watched them disappear inside as I got out of my truck.

"Back so soon? How did it go?"

"What did you tell that woman about me?" I asked, leaning against the driver door and crossing my arms.

Lizzie wore a fuzzy pink hat that was somewhere between a beanie and a beret. She pushed it up her forehead and blinked at me. "What do you mean?"

"The woman was relentless. I think she was expecting me to bend her over the café tables right then and there."

Wide brown eyes stared back at me. "What? Really?"

"She sat down and told me you were right, and I was delicious." I wiggled my eyebrows for emphasis.

Lizzie clapped her hand over her mouth and giggled, and despite myself, I found my lips tugging up at the corners. The tension from the date drained out of me, and I finally shed that panicky feeling of needing to get away.

"I can't believe that," she said.

"Did you tell her I was delicious?"

"Now how would I know something like that?" Her eyes sparkled in the cool December air, that irresistible witchy smile tugging at the edge of her lips.

I could kiss her when she looked at me like that. Feel her

part those plush pink lips and let me in. Taste her right back and find out if *she* was as delicious as she looked.

"I'll admit, Astrid was a bit of a wildcard," Lizzie said. "After Laurel, I thought maybe I'd misread you."

"I'm starting to think you might be illiterate when it comes to my taste in women, Lizzie."

"Hey, now. I'm under pressure here. You haven't given me anything to work with other than wanting someone that no one else thinks is hot."

"That's not what I said."

"No? What did you say, then?"

"I said I wanted to get to know a woman who made me feel like I was uncovering her secrets. Discovering her. Not someone who says she likes art because she enjoys getting messy."

Lizzie rolled her lips inward to keep from laughing.

"She also told me she wanted a strong coffee to get her energy up so she could drink me down later."

A gasp slipped through those lips I kept staring at, and Lizzie clapped a hand over her mouth again. "No."

"Yes."

"She's an elementary school teacher!"

"She's a sexual deviant. Or she might as well be. I've never seen anyone lay it on so thick."

A snort escaped Lizzie, and I finally began to laugh. I loved when she snorted like that, when her giggles became too much to contain. She made me feel all fizzy inside. Even the memory of that disastrous date faded into something I wanted to share with her, just to make her laugh.

The front door opened, and Aaron appeared in the doorway. He waved at us. "That was quick!"

"Oh for two," Lizzie called back.

"You're losing your touch," Aaron replied.

"No way," Lizzie protested. "I can do this. I'm good at this!
Matchmaking is one of my special skills."

"What other special skills do you have?" The question just...
slipped out of me. I hadn't meant to sound so raspy.

Lizzie glanced over her shoulder at me and narrowed her
eyes. "Wouldn't you like to know?"

Yes, yes I would.

"Come inside," Aaron called out. "Game's on. Lizzie, the
kids are in the family room if you want to check on them."

As I glanced at her profile, I saw Lizzie's smile freeze, then
brighten artificially. "Sure!" She set off toward the house, and I
had no choice but to follow.

TWENTY-ONE

LIZZIE

I WAS in the kitchen putting together a snack for the kids when Sean came in to top up his drink. He watched me arrange cut vegetables on a platter for a moment as he filled his glass with water, then nabbed a carrot stick when he thought I wasn't looking.

I smacked at his hand, and he laughed.

Sometimes it caught me unaware just how gorgeous he was. When he laughed like that, it made me feel like I was full of helium and just one fraying thread away from floating away.

Laurel's words echoed in my mind. What if he *was* interested in me? She seemed so sure of it, and maybe...

"Is all of that for the kids?"

I looked down at the plate of veggies and dip, then nodded. "Yes, but I can make up another plate for you guys to have while you watch the game."

"If it's not too much trouble..."

"Not at all." I smiled but turned away quickly to get the supplies out of the fridge again. Laurel's comments were getting to my head.

When I turned back again, Sean leaned against the counter next to me. His arm brushed mine, and his gaze followed the movement of my knife. I sliced through a cucumber and began to cut it into sticks.

"Where'd you learn how to do that?" His voice was low. Intimate.

I arched a brow. "What, chop veggies?"

"Use a knife like that."

"Mostly YouTube videos," I admitted. "Here. Let me show you." I put the knife in his hand and curled his fingers around the handle and the base of the blade. His skin was warm, his hand much larger than mine. My heart thumped at the feel of him so close to me. "You have more control holding it this way compared to just gripping the handle."

"Right," he said, and put down his drink. "And then I just..."

"Yeah. Rock the knife back and forth. Just like that."

I stood close to him, my face near his shoulder, until he'd finished cutting the cucumber into slices. He grabbed a red pepper and positioned it on the cutting board.

"Let me show you a trick," I said. "If you top and tail the pepper, you can get all the seeds out sort of like you're fileting a fish, and then you'll end up with a big strip that's easy to julienne."

"I have no idea what any of that means, but I trust you,"

Sean replied, grinning. I couldn't have stopped myself from smiling back if I tried. But I didn't try. I just stood there grinning at him over a board of half-prepared vegetables like a loon.

He smelled delicious. As I took the knife back and showed him what I meant, he leaned closer so his chest brushed my shoulder. It might have been my imagination, but I thought his hand might have floated up to brush the small of my back.

My heart rattled. My hands shook—they shook so hard the knife slipped.

Sucking in a hard breath, I pulled my finger away to see a thin line of red seeping from a fresh cut. "Ouch!"

Sean's brows slammed down. He hit the faucet, tested the water temperature, then curled an arm around my back to guide me to it. "Wash that. Where're the bandages?"

I pointed at the bottom drawer on the other side of the kitchen with my foot. "There. But it's only small. I might not even need—"

I stopped talking when Sean tore open the box, sending bandages flying over the counter. He grabbed one, then tossed me a clean dish towel and started opening the bandage's package.

Once my finger was dry, Sean gripped my hand in his much larger one and carefully, gently smoothed the bandage over my tiny wound. His fingers ran over the flesh-colored fabric a few times, his thumbs gently massaging my palms.

It was the most intimate touch I'd had with a man since my divorce, and it made me so light-headed that I had to lean against the counter.

"You okay?" Sean asked softly, concern in his eyes as he watched me.

"I'm fine. A little embarrassed that my knife-cutting skills failed me when I was trying to impress you."

He gave me one of his brilliant smiles, and my heart took off at a gallop again. My hand was still cradled in his, and neither of us made any move to pull away.

"Sean, you're missing the game!" Aaron called out.

We both jumped. I pulled my hand away and cleared my throat, making a show of inspecting the bandage. Sean tugged at his shirt and took a big step away from me.

"All right, all right," Sean answered back. He stayed there for a moment, then cleared his throat. "I should…"

I nodded. "Yeah."

Once he'd disappeared around the corner, I leaned my palms on the kitchen counter and let out a long breath. I felt silly for being so infatuated with him. I was quite literally in the process of trying to find him a New Year's kiss with another woman.

I was the opposite of special. I'd been invisible for so many years that even the scrap of attention that Sean had paid me was going to my head. So he'd touched my hand when he was tending to my wound. That was normal, wasn't it? I was the one who was being ridiculous.

Whatever Laurel had seen in him wasn't real. Or if it was, it might be some passing attraction that would fizzle out soon. For Sean to be interested in me, he'd have to broach the topic with my brother. He'd have to tell his oldest friend that he wanted to date me, and he wouldn't risk their friendship with that kind of bombshell unless he was seriously interested.

Seriously interested in *me*. With all my baggage, my past, my complications. Didn't seem likely, and indulging in these kinds of thoughts was just another way for me to torture myself.

I took a deep breath, cleaned up the bandages still strewn all over the counter, then went back to chopping vegetables.

TWENTY-TWO

SEAN

"SO WHY DIDN'T you go for it?" Aaron asked as he slouched on the couch, his feet kicked up on the coffee table beside the empty platter of veggies and dip Lizzie had brought us.

I blinked away from the TV. "Go for what?"

"The art teacher. Sounds like she would've been wild in the sack."

I scoffed and shook my head. "Trust me, it would've been a bad idea."

Aaron grinned and lifted a shoulder in a casual shrug. "Lizzie has an eye for these things. You might've hit it off if you gave it a chance. And what about the first chick?"

"Why is everyone so obsessed with setting me up with someone?"

Aaron lifted his palms. "Not obsessed. Just trying to help you out."

"I don't need help meeting women."

"Evidence suggests otherwise."

I huffed a laugh and kicked my own feet up onto the coffee table. I'd wanted to linger in the kitchen with Lizzie, but I felt awkward about doing it in Aaron's house. I was so painfully attracted to her, but he was my best friend. He was the whole reason I'd moved to this town, along with my aunts. It was for weekends like this, where we could hang out and Mikey could know what it was like to grow up with a community around him.

Could I really blow that up for a woman? For Lizzie?

Last time I'd taken a chance on a woman, she cheated on me during the one time of year I needed her most.

"You still hung up on Melody?"

I glanced over at my best friend. "What?"

"Is that why you keep brushing off these dates?"

"No. No, definitely not."

"Good. Wasn't right, what she did to you. Especially knowing what you've been through around this time of year."

A familiar ache throbbed in my chest. I rubbed the spot and nodded. "I'm over it," I said, but I wasn't quite sure it was the truth.

"Maybe we forget about the whole New Year's kiss thing and just get through the holidays. Then Lizzie can come up with some better prospects for you. You can get on the apps, see if anyone's out there. It's about time you found someone."

"Lizzie doesn't need to do anything for me," I replied a little too hotly. "She's done plenty."

Aaron hummed, eyes tracking the play on the screen. "Yeah."

"Besides, she's been divorced longer than I have, and I don't hear anyone talking about how it's time for her to start dating again."

Aaron's brows drew low over his eyes, but he didn't take his eyes off the screen. "What do you mean?"

"Why isn't anyone trying to set her up with a new guy?"

Aaron frowned harder and finally looked at me. "Who? My sister?"

"Why are you looking at me like that?"

"My sister doesn't want to date anyone."

"Oh yeah?"

"Yes," Aaron replied emphatically. "She's fine. She's happy. She's got the kids and the job and everything."

"I've got a kid and a job and everything."

"What are you trying to say?"

It was my turn to put my palms up. "I'm not saying anything. Just asking the question. She's not dating anyone, is she?"

Aaron turned back to the TV. "Not that I'm aware."

I glanced at the opening that led to the hallway and the kitchen, listening for footsteps. When I heard none, I asked, "What was up with her ex?"

"Whose ex?"

"Your sister's."

"Lizzie?"

"You got another sister I don't know about?"

Aaron snorted, then shrugged. "I think they just grew apart. That's what Lizzie said."

"She told me he was flirting with one of his coworkers."

Aaron glanced over. "Yeah?"

"Yeah."

"Huh."

"She never mentioned that?"

Aaron lifted a shoulder and let it fall. "Actually...yeah. He was talking with someone, or something? Some messages? I don't think he ever cheated on her. She just said it didn't work out and that she wanted to focus on the kids. He started dating someone new pretty quick, I think. So maybe there's something to it. Mom mentioned something about it, but I don't know."

"That doesn't bother you?"

"What?"

"That your sister's ex was basically having an affair."

"What's it got to do with me? It was years ago, man. And why do you care? Are you into my sister, or something?"

"What?" I shifted on the couch and adjusted a throw pillow. "No. I'm just asking. While we're talking about dating after divorce and all."

Aaron shook his head and chuckled. "Don't worry about Lizzie. She's happy. She always wanted to be a mom. The divorce sucked, but she pulled herself together and now she's good."

I wasn't so sure about that. I thought of her frozen smile when Aaron had called her in. The devastated look on her face when she realized no one had saved her any stuffing.

I'd meant to stay and help her, to soak up some of that sunshine she exuded, but Aaron had called me back. His voice had been a jet of ice water to the face, a stark reminder of what was at risk if I got involved with Lizzie.

He thought she was happy in her life, but I saw something different. I saw a woman who toiled without a break, who was taken for granted. A woman whose smallest desires were ignored and overlooked.

She deserved a man who saw how bright she shone despite it all. She deserved someone to tell her she was beautiful. She deserved to be held and cherished and wanted.

And I wanted to be the man to do that for her. Every time I got near her, I ached to run my hands down her curves, to feel how she'd fit against me, to get those dimples of hers to make an appearance when she graced me with a smile.

But what if it was just some temporary attraction? What if it was all this talk of matchmaking, and I ruined my friendship with Aaron? What if I acted on my desires, and it blew up in my face, just like things had with Melody?

My ex had been beautiful and vibrant and magnetic, just like Lizzie. Sure, her efforts had gone into career progression instead of childrearing. She was driven and ambitious. I'd been drawn in by her, just like Lizzie drew me in with her witchy smiles and teasing remarks.

I'd misjudged my ex so badly. I'd put my heart on the line and built a life with her, only to have it thrown back in my face.

Lizzie wasn't my ex. She was special—one of a kind. I was like some kind of rare jewel collector coveting her from afar, but I knew, deep down, that she couldn't be mine. I just couldn't risk the fallout if things didn't work out between us.

But I wanted her. I wanted her so much I could hardly focus on anything other than the sound of her voice in the other room.

When the game was over, I found myself drawn to the family room. Lizzie lay on the couch while the kids played with LEGOs on the floor, reading something on her phone. She had one knee bent and the other straight, her hip cocked up at an angle and wedged against the back of the couch. She looked relaxed and beautiful, and if she were mine, I would lift her legs and lay them across my lap so I could sit there and touch her. I'd tangle my fingers with hers and bring them to my lips to feel the silkiness of her skin against my mouth.

She glanced away from her phone and arched her brows at me. "Everything okay?"

"Yeah," I said, but it sounded like a lie. I cleared my throat. "Mikey, you ready to go?"

"Ten more minutes," Mikey protested. "We're almost done with the spaceship." He pointed to the blocks between him, Zach, and Levi.

"All right," I said. "Ten minutes."

Mikey grinned and bent his head over the toys. My gaze was drawn to Lizzie, who gave me a wry smile. "You big softie," she teased quietly.

I took a seat on the end of the couch as she bent her legs and sat up, her hair mussed, clothes wrinkled, looking perfect.

And I knew I couldn't have her.

"I think we need to reassess our strategy here," Lizzie said after a few minutes of comfortable silence.

"Oh?"

"You free this week? I have some questions for you that I think will help me narrow down some better prospects. If you're free one lunchtime, we could grab a bite and get to the bottom of this. Third time's a charm."

Lunch with the woman I should've been keeping my distance from. What could go wrong?

I shrugged. "Sure."

Lizzie grinned, then got up off the couch and gathered her kids and her things. I watched her for a few moments, then let out a long sigh and called Mikey's name.

It was just lunch. An opportunity for her to set me up with yet another woman who couldn't hold a candle to her. It wasn't a date.

So why was I already looking forward to it?

TWENTY-THREE

LIZZIE

I MET Sean for lunch on Tuesday, and I came prepared. The Four Cups Café was bustling with people who chatted and laughed over drinks, pastries, and sandwiches, the scent in the air a rich aroma of coffee, spices, and sugar. I sat at a small square table and pulled out the notepad and phone where I'd prepared more extensive questions for him.

He walked in wearing his quilted tan work jacket, jeans, and work boots. His cheeks were red from the chill in the air, and more than a few heads turned in his direction. My heart gave a leap when his eyes landed on me, and I steeled myself against the force of my attraction.

Yes, he was a beautiful man. No, I couldn't have him for myself. Repeating those thoughts like a chant was the best I could do when faced with the power of his presence.

The more attracted I felt to him, the more determined I became to set him up with someone else. I was the family matchmaker, and I would not fail. If I didn't put in a full effort, maybe someone would guess that every time he grinned at me, I felt like fainting. I wouldn't be able to stand the mortification of it. *Poor Lizzie*, they would think. *She really thinks she has a chance with him.*

So when Sean pulled out a chair across from me and dropped into it, I gave him a determined smile.

"I have a plan," I announced.

"Uh-oh." He pulled the black beanie off his head to reveal his short-cropped hair, his long fingers curling around the knit fabric as he stuffed the hat in his pocket. He had very nice hands. A man's hands, with calluses and broad palms and long fingers and—

His hands were irrelevant. I uncapped my pen.

"Laurel was a good match on paper in terms of shared hobbies, but there was no spark. Astrid turned out to want something a bit more, uh, explosive than what we'd anticipated. We're looking for someone who's in between. Someone just right."

"My Goldilocks."

I smiled. "Exactly. On that note. Physical preferences. Ethnicity? Hair? Eye color? Build?"

Sean shrugged. "Like I said before. It depends."

"I'd really like you to dig deep," I said, leaning forward. "There must be *something* you're attracted to more often than not."

"Curves," he blurted, then cleared his throat. His cheeks went faintly pink, and he glanced toward the counter as if he were reading the menu. "I like a woman with a little something extra. Something to grab." His hands made a clenching motion before smoothing out over his thighs.

I blinked at his profile, surprised and a little turned on, which was ridiculous. "Oh. I see."

"What do you want to eat?"

I plucked one of the menus from the edge of the table and pointed to one of the soup combos. Tomato basil soup with a grilled cheese on the side. "Comfort food," I explained.

He nodded and stood, shedding his jacket as he did. I ogled. I know; it was wrong. I should have looked away, but I just couldn't. He stripped that Carhartt jacket off and revealed a fitted polo shirt with Grant's company logo on the breast. The sleeves hit him at mid-bicep, so I got a nice view of the shape of his arms as he dropped the jacket on the back of his chair. The fabric wrinkled over his flat stomach before he pulled it down, covering the little strip of skin that had been exposed by his movements.

When he turned toward the counter and walked away, I stared at his ass.

"Girl, you'll want to roll that tongue back into your mouth before he catches you," a voice murmured behind me.

I turned to see a redheaded woman a little older than me clearing the table at my back. I was pretty sure she was one of the women who'd owned the place since it opened a few years back. My blush was hot on my cheeks. "I, um. Yeah. Right."

She laughed and winked at me. "Not that I blame you. He's Grant's new guy, right? Fiona—Grant's wife—told me he's been a godsend."

"Well that's wonderful," I managed, forcing a smile as I did.

"Grant didn't mention he looked like *that*, though." She laughed, picked up her bin full of dishes, and sauntered off.

I let out a heavy sigh and shook my head. If a stranger could tell I was leering at Sean, it had to be written all over my face. I needed to pull myself together, or I'd be a laughingstock. Sean Hardy was not for me. Sure, he said he liked curvy women, but when men said that they usually meant a huge rack and a tight rump with an itty bitty nipped-in waist. That was not me. Never would be.

By the time Sean came back, I had my pen poised over my pad and had written the word "curves" as my first bullet point.

"So. I was thinking about this after your date with Astrid, and I'd like to approach this in a different way."

"Okay," Sean replied, sounding unsure. He leaned back in his chair, and his foot nudged mine. Neither of us moved away, and my heart definitely should not have thumped as hard as it did.

Focus.

"Tell me about your ideal day," I said, starting another bullet point.

When I looked up, Sean's brows were raised. "My ideal day?"

"Yeah. What would be the perfect day to you? Start to finish."

"With a woman?"

"If your perfect day includes a woman, then yes."

Sean rubbed his finger over his chin as his eyes took on a faraway look. I waited, watching the way his fingers flexed and curled, and reminded myself that another woman would feel those hands on her body, and that was the way things were meant to be.

I had a full, beautiful life, and I didn't want to embarrass myself by asking for things that could never be mine. I'd learned my lesson with Isaac. With my family. With every year that went by.

"I wake up without an alarm," Sean finally replied, "in a comfortable bed, with the sun streaming through the windows. It's early, and I can hear the birds outside. My partner is beside me, and we take our time getting up. Coffee, breakfast. There'd be time for us to do things as a family, whether it's a walk or a sport or just making a meal together. In the evening, we might have friends over—a barbecue. Lots of laughs. After everyone left and Mikey was asleep, we'd spend some time together, just the two of us. Slow and easy and quiet."

My heart clenched. His vision of a perfect day sounded so peaceful and simple, and so close to what I wanted for myself. "And how does she make you feel?"

Sean's gaze flicked over to mine. His knee shifted to touch the edge of my thigh, then moved away. "She'd make me feel like there was nowhere else I'd rather be. She'd feel like home."

I dropped my gaze to my sheet of paper and tried to swallow past the lump in my throat. "So your ideal woman is someone who likes a slow pace to life, who appreciates life's small pleasures. Someone who enjoys a lot of downtime but isn't opposed to entertaining and being active."

"When you put it like that, it's no wonder Melody and I got divorced. She's pretty much the opposite."

I huffed a laugh and jotted down a few notes. My heart

ached, and I felt silly for it. I would've loved to find a man who made me feel at home. My marriage to Isaac had been fraught with stress and effort. We hadn't had many slow, easy mornings and evenings—

Well. *He'd* had slow and easy mornings and evenings. I'd spent that time making sure the house didn't fall apart.

"I'd also like someone I can spoil."

I looked up.

Sean looked a little bashful when he continued, "Not necessarily with lavish gifts and vacations, but I like to do things for people. Small things."

"Like the stuffing," I blurted before I could stop myself.

His eyes were soft when they met mine. "Yeah. I'd like to find someone who appreciates things like that. With my ex..." He gulped and ran his hand over his hair, then down to the nape of his neck where he rubbed softly for a few moments as if to soothe himself. "With Melody, I felt taken for granted. I don't think she cared about the fact that I made sure the coffee machine was prepped for her on a timer so she'd wake up to a hot cup, or how I'd—" He cut himself off. "It doesn't matter. She just didn't see those things I did, or if she saw them, she didn't let me know that she appreciated them. If I were to describe my perfect woman, it would be someone who would appreciate that side of me, and maybe...maybe reciprocate as well."

He stopped talking abruptly and shifted in his seat, as if his admission made him uncomfortable. Before I could stop myself, I reached across the table and put my hand over his, squeezing softly.

"It's not unreasonable to want to feel appreciated by your partner, Sean."

He snorted. "Yeah. I haven't thought about this stuff before. I thought we got divorced because of the infidelity, but maybe there was more to it than that."

"There usually is."

"You must think I'm pathetic, saying all this to you."

I ran my thumb along the tops of his fingers and shook my head. "Not even a little bit."

When he shifted his hand against mine, I should have pulled away. But he slid his palm forward and caught my fingers with his, and it felt so good to be touched like that, so soft and gentle, that I couldn't bring myself to stop it.

"I never felt like a priority in my marriage either," I heard myself say. In some corner of my brain, I cursed myself for the confession. This lunch meeting wasn't about me. I shouldn't have been holding hands and telling him my deepest secrets. I was supposed to find him a date. Someone who would share his perfect days. Someone who would fit beside him, who wouldn't make strangers wonder why a guy like him would be with a woman like her.

"That doesn't surprise me," Sean said, a corner of his lips tilting. "You're a giver. Selfish people take advantage of people like you."

"That's a very nice way of saying doormat and people pleaser," I answered with a wry smile, finally pulling my hand away.

"Don't do that, Lizzie. Don't put yourself down."

I opened my mouth to answer, but our food arrived. I sat back and smiled at the teenage waitress, then inhaled the aroma of my soup and extra-cheesy grilled cheese. Sean had ordered an enormous sandwich for himself. We commented on how good the food looked, and after a bite or two, talked about how good it tasted. I used those moments to walk myself back from the ledge and remember why I was here.

I dipped the corner of my grilled cheese into my soup and said, "I think I know who might be a good fit for you."

Sean chewed his sandwich and watched me. When he'd swallowed, he said, "Is that right?"

"Uh-huh. She's a mom."

"Okay."

"She's really easygoing. Her divorce was really contentious, but I think she's ready to start dating again."

Interest sparked in his eyes, and a little part of me died. Sean said, "Oh yeah?"

I ripped into my grilled cheese with my teeth to hide my disappointment, and I nodded. "Cindy Reynolds," I told him. "You'll love her."

His shoulders dropped slightly, and an emotion flashed across his face. Disappointment? It was too fast for me to read. He gave me an encouraging smile. All he said was, "Why not?"

TWENTY-FOUR

SEAN

HEART'S COVE was home to many artists, and when Cindy and I had exchanged messages, she said she was interested in one of the exhibits at a gallery on Cove Boulevard. We decided to meet outside the gallery on a clear-skied, crisp Friday afternoon.

Christmas was less than a week away; somehow, with all the excitement and distraction, I hadn't noticed the holiday creeping up on me. Melody would be in town soon to pick Mikey up for their time together.

The month of December hadn't been fraught with sleepless nights and old demons. It had been...nice. That was a shock.

I got out of my truck when Cindy arrived and greeted her outside the gallery. She was a statuesque woman that I recognized from school drop-offs and pick-ups. Her dark-blond hair was clipped at the back of her head, and she smiled at me above a knitted white scarf tucked into a black pea coat.

"Good to see you again," she said, pressing a kiss to my cheek.

I opened the gallery door for her and we stepped inside before stripping off our outerwear. Cindy wore a fitted dress that showed off her curves. She caught me staring and gave me a shy smile, then folded her jacket over her arm and tilted her head toward the artwork in front of us. "What do you think?"

"Hitting me with the hard questions right off the bat," I joked, and studied the painting. It was a landscape, and I recognized one of the lookout points that Lizzie had photographed and framed in her house. Waves crashed at the base of the cliffs, foaming white and blue. "I like it," I finally replied. "It feels like it's moving."

Cindy's smile widened. "I agree."

We walked slowly, stopping at whatever art pieces caught our gazes, and I learned that she'd lived in Heart's Cove for a little over a decade. She'd moved here with her ex before they divorced and decided to stay since her kids were settled.

"It's a great place to raise kids," she said. "You just have the one, right?"

"Mikey," I confirmed. "He's great. It's been an easy transition for him, even coming in partway through the school year. I was worried."

"You're a parent," she said.

She was kind, and I understood why Lizzie had set us up. Cindy seemed like the type of woman who wouldn't mind long evenings on the couch and easy meals with family and friends. She had a calming presence.

"I heard you went out with Astrid," she said as we admired an abstract nude figure on one of the gallery's stark white walls.

I cleared my throat. "We had coffee."

Her smile was a little teasing around the edges as she glanced over at me. "Just coffee?"

"Just coffee."

She laughed. "I've heard stories about her, you know. One of the dads got involved with her. Apparently she's got a whole room filled with whips and chains and things you wouldn't even believe."

"I'd believe it," I said, and Cindy laughed harder.

"I shouldn't laugh," she said. "Everyone has their vices."

I grunted. "I wish I'd had a little warning, is all. I don't think Lizzie knew when she set us up."

"Either that, or she was trying to figure you out."

I huffed in response, wondering.

We walked around to the back wall when a woman walked out of the back room. She chatted with us for a few moments, and we learned that she owned the gallery.

"My name is Georgia," she said with a smile. "If you need anything, just give me a shout."

"Will do," Cindy replied.

After wandering through the rest of the gallery, admiring the paintings and pieces of abstract pottery, we made our way to a nearby restaurant for a meal.

The whole date was pleasant. I enjoyed Cindy's company. She worked as a librarian and made me laugh when she went into detail about her opinion of the Dewey Decimal System.

Her divorce was difficult, and she'd only recently started dating again.

I should've wanted a second date. When we parted ways, she lingered by her car door and I knew that I could've kissed her if I wanted to. She was beautiful, funny, pleasant, and kind. Everything I had told Lizzie I wanted. It made sense that Lizzie had matched up so many couples in her life, because I'd seen Cindy around the school but we could've gone years before actually connecting with each other—but she ticked every box. Our lives could easily slide together and fit.

But there was one glaring problem.

I didn't want Cindy.

When she laughed, I found myself comparing the sound of it to Lizzie's snort. When she asked me about my divorce and commiserated over the few details I shared with her, all I could think about was how good it had felt to tell Lizzie my truths over the last few weeks. And though she was beautiful, she just wasn't Lizzie.

Sitting in my truck, I stared sightlessly out at the building in front of me. I wanted to want Cindy. I wanted to feel that spark in my gut, to feel the need to touch and tease and claim her. I wanted the simple, easy romance of someone who was perfectly good and perfectly appropriate.

Instead, I craved my best friend's little sister.

We were in our forties, but it didn't matter. She was still Aaron's kid sister. I was breaking the bro code by even thinking about her this way. I was risking blowing up the longest friendship I'd ever had. Getting involved with Lizzie was out of the question.

And getting her out of my head was even harder.

I leaned my forehead against the steering wheel and blew out a breath. Maybe I wasn't ready to date. Maybe this whole plan had been a bad idea from the start, and I should've just focused on Mikey, on work, on settling down in Heart's Cove.

My phone buzzed. I pulled it out of my pocket and stared at the screen, chest tight.

Lizzie: Cindy just texted. Said you were a charmer (which I already knew). What did you think??

What did I think? I huffed, reading her message over again. What I thought was that I was wasting my time going out with all these women when I knew exactly what and who I wanted. What I thought was that no one would measure up to Lizzie, because Lizzie was sunlight in human form. She was beautiful and generous and kind. She was a good mother. She gave and gave and gave, and all I wanted to do was lay her down and show her that she could take too. She could take from *me*.

I wanted to taste those rosebud lips. I wanted to kiss her cheeks and run my hands down her neck. I wanted to bury my face between her breasts and hear her gasp. I wanted to fuck her until her eyes rolled back and she finally let go.

A thousand perfect dates with a thousand perfect women wouldn't change my mind.

The only woman I wanted was her.

TWENTY-FIVE

LIZZIE

ELBOW DEEP IN COOKIE DOUGH, I glanced up at the sound of the doorbell. I was already late on my Christmas cookie schedule and a little on edge knowing Sean was out on a date with Cindy, so my first reaction was to sigh and hope whoever it was would go away.

But the doorbell rang again, so I washed my hands and called out, "Give me a second!" before heading down the hall toward the front door. In the long, skinny window beside the entrance, I saw the shadow of a man. A peek through the peephole made me rock back on my heels, a frown tugging at my brows.

I pulled the door open. "Sean. What are you doing here?"

His eyes were dark—darker than I'd ever seen them. His skin was red with the chill of the outdoors, and he said nothing as he crossed the threshold and closed the door behind him. "Kids here?"

I shook my head. "At their dad's."

He nodded, took a step to close the distance between us—and kissed me.

It was a shock. My hands flew up to his shoulders. My lips parted, and Sean took advantage. His tongue swept against mine and tore a groan from my throat. I felt the press of the wall at my back and realized he'd caged me against it. His lips devoured mine until my head spun circles around me. When he moved to kiss my jaw and neck, I inhaled a gasping breath.

"What—"

"Been wanting to do this for weeks," he said, his hips pressing into mine.

"You have?" The shock was evident in my voice.

Sean pulled away, his hands framing the sides of my neck while his thumbs coasted along my jaw. His eyes crinkled at the corners, but they were still dark as sin. "Yes, Lizzie."

"What's happening right now?"

"I'm kissing you."

"Uh-huh," I replied, and then he made good on his promise. He kissed me until the ground fell away from my feet. Until it was only the wall at my back and the warm press of his body at my front keeping me tethered to the earth. When we came up for air, I said, "Date was no good?"

"The date was fine. This is better."

I blinked. "Oh."

His lips coasted over my neck, lingering over the point of my thudding pulse. I blinked up at the ceiling as my hands kneaded his shoulders, then moved to trace the prickly-soft hair at the nape of his neck. When Sean let his hands slide from my neck to my collarbones, I shivered.

It had been a long time since I'd been touched like this. I leaned my head against the wall and clung to him while he stroked me, palms dragging down to feel my breasts. His thumbs stroked up along the soft flesh, and I let out a trembling sigh.

"You feel so good, Lizzie. I've been dreaming of touching you like this. Can't stop thinking about you."

"I think I might have fallen and hit my head. Am I in a coma?"

He huffed a laugh, his breath brushing against my lips. Then he ran his hands down my sides to my hips, where his thumbs ducked under the hem of my shirt to stroke against the soft flesh of my lower belly. His forehead came down against mine, and he pressed a kiss to my lips, just the barest brush of his mouth against mine.

"I want you." His voice was a rasp.

I gulped. "Oh."

"Want you so bad I can't think straight."

"I see."

"Do you?" He pulled back to meet my gaze. "Do you see, Lizzie?"

"Well, the boner makes a lot more sense now."

His laugh was just a sharp exhalation, and then he wrapped his fingers around my wrist and brought my hand down to his crotch. His erection strained against his zipper, hard and hot and throbbing. "Does this make sense to you, Lizzie?"

"Not really."

"Not really?"

I curled my fingers around his cock, stroking along the placket of his pants until I felt the base of it, then all the way back up to the tip. My own body reacted in an instant, heat and wetness surging between my legs. My skin felt stretched taut, too sensitive. I couldn't think. Then I stated the obvious. "You're hard."

"As stone."

"Yes." I stroked him again to make sure. "You are."

He was hard—for me. He'd wanted to kiss me for weeks. All those moments that I'd thought he was interested hadn't been in my imagination.

The first man in years to catch my eye wanted me. His hands coasted over my body like he thought I was the most beautiful woman he'd ever seen. He touched me like he couldn't get enough. He kissed me like he wanted to memorize the taste of my lips, like he was desperate for me.

I'd never felt anything like it. I was off-balance. I was falling.

His hand slipped from my wrist and found its way between my legs. I sucked in a hard breath when he cupped me there, pinning me to the wall with his touch. He closed his eyes as he stroked me just like I stroked him, a trembling breath slipping through his lips. "I want to fuck you, Lizzie. I'm sorry if that sounds crass. But I want to feel you come on my cock, want to taste you, want you to rake your nails down my back."

"You're supposed to be on a date with another woman."

His touch became more insistent, the heel of his hand grinding against my clit. His eyes opened. "No."

"No?" My voice was a breathless tremble.

"No."

I stood on a precipice. He was all wrong for me. We didn't fit. He was Adonis, and I was just me. I didn't have time for a man. I was terrified of giving too much to him and having my heart broken.

But he touched me like he needed me, and my body reacted. Heat swept through my stomach and down to my thighs. Everything went tight as a bowstring inside me as he stroked me through the fabric of my jeans. Even with layers of fabric separating us, his touch felt intense. I hadn't been touched like this—with raw desire and lust and need—in a long, long time.

My hand hadn't stopped tracing the outline of his hardness. A cock that throbbed because he wanted *me*. Sean dipped his head and kissed me again, stroking my tongue with his, pulling back to nibble at my lower lip.

"Do you have any idea how much I want you?" he asked.

"I—" I gripped his cock through his pants. "I think I can tell."

He huffed again and shook his head, his lips coasting against my cheek, down to my jaw. "No, Lizzie. You have no idea. I dream about you. I've been thinking about your body since Thanksgiving. Every time you set me up with someone else, I compare her to you. Every time you laugh, I want you more. I can feel how hot you are," he continued, squeezing between my legs. "So fucking hot, Lizzie. You drive me insane."

"I do?" I blinked.

"Yes." His eyes were fully dark, just a blown-out pupil surrounded by the thinnest ring of color. He stroked between my legs again, and suddenly it wasn't enough. I didn't want just his hand on top of my pants. I wanted his hands on my skin. I wanted his mouth. His cock. I wanted all that attention, all that lust, to bear down on me and make me forget that this was a terrible, terrible idea.

His breath ghosted over my lips. "Let me fuck you, Lizzie. Please, baby. Please." His voice trembled as he begged, and I'd never felt so powerful or so turned on in my entire forty-one years of life.

I nodded, unable to form words.

"Yeah?" he asked, breathy and low.

"Yes," I managed.

Sean's fingers were quick. He unbuttoned my jeans and shucked them off with a flick of his wrist, underwear and all. I stepped one foot out of them, holding his shoulders for support, while his hand slid between my legs. Groaning at the feel of my arousal, Sean swore under his breath and stroked me until I was a trembling mess.

Need ripped a gash through the very core of me. I leaned against the wall and spread my legs, holding onto him for stability while he stroked me until I was a quivering mess. I made little breathy noises, gasping and moaning with every touch of his fingers against my clit. And when he slid his fingers inside, the sound of his groan nearly undid me.

He was on the brink of wildness because of me. My body. My sex. My skin.

"Need you," he gasped, lips against mine. "Need you so bad."

My mind spun. I couldn't figure out how we'd gotten here. Didn't know what path I'd taken that had led to this moment. But his fingers teased my folds and rubbed against my bud, and any attempt at thought went through my head like sand through a sieve. My body was on fire. I panted as he curled the fingers of his free hand around my thigh to spread me wide. We both looked down to watch when his fingers slid down to my opening and thrust inside me once more.

"Oh," I said, and Sean groaned. His teeth ran along my jaw until they found my earlobe, and he bit me while his fingers drove in and out of me. I balanced on one leg, the other curled high on his hip, while my breaths became big gasping pants.

"You're so wet and hot and so fucking soft, Lizzie." His voice was a growl at my ear. "Can't wait to feel that all around my cock."

"Really?"

"You don't believe me?"

"I'm—"

"You're what?"

"I just... My body..."

"Is perfect." His fingers slid inside me as he pulled his face away from mine. The heel of his hand ground against that sensitive bundle of nerves. I bucked, and Sean exhaled. "Your body drives me crazy, Lizzie. Watching you makes my mouth water. Touching you is making me lose my mind."

"Oh."

"So when I tell you I can't wait to feel all of you around my cock, do you believe me?"

He added another finger. The stretch of it was the best thing I'd ever felt. "Yes," I breathed. "I believe you."

"So you'll be good and let me fuck you like I've been needing?"

I nodded, lips trailing kisses on his cheek while my fingers fumbled with the buckle of his belt. I pulled it loose while he pleasured me with his fingers, his other hand gripping my thigh so hard I wondered, distantly, if it would leave a bruise. I wanted it to. I wanted to be able to press my fingers to it and remember how it felt to have him spread me open like this.

We were still just a couple feet away from my front door. Moving was out of the question. Moving would require him to stop touching me. It would require me to use my legs to walk.

Sean swore again and helped me with the fly of his pants, then dug through his pockets until he found his wallet. He pulled out a condom and dropped the wallet. Credit cards and cash went tumbling across my entryway. Neither of us paid them any attention.

My hands shook, so it was difficult to help him with his pants. We managed to get them down to mid-thigh before he gave up and tore the foil packet with his teeth. I watched him sheathe himself, my breath shaky, loving the way those big hands wrapped around his thick cock.

There was no romance. No preamble. Nothing but raw, animalistic need between us. Sean grabbed my thighs and hiked me up the wall. I was shocked at his strength, and another wave of lust and longing tore through me. I'd never been manhandled like this. Never knew I wanted it quite this badly.

"Lock your ankles behind me," he commanded, and all I could do was obey. Then his hand was between us to position him where he needed to be, and his eyes rose up to meet mine. His lips were parted, wet from our kisses, and I heard his soft exhale the second before he drove himself inside me in one long, steady, inexorable thrust.

I moaned. The back of my head hit the wall as my fingernails dug into his shoulders. He held my thighs and rocked into me until his hips locked against mine. The stretch of him inside me was so intense I saw stars. My breaths were short and sharp, and I could think of nothing at all except the feel of his body joining with mine.

"Lizzie—" He shuddered. "Lizzie, you feel so good."

"Yes," I panted. "Yes."

Then he began to move. His head ducked down to the crook of my neck, teeth rasping against my pulse, and the only sounds in the house were our mingled moans and the slap of wet flesh against flesh. His hands dug into my thighs while his mouth gusted harsh breaths against my neck.

I'd never had sex like this before. I'd never been picked up and fucked against a wall. I never knew I wanted it so damn bad, to be pinned and used and cherished all at once. To be wanted so desperately that I could feel him coming undone with every stroke of his cock inside me. I found his mouth with mine and scraped his bottom lip with my teeth. He paid me back by thrusting into me hard and fast, the press of the wall behind me making every rock of his hips more intense.

This was not the staid, routine lovemaking I was accustomed to. It wasn't even like the hard quickies I used to enjoy at the start of my marriage, before things fell apart. This was wild and rough and mindless. It was something more than sex. It was raw need, stripped of everything that could blemish it. Pleasure in its purest form.

I loved the way his hands sank into the soft, dimpled flesh on my thighs. Loved the way he bit my jaw, my lips, my neck. Loved the way he rasped my name like he could imprint it against my skin with his voice.

I came like a supernova. Crying out, I could do nothing but cling to him and ride it until the end. Distantly, I heard Sean groan. I heard him praise me, tell me how good I felt, how much he'd dreamed of this, how much better it was than he'd imagined. I heard him tell me he loved my body. That he was obsessed with the feel of me pressed up against him. His voice drove me on until my body was made of light and heat and pressure, and then I felt him go still and tense with one last hard jerk of his hips against mine.

Aftershocks of pleasure coursed through me as I felt him reach his own peak. I was dazed, mindless.

When Sean went still and loosened his grip on my thighs, I unhooked my ankles and let my feet fall to the ground. That's when I realized there was no strength in my legs, and I slid down the wall until I was seated on the floor, stunned.

Sean leaned a shoulder on the drywall above me, then rolled to his back and slid down beside me. His breaths were deep and harsh, and I glanced over in time to see that his head was tilted back against the wall and his eyes were closed. He swallowed and peeled his eyelids open, blinked a few times, then turned his head to look at me.

I don't know what he saw. My mind was in pieces, and I was sure I looked like a mess. My hair fell down in clumps around my shoulders, half of it still in the messy bun that had previously kept it out of my face. My shirt was askew, and my pants and underwear were still hooked around my left ankle.

Thought was difficult; speech was impossible. I licked my lips and tried to form words, but I had no idea what I was supposed to say.

Sean saved me by reaching up to tuck a strand of hair behind my ear. He angled my chin up and kissed me, soft and tender, with one thorough lick of his tongue against mine. That kiss shocked me more than the sex did. It made me wonder what, exactly, had just changed between us.

Then he leaned his forehead against mine and said, "Something smells like it's burning."

TWENTY-SIX

SEAN

LIZZIE LEAPED OVER MY LEGS, caught herself against the wall, then sprinted down the hallway with her pants still strangling one of her ankles. "My cookies!" she yelled as she skidded around the corner and into the kitchen.

Meanwhile, I picked myself up off the floor and dealt with the postcoital mess and the exploded wallet I'd tossed before following her. When I turned the corner, I got a wonderful view of Lizzie's fabulous ass pointed in my direction as she pulled a tray of charred, smoking cookies out of the oven.

The smoke alarm began to blare in protest.

"Ahh!" Lizzie yelled, shoving the cookie sheet on top of the stove. She grabbed a dishtowel and started waving it wildly in the general vicinity of the smoke alarm while I flung the patio doors open to clear some of the fumes.

When I turned back around, Lizzie had given up on the dishtowel strategy and had resorted to glaring at the smoke alarm with her hands on her hips. Her pants and underwear were still caught around her left ankle.

I laughed, which made her turn that ferocious glare onto me. I threw my palms up. "Sorry."

"Stupid thing," she grumbled, and it went blessedly silent. Seeming to realize she was still naked from the waist down, Lizzie sighed and bent over, then struggled with the tangle of clothes until a cute little growl slipped through her lips.

I closed the door on a gust of cool wind, crossed the space between us, then slid my hands over her hips until she straightened and leaned against the counter. Her hands landed on my biceps, and I'd be lying if I said it didn't feel like heaven to be touched by her.

"You seem frazzled," I noted.

"A lot has happened in the last few minutes."

"That's true." My thumbs stroked over the soft curve of her hips. Touching her was a dream. "Are you upset about what happened?"

"Those cookies have been chilling in the refrigerator for two days. What a waste."

"I wasn't talking about the cookies, Lizzie."

Her cheeks were red. Catching her bottom lip between her teeth, Lizzie flicked her dark-brown eyes up to meet mine. "Right. The other thing."

"Yes. The other thing."

"That was...nice."

"Yeah?"

"Uh-huh."

I leaned forward and brushed my lips against hers. "I thought so too."

"So your date with Cindy didn't go so well, huh."

"It went fine."

"Right. I just assumed, you know, since you broke my door down and then screwed me up against the wall, and all..."

My cock gave a twitch, which had to be some kind of record for speed of recovery past the age of forty. Then again, I'd never been attracted to a woman the way I was attracted to Lizzie. I let my hand slide from her hip to her mound, then lower. "That was something I've been wanting to do for a while."

Her breath trembled as I touched her, softly at first, delving into the soft, wet, wonderland between her legs. "Sean—"

"You want me to stop?" I slid my fingers up to tease the little swollen bud at the apex of her thighs, loving the way her eyelashes fluttered when I did.

"No," she admitted, voice breathy. "Not really. But..."

I stroked her again and bit back a groan when her nails curled into my biceps. "But?"

"What's happening right now?"

"I'm touching you." I slid my fingers lower so I could tease her opening, loving how wet and plush she was against my hand. She was made for sex.

"Right," she said, widening her stance another inch or two. "I meant in a broader sense. Like, what's happening here, with us." Her eyes, which had closed, blinked open again. I loved her hazy, pleasure-drunk look. Loved the way her rosebud mouth parted when I coaxed a finger inside.

"I'm touching you so I can watch you come on my fingers," I clarified. "So I can enjoy the look on your face when you do."

Her laugh was little more than a puff of breath. "Okay. I still don't understand, but okay."

I took my time. The kitchen was warm and smelled like burnt sugar and Lizzie. She let her hands roam over my shoulders and arms, and I learned the way a hitched breath or a twitch in her fingers told me what she liked. I drank in the flush on her cheeks like it was sustenance, then let my lips roam over her soft, soft skin. When I bit her earlobe, she let out a shudder and a moan.

"Love how wet you feel," I told her.

"You do?"

"Uh-huh. Does that surprise you?"

"It's just..."

"Just what?"

"I didn't think you were into me that way," she finally said, her voice small.

I pulled back to watch her face, my hand still busy exploring between her legs. "I'm into you, Lizzie. Haven't been able to stop thinking about you."

Her brows tugged the slightest bit.

I paused my movements and stroked her thigh, glancing from one dark eye to the other. "You don't believe me?"

"I... Well, no. Not really."

"I thought we covered this."

"We were kind of in the middle of something when we did."

I wanted to laugh, but all that came out was a soft snort. My lips curled as I pressed a kiss to her mouth. My hands stroked up the curve of her hips to the little pouch below her belly button. There was something so unbearably erotic about that part of her body, something womanly and irresistible. I brushed her skin there and felt her stiffen, then looked up to meet her eyes again.

"My stomach—"

"I love the shape of you."

She blinked.

"The way you move. You're all curves, all softness." With the tips of my fingers, I began to lift her shirt. Lizzie bit her lip then lifted her arms, and I let out a shuddering breath as it came free and I saw the length of her. She inhaled as I reached for the strap of her nude-colored bra, brushing it down the slope of her shoulder before reaching behind her to unclasp the last garment clinging to her body.

"Let me see you."

She gulped audibly, then removed her bra. Her hands moved to the counter at either side of her hips while I stood before her, running my hands from her shoulders down to her breasts. She didn't have the pert breasts and small nipples of a woman half her age, but the feel of that flesh against my palm made my head spin. I squeezed gently, watching the way she overflowed around my grip. I couldn't resist the urge to plump her breast and bring my lips to it, clasping her nipple between my teeth in a soft scrape. Her chest rose as she inhaled, and her hands finally released their tight grip on the counter to reach for me. I groaned as she ran her fingers through my short hair, body undulating against me as I lavished her with all the attention I'd been craving for weeks.

SEAN

"You're so beautiful, Lizzie," I rasped against her skin, moving to the other breast.

Her laugh was shaky, but she didn't protest. Instead, she reached for my shirt and tugged it up. When it landed on the floor beside her own garments, Lizzie shook her head as she watched her palms spread over my pecs and across my collar-bones. "You're the beautiful one," she said.

When she looked at me like that, it became hard to think. I'd seen so many expressions on her face since we'd run into each other at the pharmacy. The soft joy of watching her kids play. The tight smiles around her family at Thanksgiving. The unbridled joy at decorating a Christmas tree or a gingerbread house.

But this look—the one that looked pleasure-drunk and a little greedy—was my favorite.

For the first time in years, my shoulders were free of the usual weight of responsibility and expectations. All the bitterness of my divorce and the years of struggle as my son's primary caretaker took a back seat to watching a beautiful woman explore my body with soft touches and desire written on her features. She made me feel powerful. She made me want to lay her down and cherish her the way I knew she deserved.

As her fingers traced the trail of hair leading south from my navel, I sucked in a hard breath and wondered just how fast it was possible to fall for someone—and if it would hurt when I finally hit the ground.

TWENTY-SEVEN

LIZZIE

I WAS LIVING IN A DREAMLAND. A place where the hottest man in existence looked at me like I was some kind of supermodel. Where he touched all the parts of my body I'd spent years trying to hide like they actually turned him on.

And the crazy thing was, I believed it. When a rough palm slid to the back of my thigh and squeezed, a jolt of lust went through me because I could feel Sean's harsh breath against my skin. If I followed the path of my hand just a little farther down, I knew I'd feel something hard behind the fabric of his pants.

There were so many reasons not to do this. He was my brother's best friend. We both had kids. I was trying to set him up with someone else. Whatever lust had driven him here tonight wouldn't last—it couldn't. Not when I was Lizzie Butler, designated mom and babysitter extraordinaire.

But for right now, for *this moment*, wouldn't it be nice to enjoy it?

So, when Sean threaded his fingers through mine and tugged me across the room to the couch, I let him. When he pressed me onto the cushions and huffed a laugh as I extricated a kid's toy from under my butt, I smiled right back at him and extended my arms for him to drape himself over me.

This would end; I knew it would. But it had been so, so long since I'd done something for myself. Since I'd done something *bad*.

This was bad. I knew it would blow up in my face. But it was also intoxicating, to have a handsome man run his hands over my hips and let out a shuddering breath like he'd never felt anything so good as my body beneath his.

And when he kneeled on the floor in front of the cushions and had me hook my knees over his shoulders, I was too far gone to push him away.

Truth be told, I wanted to see what would happen when his mouth touched my core. I wanted to feel the rumble of his groan against my flesh and reach the peak of another long-overdue orgasm. I wanted to be selfish, for once. To be seen.

The blaze of pleasure still took me by surprise, though. My fingers curled into the cushions as my back arched, and Sean used his lips and teeth and tongue to make me forget about everything other than the feel of my own pleasure. His hand slid up my stomach to my breast, and I placed my hand over his to keep it there.

My vision went white with pleasure, but I wasn't ready for this to be over. On the heels of my orgasm, I found myself clawing at his pants and tugging them down. I sat on the edge of the sofa and took him in my mouth, and Sean swore above me and curled his fingers into my hair.

Just like I'd imagined—but better.

Pleasure sparked inside me as I sucked him, glancing up to watch the way his head fell back on a gasp. I loved the feel of him against my tongue, the flared tip, the throbbing veins. I loved the way his hand spasmed against my scalp, the breathless, desperate way he said my name.

This wasn't a moment to think about consequences. It was a decade of repressed desire finally breaking free.

"Lizzie," Sean panted. "Fuck, Lizzie that feels so good."

I hummed around his cock and reached down to touch his sac. His groan was strangled, and I pulled back to grin at him. When he met my gaze, his eyes were wild, his cheeks flushed. I hadn't had this much fun being intimate with a man in a long time. Truthfully, I'd forgotten that it *could* be fun. That I could lose my inhibitions and get out of my own head. That a man could look at me the way Sean did and make me forget that anything else existed.

"Get up," he commanded, then reached down to grab my hand. He hauled me up and wrapped an arm around my waist, then kissed me so deeply my head began to spin. Then it was my body that was spinning, my back to his front, his hands running down to stroke between my legs. I felt the press of his free hand on my shoulder, and I bent over to grab the back of the couch.

He entered me in a swift thrust, and I moaned in response. My legs began to tremble a minute later. A minute after that, I was shouting his name and feeling the hard grip of his hands on my hips.

Any control I might have had slipped my grip, and I lost myself to the pleasure, to the feel of him, to the moment. My consciousness was reduced to a series of snapshots. The feel of the couch's fabric against my palms and shins. The trembling weakness that overtook my limbs. The way Sean stroked down my spine with a broad, hot palm. The feel of him stretching me as he thrust inside again and again and again.

My orgasm was a series of waves that ran into each other, shredding thought as it grew. I collapsed onto my elbows and sobbed into the climax just as Sean pulled out of me and moaned, his release warm on my ass and thighs. I panted wordlessly, body twitching, until Sean shifted behind me.

"Towel," he gasped. He sucked in a hard breath. "Stay."

"Yeah," I mumbled back, collapsing onto my side. Full sentences were evidently beyond us. A moment later, the sink in the kitchen turned on, and a moment after that, Sean was wiping up the mess from my skin and collapsing onto the cushion beside me.

I struggled up to my elbows and laughed as he tried to help me, finally giving up and flopping into his arms. We stayed there like that for some time as our breathing returned to normal. I closed my eyes and enjoyed the feel of his fingers drifting down my arm and back up again, listening to his heartbeat slow as the minutes trickled into one another.

Finally, the reality of the situation entered my addled mind. I had one hand hooked over his shoulder, the other trapped between our bodies. Our naked bodies. I blinked against his skin and unmashed my face from his chest to glance up at him.

I'd just had sex with my brother's best friend. Multiple times. There would be a reckoning.

He met my gaze, a soft smile on his lips. "Don't," he said.

"Don't what?"

"Don't say whatever you're thinking right now."

Slightly offended, I frowned. "How do you know what I'm thinking?"

"You're going to say something about how we shouldn't have done that, and I don't want you to."

"You don't want me to?"

"No."

"Why not?"

"Because I think we absolutely should've done that."

"Is that right?"

"Yep."

"What about now?"

"Now?"

"Yeah," I answered, narrowing my eyes. "What happens now?"

"Well," he said, "we could have a snack."

"A snack."

"That was a lot of energy to expend, and I'm feeling peckish."

"You're unbelievable."

"Thank you." His lips twitched.

"I'm not feeding you until you tell me what the hell just happened."

"Well, Lizzie, when two people are attracted to each other..."

"Stop it," I said, biting back my laugh as I smacked his chest. "You know what I mean."

He let out a breath and pressed his lips to my temple. "Do you regret it?"

"I..." Trailing off, I closed my mouth. "No," I finally answered.

"Good."

"That doesn't mean I understand what we just did."

"We just had sex, Lizzie. Hot sex. Unbelievably, mind-blowingly hot sex."

A little zip of pride went through me. It *had* been unbelievably hot, and I was glad he thought so too. "Twice," I pointed out.

"Twice," he agreed.

"Maybe we've earned a snack."

He huffed, then dipped down to kiss me. It was tender, just a brush of his lips against mine while his fingers stroked my cheek, and it made me feel more off-balance than when he'd bent me over the couch and had his way with me.

"Why are you looking at me like that?" he asked gently, gaze flicking between my eyes.

"You kiss me like this was more than just hot sex to you."

His throat bobbed. "I like you."

A denial was on the tip of my lips, because what did that mean? How could he like me? My life was complicated. I was busy—really busy—and I didn't have time to date. Besides, he was possibly the worst option in terms of dating prospects.

There were a thousand reasons that made dating Sean more complicated than someone else, mostly because my family would go bananas if they found out.

And then what would happen if this fizzled out? Aaron would keep being friends with Sean, probably. Would I have to see him at every family gathering? He'd been a fixture at every Butler event growing up, and I knew my parents and brothers wanted the same thing now that he was back in Heart's Cove.

How would they react if they found out I'd just messed it all up? Would they blame me, just like they'd blamed me for the failure of my marriage?

I cleared my throat. "I'm supposed to be setting you up with one of my friends."

"No," he said.

"No?"

Sean shook his head, and his lips began to curl. "No. You're not going to do that anymore."

"But—"

"I'm not going on any more dates, Lizzie. I want you."

Wow. All I could do was stare at him and blink for a minute, because the thought of this beautiful man eschewing all other women for the sake of me was so mind-bogglingly, intoxicatingly flattering that I just had to breathe through the feeling for a minute or so.

"You want me?" I finally asked in a small voice.

His smile grew. "You're asking that now? After everything we just did?"

"That might've been a fluke," I pointed out.

"Give me an hour to recharge, and I'll prove to you that it wasn't."

I rolled my lips in to bite back my smile, my heart aglow. "Maybe we should have a snack to help you along."

He laughed as I got up. We got our clothes back on and shuffled to the kitchen. Sean chose a bottle of wine while I threw the charred remains of my Christmas cookies in the trash. Then I opened the fridge and put together a poor woman's charcuterie board, which was a packet of Slim Jims, leftover grapes from one of the kids' lunches, and some sharp cheddar plonked onto my cutting board.

We ate and drank wine. I watched Sean over the rim of my glass, and he watched me over the rim of his.

"Are you going to tell my brother about this?" I finally asked.

Sean finished chewing his bite of cheese and took a sip of wine. He set the glass down, shrugged, and met my gaze. "I don't know. I hadn't thought that far."

"I thought you'd been planning this for weeks."

He arched a brow. "I said I'd been wanting you for weeks. None of this was planned."

I took a sip of wine and nodded. "I see. Aaron might be upset."

"I know he's protective of you, but—" Sean frowned when I started laughing.

I shook my head. "He's not going to be upset at you. Well, he might, but he'll forgive you. He'll be upset at *me*."

"What?"

"My brother..." I took a deep breath. "Both brothers, and to an extent my parents..."

How could I put it into words without sounding like I was wallowing in self-pity? I wanted to tell him that my role in the family had been etched into permanence over the past decade— or even longer. After my divorce, there hadn't been questions about me dating again. It had been a given that I would focus on the children, that I would put myself second. And I did. But to show up at Christmas dinner on Sean's arm...

That would upset the balance of things.

"They don't see you," Sean said quietly.

I blinked and glanced up at him. "What?"

"They see you as free childcare, as someone who will do the grunt work at family events. But they don't appreciate that you might want more from your life than that."

My throat was suddenly tight. "They're not bad people."

"I never said they were. But they use you, Lizzie."

"They—" I shut my mouth, because what was I supposed to say? The little voice in my head that had piped up when no one saved me any stuffing at Thanksgiving, when my brother had called me and expected me to drop everything to go babysit for him when he needed it—that voice agreed with him. And it had been getting louder. When my bottom lip began to wobble, I shoved a grape in my mouth to hide it.

"Lizzie," Sean said, moving closer. He let his fingers drift down my arm, then dropped his hand. "I didn't mean to make you upset."

"You didn't. It's just..." I took a deep breath, slugged some wine, then shook my head. "It's just been a long time since someone saw me as something more than just a mom."

He let out a sigh, and I didn't have the courage to look at him. I didn't want to see the pity in his eyes. And I didn't want to glance over and see all that intoxicating attraction fade away when he realized who I really was. What if I was just a mom? What if I was just good at grunt work?

Then strong arms slid around me, and my face was mashed against his chest. I curled my fingers into the fabric of his shirt on either side of his spine as he held me, deep shuddering breaths moving in and out of my lungs.

"You want to know what I see when I look at you?"

I inhaled the scent of him and shook my head. "Not unless you're about to tell me I'm a goddess among women."

He huffed a laugh as his hand made a slow sweep down my spine. "That's pretty close to what I had in mind."

I snorted and finally flicked my gaze up to meet his. "Sorry."

"For what?"

"This isn't why you came here tonight."

"How do you know what I came here for?"

I arched a brow. "I think you made it pretty clear when you started kissing me two seconds after walking in the door."

He grinned. "That's one of the reasons. You want to know the other?"

I licked my lips. Nodded.

"You make me feel good, Lizzie. Every time I'm around you, it's like life is suddenly easier. Problems don't seem so bad. My thoughts are peaceful. I can't get enough of it. Of you."

Swallowing thickly, I held his gaze. "Oh."

"When I look at you, I see a woman who's strong. Someone who's been battered by life and come out the other side. Yes, you're a mom. But you're also a survivor. You're funny, and sweet, and smart. You keep everyone around you afloat, and you do it without them even realizing it." He stroked my cheek with his thumb, and any defense I had against him crumbled. "You deserve someone who will carry some of that load for you, Lizzie. And I... I guess for the past few weeks, I've been fantasizing about that man being me."

His words were too big for me to carry. I couldn't process them all as he held me so tenderly, couldn't accept that a man would look at me and see all that.

"Can I ask you something, Lizzie?"

"Sure."

"Will you show me some of your photos?"

I pulled back, frowning. "My photos?"

He nodded to the image on the wall—the one I'd taken years ago of a bluff overlooking the ocean. "Laurel told me you took that. She said you used to be into photography, before life got in the way. The snaps you took of me and Mikey putting up the Christmas tree were amazing, and you just took those with your phone."

"And that makes you want to see what else I've done?" I stared at him like he was crazy, which made him laugh.

"Yes, Lizzie."

"Why?"

"Do I need a reason?"

"Yes."

He laughed again. "Fine. Because I find you interesting, and

I want to get to know you better. All the parts that you've kept hidden."

"I think I *am* in a coma. There's no way you're real."

His grin was a little wry. "If you're in a coma, then there's no reason not to show me your photos."

My heart thumped and I knew by the heat burning in my face that my cheeks were red. But I shrugged and led him to the office just off the living room where I kept my laptop. I grabbed the device and headed back to the couch, waiting until the cushions dipped as he took a seat beside me. Glancing at him, knowing I'd show him the product of a hobby I'd abandoned years ago, I felt exposed.

But I also felt seen, and heard, and appreciated in a way that I hadn't felt in a long, long time.

So I opened the laptop and found my old photographs, then settled into the crook of his arm to show them to him. When he asked me to send him a few of his favorites, the flush of pride that went through me washed away all the vulnerability and left me feeling clean and cherished.

TWENTY-EIGHT

SEAN

WE STAYED up late looking at her photography work, and I enjoyed the spark that entered her eyes when she told me about trips she'd taken before the kids, anecdotes about certain shots, the soft smile that tugged at her lips when she lingered on a favorite photo. She was proud of her work, and she had good reason to be.

We ate again after that, then cleaned up the kitchen and went upstairs. I made love to her in her bed, intoxicated by the smell and feel and taste of her.

Afterward, when we were lying in a tangle, I stroked her skin and let out a long breath.

"Finally worn out, huh?"

I huffed. "I was just thinking about how different this year's holidays were from every other year."

"Because of the move?"

I glanced down at her. "Because of you, Lizzie."

She swallowed, blinking. "What do you mean?"

"Do you remember my dad?"

Her eyes flicked between mine, and she tilted her head back and forth. "Vaguely. He wasn't around much, was he?"

"He left when I was fourteen."

"I'm sorry."

"Don't be. We were better off. He drank a lot. And it always got bad at Christmas."

Lizzie was quiet, but it wasn't the tense, expectant silence of discomfort. She was patient and open, waiting for me to share. This was her magic: it was the quiet peace of her presence, the balm that she smoothed over everyone's wounds without them even noticing. I felt a swell of emotion for her, and a desire to protect and cherish her. I wanted to know her—and for her to know me.

"Most of what I remember from early Christmases was tiptoeing around my dad," I admitted. "Mom would be stressed and Dad would find any excuse to nitpick and poke at her. There would inevitably be screaming matches. My mom would cry. It wasn't a happy time."

"And that's why you don't care for Christmas?"

"Among other reasons." I gave her a tight smile, and she moved her hand to stroke my chest, my shoulder. Her fingers were like little fluttering butterflies over my skin, and I relaxed into the pillows, the scent of her all around me. My eyes closed as I enjoyed her touch.

"Your mom passed away around this time of year," Lizzie said. "That was so hard."

I nodded. "Yeah," I replied, and it came out as a croak.

"It's no wonder you let your ex-wife get Christmas. You probably like to have the time to yourself."

My throat was tight. I ran my hand up and down her side, stroking her skin like it would heal the hurt in my heart just by touching her. "I'm starting to wonder if that was a bad idea. Mikey asked me to spend Christmas together."

"Oh."

My lips turned down. "Sometimes I wonder if Melody cheated at her office Christmas party just to twist the knife a little bit more. She knew everything I'd been through, knew how I felt about this time of year. But then again, maybe I'm the one who withdrew."

"That's understandable."

"You're too nice, Lizzie." I stroked her back, letting my fingers run up beneath her hair to tease her nape. "All this stuff is supposed to scare you away from me."

Her eyes sparkled. "Well, I absolutely love the holidays, so this could be a problem long-term."

I huffed a laugh and shook my head. "This year felt different. Lighter."

She licked her lips and swallowed thickly, then inhaled. I could tell she was bracing herself to ask something, so I stayed quiet. When she finally spoke, her voice was steady. "Do you think this"—her fingers flicked between us—"was a result of all these feelings you're having? They just bubbled over and kind of...landed on me?"

"No."

Her brow arched. "No? Not even going to consider it?"

"What, like me wanting to be with you is some sort of over-correction?"

"You just said that I've made you feel good around the holidays for the first time in..."

"Since I can remember."

"Right. So maybe how you feel about me is getting inflated."

"Why do you do that?" I frowned.

For the first time since we'd started talking, Lizzie stiffened against me. "Do what?"

"It's like you don't believe that I might actually like you."

Her cheeks flushed as her eyes slid to the side. "I just... I've spent a long time feeling invisible. You've caught me by surprise, is all."

"You find it hard to believe that I'd want to be with you?"

Her flush deepened. "Sean, I—" She sucked in a hard breath. "Yes, okay? Yes, I find it hard to believe. I've spent more than a decade feeling like nothing more than a mother and a maid. And now this incredibly hot man is telling me I'm the best thing since sliced bread? Come on."

I flipped her onto her back and propped myself on top of her, using the tips of my fingers to push her hair off her temple. "What's it going to take for you to believe me, Lizzie?"

She let out a breath. "Look, just like you have these deep-seated feelings about the holidays, I have some insecurities about myself. Those things don't just go away within the space of a few hours."

I didn't know what to say to that, so I responded by pressing a kiss to her lips. Her arms slid across my shoulders and around my neck, and I sank down against the heat and softness of her.

She relaxed beneath me, and we shifted against each other so that our bodies were slotted against each other and nestled in the comfort of her pillows and blankets. I hadn't felt this comfortable in a long, long time.

We were too tired to make love again, but it didn't stop me from kissing and stroking and cuddling her until we both fell asleep. When I woke up, our bodies were tangled together like we'd spent the whole night not wanting to miss a second of each other.

Lizzie nuzzled into me as she woke, then stretched against me so all my favorite parts of her rubbed up against me. I never wanted to wake up any other way again.

"Morning," she said, drowsy and smiling. "You're still here."

A dart of annoyance speared me. When would she really believe that I wanted to be here? "Did you think I'd disappear?"

"I thought it might've been a fever dream."

I huffed a laugh, then curled my body around hers. "It wasn't."

She shook her head, then glanced over her shoulder. She bit her bottom lip, let it slide out, then said, "This doesn't feel like a one-time thing."

"No, it doesn't," I agreed.

"So we'll have to tell people."

"Doesn't sound like you want to."

"Maybe it would be better to wait until after the holidays?"

I let my hand drift over her breast and nuzzled into her hair. "Is that what you'd prefer?"

"I just think it might be a lot for my family to take. And the holidays are so chaotic to begin with."

I nodded, but I wasn't able to ignore the sting of her words. I understood, but it felt similar to the way Melody used to brush me off and tell me she didn't want me at her work events. Like I was something to be hidden away instead of shown off.

But this was different, and I knew Lizzie was right. It was a delicate situation, and we didn't need to rush. We had an easy breakfast and then said our goodbyes, and I headed over to Aaron's house to pick Mikey up from his sleepover.

Emily opened the door and smiled at me, her eyes sparkling. "Good night?"

"Can't complain," I replied, knowing she thought I'd spent it with Cindy. "How were the boys?"

"They're great. Built another LEGO project last night, watched a movie, and had spaghetti for dinner. They're in the basement now. I'll go grab Mikey if you want to say hi to Aaron?"

"Sure," I answered, and made my way to the kitchen where she gestured.

My oldest friend was sitting in the breakfast nook with a cup of coffee. He leaned back in his chair when he saw me, grinning, "Success?"

I shrugged. "Mikey behave himself?"

"You know he did," Aaron said. "Now come on. How was she?"

My throat tightened. I didn't want to lie to him. Aaron had been there for me through my father's drinking and my mother's illness. When my marriage fell apart, he was the one I called. For decades, he and his family had been a constant in my life.

I'd moved my son—my whole life—back to this town to be closer to him.

And now I was lying to him.

It wasn't that I regretted what had happened last night. Lizzie was something special, and I was beginning to realize that my feelings ran a lot deeper than even I'd anticipated. It wasn't just lust. I was intrigued by her. Captivated.

But Aaron was my best friend.

I gulped. "Cindy was nice. We went to the gallery, had dinner, and then parted ways."

Aaron's brows jumped. "That's it?"

I poured myself a cup of coffee and avoided his gaze. "That's it," I confirmed, which wasn't technically a lie but still felt like one.

Leaning against the counter, I sipped my coffee and searched for the right words. The problem was, I didn't know what I wanted to say.

"Hey, my parents are hosting Christmas this year," Aaron said, pushing his chair back as he got up. He topped his own coffee up and leaned against the counter opposite me. "They asked me to invite you and Mikey."

"Mikey'll be with his mom," I said.

"Just you then."

My ribs tightened around my lungs. I dipped my chin. "I appreciate that. You and your family have always been welcoming to me. I hope you know how much it means to me."

Aaron gave me a confused smile. "You're my best friend. How else would I treat you? Besides, my mom basically told me she'd disown me if I didn't invite you over. She said your aunts are welcome too, in case that stopped you from spending the day with us."

The tightness in my chest expanded to my throat and stomach. I'd gone about this all wrong. Whatever my feelings for Lizzie, I shouldn't have acted on them without talking to Aaron. But there'd been no stopping last night. Not when I'd finally admitted to myself just how much I wanted her.

Had I made a mistake? If things ended between me and Lizzie, I'd have to spend holidays and social gatherings with her and her family, knowing that she was the first woman in years to make me feel whole.

I was torn between my friendship with Aaron and my growing feelings for Lizzie. It felt selfish to put a woman ahead of my oldest friendship. It felt like a betrayal, and I hated myself for it.

"You okay?" Aaron frowned at me. "If you don't want to come over for the holiday, you can just say so. I know it's a tough time of year for you. I just figured you might want a distraction."

I shook my head. "It's not that."

"No?"

I huffed. "Honestly, Christmas hasn't felt so bad this year. I even found myself humming along to 'Rudolph, the Red-Nosed Reindeer' on the radio yesterday."

Aaron laughed. "Wow. Christmas music used to send you into a rage."

It did—before Lizzie. Before her flushed cheeks and her sunny smile. Before she showed me how good it could feel to create memories with my son. With her, and her kids, and her family.

But could I put a few weeks of intense emotion ahead of a friendship that had lasted decades? What if I jeopardized my relationship with Aaron for something so new?

"I'll talk to my aunts. We'd planned a big meal for when Mikey's back from his mom's, so I don't know if they're doing anything the day of."

"Let me know. My mom's already got your gift."

Gifts. Oh, God. I was so used to spending the holiday alone that I hadn't considered the fact that a community and circle of friends would require me to shop for presents. The sheer panic must have shown on my face, because Aaron began to laugh.

"Get my dad a nice bottle of Scotch and my mom a scarf or some fancy soap. It'll be more than enough."

"Right." I gulped. "Right, yeah. I just—I haven't done the whole holiday thing in a while."

"Well, you've got four days. Plenty of time."

I shoved my hand through my hair and was grateful for Lizzie's foresight. She was right to delay any big decisions or announcements about us until after the holidays. A lot had happened in a short period of time, and I owed it to her—and to Aaron and his family—not to mess this all up.

The sound of footsteps pounding up the basement steps alerted me to my son's arrival. He was bright-eyed and messy-haired, with a face-splitting grin on his lips. "Dad! Levi said he'd let me build one of his *Star Wars* LEGO sets as long as I did it here. Can I?"

"Sure," I said, glancing at Aaron, who shrugged and nodded. "But we might have to wait until you get back from seeing your mom."

Mikey's shoulders dropped. "What if I want to stay here?"

His words caused a pinch in my chest, but I forced a patient smile onto my face. "Your mom has a nice week planned for you, buddy. She's taking you skiing, remember?"

A pout pushed out my son's bottom lip. "O-kay," he said, like a ski holiday in Tahoe was the chore of the century. I huffed a laugh. I ruffled his hair, thanked Aaron and his family for taking care of him, and then loaded him up into my truck. As Mikey got settled in his seat, I waved at Aaron and watched my best friend close his front door.

Was I really ready to risk his friendship and support for a woman who had meant next to nothing to me just over a month ago?

TWENTY-NINE

LIZZIE

EVERY YEAR, I told myself I'd be a better planner so the holidays would go off without a hitch. And every year, the last few days before Christmas ended up being a mad panic of last-minute shopping, buying and prepping way too much food, unexpected school or work commitments, and one too many events.

I got to sit down for what felt like the first time in days when the lights went down on the school stage and Hazel's play started. I'll be honest, I zoned out for most of it. My eyelids had little weights attached to them, and I kept having to blink my eyes open. It wasn't until the candy canes came out to do their dance that I perked up, smiling at the beaming happiness on my daughter's face.

The thought that she'd choreographed and pitched the dance to the teacher made it all the sweeter. I couldn't wait to see what she accomplished as she grew up.

The kids got a standing ovation, of course. Zach clapped to one side of me, and June and Isaac on the other. We waited for Hazel to come out once the play was over, and I didn't even mind the stilted conversation with my ex-husband and his wife.

"Good job, kiddo," Isaac told Hazel when she bounced up to us with red glitter all over her face.

"Did you see me? Did you see the dance?"

"Got it all on video," Isaac confirmed, nodding at June.

I smiled as Hazel beamed. She wrapped her arms around me while her brother whacked her on the back. I nodded at my ex.

"I'll drop them off tomorrow after school," I said, and even managed a smile.

"Can't wait," June replied, and Isaac put his arm around her.

For once, I didn't feel the bitterness of being alone in the face of their companionship. I'd never been jealous of June—I didn't want Isaac back—but I'd always felt like the odd one out. This time, as we parted ways, I felt a little taller than I had before.

I wasn't the invisible mother and maid toiling away behind the scenes. I had something to look forward to. And, after Sean had left on Sunday morning, I'd actually gotten my camera out of its case and charged the battery. There were old photos on the SD card that I'd forgotten about, and I'd made plans to go for a walk along the coast while the kids were at their dad's to take some photos. Maybe Sean would join me. Maybe I could try to capture that light in his eyes when he laughed, the crinkles around his mouth.

For the first time in years, I was making plans for myself. And yes, that time could be spent doing chores or prepping meals or completing one of the million tasks that always landed on my plate. But I wasn't going to let myself miss another well-deserved bubble bath.

I'd earned some time for myself. And if Sean wanted to spend some of that time with me, then all the better.

As the kids walked ahead of me toward our car and I watched Hazel skip beside Zach's steadier pace, I realized with a start that they were growing up. Neither of them believed in Santa Claus anymore. The past eleven years had gone by in a flash, and in even less time, Zach would be off to college or trade school or whatever he decided to do. Hazel wouldn't be too far behind.

Where would that leave me? I couldn't keep letting myself be shoved into the role of mother and nothing more. I was a woman. I was an amateur photographer. I was a trashy reality TV show aficionado. I could be all those things and still take care of my kids and my home and my life.

Maybe, I could one day be a wife and partner. A lover.

Glancing in the rearview mirror to make sure the kids' seatbelts were on, I let a smile curl my lips. I felt ready for change, and I knew that Sean's attention was a big part of it. He'd seen parts of me that I'd hidden even from myself.

And I couldn't wait to show him just how much I appreciated it.

My heart skipped a beat when I drove up to our house and saw Sean's truck idling next to the curb. He and Mikey got out as we pulled into the driveway.

"Hope you don't mind us dropping by," he said. "Mikey's off with his mom tomorrow, and he wanted to stop by before he left."

Mikey smiled as he lifted his hands, bearing a gift in each. He gave one to Zach and the other to Hazel. "We went shopping this weekend. I wrapped them myself."

Hazel hopped on the spot with excitement. "Can we open them, Mom?"

"Come inside," I said. "Don't you want Mikey to have something to open too?"

Zach smiled and ran ahead with Mikey, whose eyes began to sparkle. I herded them all inside as Sean took up the rear, and the kids tromped off to the living room where Mikey's present had been stashed under the tree. Zach had picked it himself, a complicated robotic thingamajig that he promised Mikey would love.

"Stay for dinner?" I asked. "I was thinking takeout." I cringed slightly and felt the need to explain. "I've been prepping for Christmas dinner all week. Don't feel like cooking tonight."

Sean's smile was soft. "Sounds perfect," he said, and I believed him. It was such a small thing for him to genuinely not mind that I wasn't cooking, but it still resonated through me like the tolling of a big bell. My ex-husband had always given me the sense that I should be feeding the kids home-cooked meals all the time. He'd cluck disapprovingly whenever I said I was too tired to cook, but never once did he volunteer to get in the kitchen himself.

As Sean moved closer to me, I wondered how many of these

moments would happen as we kept spending more time together. How often would I realize that my needs had been cast aside for the sake of my ex's ego, or his unrealistic standards, or his own needs? How deep had my self-sacrificing streak burrowed into me, to the point that a rare takeout meal set me on edge?

It felt like a part of me was unfurling. It wasn't just my interests and hobbies that were poking their heads above ground for the first time in years, it was the part of me that said, *I'm tired, and I need a break.* The part of me that was so used to being ignored and dismissed.

Sean glanced down the hall, then lifted his hand to stroke my cheek and press a soft kiss to my lips.

I flushed and glanced over my shoulder again, then shot him a half-reproachful look. "Not with the kids here."

"Sorry. Couldn't resist." His smile was roguish, and I forgave him in an instant. We made our way to the kitchen to watch the kids open their presents, then I made a call to a local Chinese restaurant and put in our order. Sean went to pick the food up, the kids set the table, and I got the drinks ready.

We ate together, and when I glanced across the table to meet Sean's eyes, I felt like the world was full of quiet, happy possibilities.

THIRTY

SEAN

THE NEXT MORNING, I helped Mikey pack his suitcase and hauled it down the steps for him. We ate breakfast, then we hung out in the living room next to the lit-up Christmas tree and waited.

Melody arrived an hour later. A BMW SUV boasting a roof rack laden with ski gear pulled up outside the house and she got out of the passenger seat, while her boyfriend got out from behind the wheel. She hurried toward the front door while I braced myself and got to my feet.

Mikey lifted his gaze from the robotics set Zach and Hazel had gifted him—which had consumed his attention since he'd opened it—to look out the window. A moment later, the doorbell rang.

Mikey glanced at me, and I forced a smile onto my lips. "Your mom's here."

For three years running, the Christmas handoff had been

one of overwhelming relief. Around this time, I would've spent weeks gritting my teeth against the assault of holiday music and well wishes, averting my eyes at the sight of every Christmas tree, and counting down the days until I could hole myself up in my house and wait for the world to come to its senses so I could emerge again.

This time was different.

When I opened the door and invited my ex-wife inside, I glanced down at Mikey's suitcase and felt a pang of regret. The time I'd spent in Heart's Cove had been marked with happy, calm memories of this year's holiday season. With Lizzie's smile, and her kids' exuberance, and the rest of the family's warmth.

For the first time, I wanted to share more of those moments with my son.

But we had a custody agreement, and there was nothing I could do about it now. "Hi, Melody."

She smiled at me, looking glossy and slim and expensive. She wore a tan woolen jacket and a plaid scarf, her long hair curled in soft waves beneath the fabric of her hat. She'd always been a beautiful woman, and as time passed, that hadn't changed. Her brows lifted. "You have a tree."

I glanced into the living room and nodded. "We have a tree."

"That's a surprise. Getting you to even buy Christmas presents used to be like pulling teeth."

"Dad likes Christmas now," Mikey announced, moving to wrap his arms around his mother's waist.

She combed her manicured fingers through his hair and

smiled. "Is that right? What I would've given for him to put one tenth of that effort in a few years ago..."

I flinched. It was an old insult, one she'd flung at me many times as our marriage broke down. She'd been driven to cheat because living with me was too difficult. Every year when the holidays came around, I turned into a different person. Could I blame her for seeking comfort elsewhere?

I'd never been able to answer that question in a way that felt right. Because, yeah. She was right. She'd deserved better than someone who sank into his own darkest thoughts the moment sleigh bells started ringing at the start of the holiday season.

Mikey nodded. "Dad said maybe next year I could spend the holidays with him."

Melody's brows shot up.

I cringed. "I said we'd talk about it."

Mikey threw me a glance like he knew exactly what he was doing, and I rubbed the back of my neck as I met Melody's gaze. "I know that's not what we agreed. We don't have to talk about it now."

"No, I'm just surprised, that's all." She cleared her throat. "We can talk about it later. Come up with something that works for both of us."

"For now, you need to get your jacket on," I said to Mikey. "I'll bring his bag out to the car."

"Thanks, Sean." Melody smiled at me and let me pass.

I walked down the pathway and watched the BMW's trunk open. Melody's boyfriend opened the trunk while I hauled my son's bag into the back. I cleared my throat and forced myself to meet his gaze as I nodded at him. "Todd."

He pressed a button on the trunk, which began to lower automatically, then turned to me and extended his hand. "Got any plans for the next week?"

"Just catching up with family and friends," I said as we shook. "You must be looking forward to getting to Tahoe."

"Snow's supposed to be great this year."

It was a perfectly pleasant conversation between two people who shared a slightly uncomfortable relationship. I had nothing against him, and usually at the Christmas handoff, I'd be glad to see him and Melody arrive. This year, I resented his presence more than I wanted to admit.

I nodded and glanced over my shoulder to see Mikey emerging from the house. I turned to Melody's boyfriend and gave him another tight nod, then said my goodbyes and watched them all load up into the car and drive away. Mikey waved at me through the window, and I waved back with a big fake smile on my face. When I closed the door and stood in the silence of the house, the regret I'd felt earlier only got stronger.

Had I been a bad father to Mikey all these years?

And if things didn't work out with Lizzie...was I just setting him up for an even bigger disappointment? What if Melody was right to be surprised? She knew me well, after all. What if her doubts about me were well-founded? Maybe this was a temporary reprieve, and I'd be back to hating the holidays next year.

Sighing, I shook my head. There was nothing I could do about it now. If I wanted to spend the holidays with Mikey in the future, that was something Melody and I would have to negotiate. Still, the house was too quiet and my thoughts were too loud.

And then my phone buzzed. I pulled it out of my pocket and immediately felt my shoulders soften.

Lizzie: Just dropped the kids off at their dad's and feeling like drowning myself in a vat of mulled wine. Any chance you want to join?

Ten minutes later, Lizzie opened the door with red-rimmed eyes and a self-deprecating smile on her lips. "I don't know why I still get emotional about this. It's been years."

I kicked the door closed behind me and wrapped my arms around her, inhaling the scent of warm spices and sugar that seemed to cling to her. Then I kissed her, and everything felt a little better.

"I didn't want to let Mikey go with his mother," I admitted. "I wanted to keep him for myself."

Lizzie pulled away and stroked the edges of my stubble, where the prickly hair met my cheekbones. Her soft smile eased some of the sharpness around my heart. "I know exactly how you feel. Every time I have to do a handoff for a special event, it feels like part of my heart goes with them."

"They'll be back soon."

She nodded, swallowing thickly. "Yeah. And they deserve time with their other parent."

"Yes."

"But it sucks."

"A lot," I agreed. Water gathered on the lower rim of her eyes, and I kissed away the first tear that spilled. Then my lips moved to her mouth, and I lost myself in the feel and taste of her. She softened against me, her arms pulling me closer in a desperate movement, and I couldn't help but kiss her harder.

"Silver lining," I said between kisses, "is that now I get to do this with you."

Her lips curled against mine. "Make me feel good, Sean," she whispered.

"Always," I promised. My limbs trembled as I framed her face with my hands, and without quite knowing how, we teleported to the bedroom and lost all our clothes along the way. Then we made each other feel better a few times over.

THIRTY-ONE

LIZZIE

MY PARENTS WERE HOSTING Christmas this year, and I arrived bright and early with bags of food and presents. I rang the doorbell and immediately pushed the door open, calling out a "Hello!" as I set my bags down in the foyer.

"In the kitchen!" my mother called back.

I kicked off my shoes and shed my jacket, then made my way toward her voice. I passed the living room along the way, where my dad and aunt were sitting beside the Christmas tree with glasses of eggnog in their hands. I greeted them with smiles and kisses, then headed on to the kitchen.

"Good, you're early," Mom said, wiping her forehead with the back of her wrist. "I've got the roast beef and ham prepped. You mind peeling potatoes while I work on a pie?"

"On it," I replied, shoving some of the desserts and side dishes I'd prepped earlier into the fridge. I grabbed a dark-blue apron from the back of the pantry door, tied it around myself, and got to work.

"Have you spoken to the kids this morning?"

"Called them when I got up," I replied. "Isaac got Hazel a new bike. Sparkly pink with streamers on the handles. She was over the moon. Zach showed off his new baseball mitt and a computer game he'd been asking for."

Mom glanced over at me and smiled. "That's nice."

I nodded and forced my own lips to curl. I didn't mention that when I'd hung up the phone, it had taken me a few minutes of deep breathing to ease the tightness in my chest. Missing these moments with my kids never got easier, but I had to remind myself that I got them most of the time. Their father had been a terrible husband, but he did love them. And June was as good a stepmother as I could hope for. It was just my selfish desire to hoard every moment, every holiday, every memory with my kids for myself. They deserved better.

Besides, wasn't I trying to enjoy this time to myself? Wallowing in self-pity wasn't going to help anything.

"Well, I'm glad you're here with us," Mom said. "We'll have a nice day, and then we spend a nice week until New Year's when we celebrate with everyone together."

"Exactly." I focused on the potato in my hands, peeling its skin off in long strips. It wasn't the first holiday I'd spend without my kids, and it wouldn't be the last.

My mom went over to the old stereo in the corner of the kitchen and started up some Christmas music. I smiled at the old folk CD she'd been playing for decades and sang along as we cooked side by side. Every time the doorbell rang, my ears pricked.

Cousins arrived with their kids. Aunts and uncles came through the door. My brothers blew in with gusts of cool air.

Finally, in the early afternoon, the doorbell rang and wasn't immediately followed by the sound of the newcomer's voice. My heart skipped a beat, because I knew that the only person who wouldn't let themselves in without hesitation was Sean.

Sure enough, a few moments later, I heard my father's voice greeting him, followed by the familiar rumble of Sean's response. My pulse rattled, and I was sure my cheeks were flushed. Grateful for the hot stove in front of me that could be used as an excuse, I kept my head down until I heard the familiar cadence of Sean's footsteps on the tiles behind me.

"Sean!" Mom exclaimed. "Merry Christmas."

"Same to you, Mrs. B."

"You're not a teen anymore, Sean. Will you call me Sandra?"

I glanced over my shoulder in time to see Sean grin. "Probably not. You'll always be Mrs. B to me."

Mom laughed, delighted, and wrapped him in a warm hug.

I put the lid on the gigantic vat of potatoes and turned, wiping my hands on my apron. Sean glanced up and met my gaze. Just a few hours ago, he'd been in my bed. He'd left so we could both get ready for dinner at my parents' place, but the sight of him here and now reminded me that our naked bodies had been pressed together not too long ago.

"Merry Christmas," I told him, and I smiled. I hesitated for a brief moment, then closed the distance between us, got on my tiptoes, and pressed a kiss to his cheek.

Sean's hand skimmed down my side and over my hip, sending wild flutters through my stomach. "Merry Christmas, Lizzie," he said quietly in my ear. We'd already wished each other a happy holiday this morning as the sun came up, but I could feel my mother's eyes on me and it would be weird not to say it to him again.

Pulling away, I cleared my throat. "How was your morning?"

As soon as the words left my lips, my cheeks flamed. Sean grinned. "My morning was great."

I could sense my mom hovering beside us, so I took another step away from him and gave them both a bright smile. "Drink? Mom's special eggnog? Or we have mulled wine, soda, water, beer..."

"Can't say no to a bit of eggnog," he said, eyes lingering on me for a moment before turning to my mom. She beamed at him and poured him a glass, and I busied myself cleaning up the counter where the potato peels had left starchy water splattered all over the granite.

Sean stayed long enough to compliment my mother on her eggnog, then made his way to the living room to greet the rest of the guests.

Mom was quiet for a few long moments, and I began to breathe easier. Maybe the tension between me and Sean hadn't been as obvious as it had felt.

Then my mother said, "You've been spending an awful lot of time with Sean lately, haven't you?"

I jumped. "What?"

She chopped a carrot and shrugged a shoulder. "How goes the search for that date to New Year's? Just a week to go now."

"He's been on three dates," I told her, which, strictly speaking, was the truth. "None of them worked out as far as I know."

My mother glanced over at me, with those all-seeing eyes that used to strike fear into the very depth of my heart. I discovered, in that moment, that even at forty-one years old, her eyes still had that ability. All she said was, "I see. Tougher nut to crack than your usual matchmaking prospects, then?"

"I guess so," I replied. "Everything seems to be under control here for a bit, huh? I'll go say hi to everyone and see who needs a fresh drink."

Mom nodded and took out a tray of hors d'oeuvres that had been warming in the oven. "Pass these around, and bring that veggie platter out while you're at it."

I did as she asked and scurried away from her penetrating gaze. The living room was full of chatter and laughter. The kids had disappeared into the den just around the corner, and I could hear the excited noises of the kids sharing what presents they'd opened this morning when they woke up. I passed around the platter of tiny samosas and mini quiches, greeting everyone and wishing them a happy holiday, and finally set the plate down on the coffee table and took a seat next to my dad.

Sean was seated across the room from me, and I couldn't resist the pull of his gaze. His blue-green eyes seared into me across the space, and I did my best not to squirm where I sat. Even with what little time we'd spent together as an intimate couple, I could tell by the spark in his eyes and the tiny curl at the corner of his lips that he was thinking about things that had no business at a family holiday event.

And it was thrilling.

Here, in this house where I'd always just been little Lizzie, surrounded by people who saw me as a glorified babysitter and failed wife, there was one man who saw me as a woman. He saw me as someone interesting, captivating. He made me feel more beautiful and more precious than I'd ever felt before, and he did it with little more than a look.

Then my brother dropped into the seat beside him, and my dad nudged me with his shoulder, and I smiled at him as he curled his arm around my shoulders.

"How's my favorite daughter today?"

"I'm good, Dad," I replied, and was surprised to find I was telling the truth.

His arm tightened. "Not too sad about missing the day with the kids?"

I knew he was trying to connect with me. Knew he'd seen how in years past, I missed my kids like crazy on days like these. Usually, a comment like that would make me feel understood. Today, it made me feel like there was space between us that couldn't quite be bridged. It was always Lizzie, mom of Hazel and Zach. It was never Lizzie, a person in her own right.

And, yes, fine, I wanted my kids around me at Christmas. And I'd be happier if I got every holiday, every birthday, every weekend, and every event.

But as the days passed and my family's comments stacked up on top of each other, I realized that I also wanted to be seen for being me. A person with hobbies and a career and a life beyond just her kids.

I wanted what Sean gave me: a view of myself like I used to be before I sacrificed everything I was for the sake of my children.

I wanted to be Lizzie *and* a mother. Both—not one or the other.

"I don't feel sad right now," I finally replied, and smiled at him.

"Good," he replied with a nod. My mom appeared at the edge of the living room with fresh drinks, and she beckoned me back into the kitchen to get back to work. I followed her and busied myself with the thousand and one tasks required to pull off a big meal, trying not to dwell on the shift in my identity that seemed to be happening within me with every minute that passed.

An hour later, when dinner was in good shape and everyone had fresh drinks, I realized I was desperate for the bathroom. I ducked to the downstairs powder room, which was past the den, tucked through the laundry room around the corner from the stairs. The sound of conversation was muffled at the back of the house, and I let out a deep breath as I tried the doorknob.

Locked.

Sighing, I leaned against the doorjamb leading out of the laundry room and stretched my neck from side to side. I wondered what my kids were up to, and how Sean was enjoying himself. I wondered just how long we'd have to dance around each other before we'd tell people we were seeing each other.

If he decided he wanted to take that leap with me.

My heart jumped at the thought. An illicit little affair had been thrilling, and he'd made me feel like I was worth so much more than I'd previously allowed myself to think, but to actually date each other, in the open...

That would mean he really wanted me. It would mean this wasn't just about sex. It wasn't just the excitement of doing something naughty, something that felt a little bit dangerous and wrong.

Once the holidays were over, I'd know if Sean really wanted me for me. If all those pretty words had meant something, and if these feelings mushrooming inside me were real.

Then the powder room door opened, and I lifted my gaze. Sean appeared in the doorway as I straightened, our eyes clashing across the laundry room.

"Hey," he said.

"Hi."

I felt like a trapped, trembling little rabbit caught in a snare. My eyes darted down the hallway then back to the laundry room, and I found Sean prowling toward me. He stood on the other side of the doorway, eyes roaming over my face as a soft smile graced his lips.

"You look beautiful, Lizzie."

"You've got to stop saying things like that to me," I said, glancing over my shoulder to see if anyone was in the hallway behind me.

"I won't."

I gave him a flat look. "We shouldn't even be talking to each other."

"That's a ridiculous statement," he said, grinning. "Besides..." He lifted his finger and pointed directly up.

I followed the motion with my gaze, heart jumping at the little bundle of mistletoe hanging in the laundry room doorway. "Sean..."

He stepped toward me and wrapped an arm around my waist, tugging me close. Then I was pinned to the inside edge of the doorway, the length of my body pressed to the length of his. I let my hands settle on his chest and felt the rioting of his heart beneath his breastbone.

With one hand around my waist, Sean lifted the other to sweep back a sheet of my hair. He stroked my jaw with a calloused palm, his thumb stroking from the corner of my lips to the edge of my cheek.

"Merry Christmas, Lizzie," he said. "You've made this year's holiday season one of the best of my life."

My throat was so tight I could barely swallow, and I blinked back moisture from my eyes. "You've made me feel like myself again," I admitted.

"I'm glad we found each other," he whispered—and he kissed me.

We'd spent entire nights in each other's arms. We'd kissed countless times now, tenderly and passionately and roughly and everything in between. I'd seen him naked and partially clothed, and I'd explored every inch of his body with my hands and my mouth.

But this felt different. It felt like the ground swelling beneath my feet, like a seismic shift in the very depth of me. This man had crashed into my life, and he kissed me like he wanted to pick up the pieces with me and make something new together.

We weren't supposed to be kissing here, like this, but the moment got away from me—from both of us. His grip on my jaw tightened as he deepened the kiss, tongue sliding against mine as he let out a soft moan. I lost myself in the feel of his strong body pressed against mine, the strength of him holding me, the way his hand on my waist stroked me through my shirt like he was wishing he could touch my skin.

My hands skimmed up his shirt and teased the stubble on the sides of his neck as I nibbled his upper lip. I loved the warmth of his skin, the hard press of his muscular frame against my much softer one. I loved the curve of his neck as he bent down to kiss me.

I loved the way he made me feel like I deserved all this and more. In that moment, I realized that I was falling in love with him.

As if he could sense the shift in my emotions, Sean's grip on me tightened. He deepened the kiss and held me so close all that existed were the points of contact between our bodies. His hands on my face, and my hands on his. His chest against my chest. His legs trapping mine.

I loved him. I loved how he made me feel. I loved how he touched me, how he kissed me, how he made love to me. I loved how he treated my children, and I loved watching him parent his son. I loved how he *saw* me.

That one kiss under the mistletoe was like pulling the curtains on a darkened room to find a blazingly bright sunny day beyond. Suddenly, I could see every dusty detail of the life I'd been living—and all the ways he could make it better.

I loved him. I was in love with him. Desperately, foolishly, in love.

Then I heard my brother's voice say, "What the fuck?" and all the heat and magic and love inside me turned to ice.

THIRTY-TWO

SEAN

IT TOOK me a second to realize what had actually happened. I was so consumed by Lizzie, so caught up in the feel of her in my arms, that the sound of her brother's voice didn't actually register until she stiffened and pulled away from me.

The feeling of that moment was familiar, but it still caught me by surprise. It was that gut-plunging, rug-pulled-out-from-under-me moment of pure horror that I'd felt when I found out my ex-wife had been unfaithful.

It was the pit in my stomach when I heard my father stumble through the door when I thought this Christmas, finally, would be different.

It was the sound of Christmas music in the hospital lobby moments after my mother had passed.

I turned to see Aaron staring at us with a look of shock and disgust on his face. My arms were still wrapped around his sister and my mind was still on the kiss. The kiss that had made me feel like I was flying. The kiss that made me feel whole for the first time in years.

The kiss I wasn't supposed to be having with the one woman who was meant to be off-limits.

"Let me say that again," Aaron said, face going red. "What the fuck?"

"Aaron," Lizzie answered, voice strangled and breathless.

I cleared my throat and turned to face him. "I—"

"Don't tell me this isn't what it looks like," Aaron snarled at me, and I deserved it. I deserved his anger. I'd taken his friendship and thrown it back in his face.

If I'd been less of a coward, I would've talked to him about this. I would've admitted that I was interested in his sister. I would've protected the one precious relationship that had lasted through my whole life. The only person who had been there beside me when everything fell apart. The best man at my wedding. My best fucking friend.

Instead, I let these heady, addictive feelings get away from me. I hurt him, and I realized that gut punch of a feeling wasn't something I was receiving this time—it was something I was causing *him*.

Aaron stared at me, wide-eyed and red-faced, waiting for me to answer.

"I'm sorry," I said.

Lizzie turned toward me; I could feel her gaze on the side of my face. I couldn't look at her. My head was too full of noise. Panic raced through me and burned every nerve ending, making it hard to focus on anything except the jittering in my legs and the pounding of my heart.

"My *sister?*"

"It's not—Aaron, I made a mistake. I'm sorry."

In my peripheral vision, I saw Lizzie flinch. Her gaze left my face, dropping to the ground in front of us.

"A mistake." Aaron scoffed.

"I…" I couldn't take my eyes off him, off the anger and shock blazing in his expression. "Yes. It just happened. I can explain."

I was flailing, and my words were making Lizzie flinch and crouch away from me, which made the panic inside me rear up taller and stronger and scarier.

Then Aaron's eyes moved to Lizzie, and his lips curled. "So, what, you used the whole matchmaking thing as an excuse to—" He cut himself off and shook his head. "I don't even want to say it."

"It's my fault," I said.

"You weren't the only one participating in that little display," Aaron shot back. "I didn't see Lizzie fighting you off."

"We're both adults," Lizzie finally said. "What's your problem?"

My mind was torn between them. Between the friendship that had gotten me through every significant moment of my life —my father's antics and his final departure from our lives, my mother's illness and death, my wedding, the birth of my son, the breakdown of my marriage—and the woman who made me feel like I was alive again.

How could I choose between them? How could I have been so stupid to think I could have both?

"My problem?" Aaron shot back. "My problem is that my

best friend *just* moved back to town and you wasted no time in spreading your legs for him. My best friend, Lizzie!"

Lizzie's face went white, and the panic inside me snapped. "Don't talk to her like that."

"Like *what*." Aaron's vitriol turned back to me.

"What's going on here?" Mrs. B's voice called out. A moment later, she appeared behind Aaron, frowning in confusion. "I heard shouting."

"What's going on is that Lizzie and Sean were making out," Aaron said, flinging his arm toward us.

Mrs. B's eyes went wide. She glanced at me, then at her daughter. All she said was, "Lizzie!"

Lizzie flinched again and shook her head. "I have to go."

"Oh, you're going to run away?" Aaron said as she hurried past him. "Like you ran away from your marriage? No wonder Isaac left you."

The sob that left Lizzie's throat was the only catalyst I needed. I took two steps and was on Aaron, but he saw me coming. I tried to punch him, but he caught my arm and got me off-balance. What followed was the most pathetic few minutes of red-faced grappling I'd ever been involved in. Suddenly we were fifteen again, tackling each other to the ground, pulling each other's shirts over our heads, getting body punches in between snarled curses.

Mrs. B yelled at us to stop, and pretty soon the space filled with enough people that I was hauled off Aaron's body by Kyle. Aaron was pulled to his feet and held back by his father and uncle. I touched the side of my jaw and found I was bleeding.

There was shouting. Kids poked their heads around corners,

and as the adrenaline faded, shame began to gurgle its way to the surface. I stood in front of the mistletoe where a kiss had nearly undone me, surrounded by the only family I had left, and I knew that I'd made a mess out of everything.

And I'd done it for a woman that had meant very little to me only a couple of months ago.

As the ringing in my ears subsided, I realized Kyle was telling me to get myself together. He was asking me what the hell happened, demanding explanations. I shook him off. "I'm leaving," I mumbled.

"Go," Aaron snarled across the room. "Unless there's someone else here you'd like to fuck? Another family member of mine you have your eye on?"

"Aaron Thomas Butler," Mrs. B snapped. "You cut it out right now. It's Christmas!"

I let out a bitter scoff. It was Christmas, all right. It wouldn't be Christmas without an alcohol-fueled fight. Without chaos and shouting and disaster. What was a holiday without a few tears?

"Sean," she said, turning to me. "Hold on. You don't have to leave."

"I do," I said. I pushed past a few bodies in the hallway and stumbled to the front door. Stabbing my feet into my shoes, I grabbed my jacket and flung open the door.

"Merry Christ—" My aunt Dorothy snapped her mouth shut and frowned at me from where she'd stopped short on the stoop. "Good Lord, Sean, what happened to you?"

I mumbled my apologies and near-sprinted past her, Margaret, and their partners. When I got behind the wheel of my truck, I was shaking so hard I couldn't get the key in the ignition. Out of the corner of my eye, I saw people gathering on the front porch, heard my aunts' questions, saw Mrs. B put a hand to her forehead as she glanced my way.

Finally, the truck rumbled to life. I stepped on the gas pedal and got the hell out of there.

If there was one silver lining in the disaster I'd just made of that event—of my life—it was that my son wasn't there to see it. That thought was cold comfort as I left the Butlers' house in my rearview mirror. I'd chased after a woman I knew was off-limits, and I'd ruined one of the most important relationships of my life.

Just like I knew I would.

THIRTY-THREE

LIZZIE

I WASN'T one for drinking by myself, but the first thing I did when I got home was rinse out one of the mugs I'd left in the sink this morning, then fill it to the brim with white wine. I chugged half of it down and spluttered over the sink, my eyes watering as I dumped the rest of the drink down the drain and sucked in a deep breath.

I didn't cry. It felt like I was living in a funhouse, where the world was distorted and nothing was where it should be. The shock must have kept the tears at bay.

It wasn't that we got caught. That wasn't ideal, but getting caught kissing Sean wasn't the end of the world.

No, what made me feel like the sun had just gone out was that he'd called it a mistake. Without even hesitating, he'd told Aaron that kissing me was a mistake.

That *I* was a mistake.

I wasn't the wonderful, magical, mystical woman he'd

pretended I was. I wasn't a woman worthy of love and devotion. I wasn't fucking *special*.

I was a mistake.

My chest was an empty pit, a crater. I stared at the wine splatter in the bottom of my sink and tried to breathe through the pain. When I closed my eyes, I heard Sean's voice. I saw my brother's disgust. My mother's disappointment.

I never deserved to find love again. I was never supposed to get a second chance—not to them. I was just Lizzie, who scurried around making everyone's life easier. And for Sean, I was just some sort of plaything, a distraction.

I should've stuck to being the family babysitter and then done what was expected and adopted twenty-seven cats once my kids grew up and moved out.

When my doorbell rang, I didn't realize I'd walked toward the front door until my hand was on the knob. I was moving through a dream, and as I pulled the door open, I wasn't even surprised to see Sean standing on my stoop.

"Can I come in?" he asked, his eyes feverish.

"No."

He sucked in a breath and dipped his chin. "Yeah. Okay. I—I'm sorry, Lizzie. I didn't mean for that to happen."

"For what to happen?" My voice was flat. It would've been impossible for me to put any sort of emotion into it, because nothing made sense.

I actually thought I loved this man? The man who stood beside me and instead of protecting me from my brother's anger, had stepped aside and let me take the brunt of the blame?

He'd done exactly what my ex-husband did. He protected

himself while leaving me out in the cold. I'd been such a fool to think he was different. To think I deserved better.

Better didn't exist. Not for me.

"I didn't mean for us to get caught like that."

"Well, you said it yourself. It was a mistake."

Devastation etched itself into his features. "Lizzie—"

"I think you should leave, Sean."

"Lizzie, I care about you. I'm not—that wasn't—"

"I spent a long time married to a man who used me as cannon fodder," I told him. "I made myself small to make his life easier. I still do it. I still let people walk all over me in the name of keeping the peace and being the glue that holds the family together." I shook my head. "I'm done, Sean. I just realized what I mean to my family, what I mean to you, and it's a whole lot less than I thought. I'm not going to let another man treat me the way my ex-husband did. You used me, just like everyone else does."

His lips parted, but nothing came out. I closed the door slowly, and maybe a part of me was hoping he'd stop me, that he'd say something to make it all better, but he just stared at me with those blue-green eyes and that stupid handsome face, and he let me close the door without putting up a fight at all.

I told myself it was better this way. When the dam broke and I finally started crying, I was glad it happened when I was alone.

THIRTY-FOUR

SEAN

I SLEPT ON THE COUCH, in the shadow of the Christmas tree that Lizzie had helped me choose. When I opened my eyes the next morning, I looked at the deep green branches and the twisted wire of the lights I hadn't bothered to turn on, and I felt like a hollowed-out version of myself.

My back hurt. My legs were stiff. I dragged myself to the kitchen and watched the coffee drip into its pot, my mind completely blank.

I'd messed up. But the worst of it was, I didn't know how to fix it, or even what I wanted the outcome to be.

Choose Lizzie? Choose Aaron and the rest of the family? Slink back into oblivion and move away from Heart's Cove with Mikey?

The last made me close my eyes in disgust. My son loved it here. Within days, he'd been smiling more than he had in San Fran. He had more friends here than he'd had in the city. He was excited about joining clubs and doing sports. That was exactly what I'd come here to give him: community, support, a richer life.

And instead of being satisfied with that, I'd gone and ruined it.

As I filled my mug with black tar and drank down the bitter sludge, I thought of Lizzie's face last night. It had been like staring into the eyes of a stranger. Like she'd closed the door on all the parts of her that I'd come to admire. I didn't have the right to see them anymore.

I drank my coffee and stared at my phone, which was blank and silent. No message from Mikey or my ex, no anger from Aaron, no word from Lizzie.

Why had I thought I deserved a woman like Lizzie? What had possessed me to pursue her, when I knew that she never would've made the first move? I'd been so caught up in my own needs that I pushed her into an impossible position. And then when she told me she wanted to wait until after the holidays to broach the topic with her family, I'd ignored that too.

I was the one who'd kissed her. I was the one who'd called it a mistake, who'd ruined her family's Christmas dinner. Maybe I was no better than my father, after all.

She deserved so much better than me.

The doorbell rang, pulling me from my thoughts. I shuffled to the front door and opened it to see my aunt Margaret standing on the other side. Her silver hair was pulled back into a bun at the nape of her neck, and she wore a deep burgundy jacket with a cream silk scarf. Her ears were adorned with smooth, white pearls.

"Hello, Sean."

I moved aside to invite her in. "Merry Christmas."

She arched a brow at me and stepped inside. I gestured to the kitchen and offered her a drink, then apologized for the state of the coffee when she made a face after her first sip.

I sat down across from her and stared into the dark liquid in my mug. "What happened after I left last night?"

"Oh, everyone was aflutter with excitement, as was to be expected."

I lifted my gaze to meet hers and caught the wry look in her eyes. "Aflutter, huh?"

"Aaron vowed to do some unpleasant things to you when he saw you next. Then he called his sister some unsavory names. Sandra got upset. Dorothy opened half a dozen bottles of wine and insisted everyone calm down by screaming at the top of her lungs, which was surprisingly effective. Then we ate dinner and pretended everything was fine. Sandra got me a lovely new jewelry dish for my vanity."

"Sounds like Christmas."

Margaret sipped her coffee and managed not to make a face at how disgusting it tasted.

"Let me make a fresh pot. I know it's terrible."

"Sit down, Sean."

I lowered myself back onto my chair and cleared my throat, "It's my fault everything went wrong last night," I blurted.

It surprised me to see sadness enter Margaret's kind eyes. She'd taken her jacket off and hung it on the back of her chair, and as she pushed up the sleeves of her cashmere sweater, I stared at the watch she'd worn for decades. She'd always been a steady presence that seemed a little uncomfortable compared to the chaos of my childhood home.

"It wasn't your fault, Sean."

I scoffed. "No? I'm the one who kissed Lizzie right there where anyone could see. I'm the one who pursued her. I'm the one who tackled my oldest and best friend to the ground."

"You used to do that every second day when you were teenagers."

"Yeah, when we were teenagers."

Margaret let out a long sigh. "Fine. I'll amend what I said: you weren't *solely* responsible for what happened yesterday."

"It wasn't Lizzie's fault, Margaret."

"I never said it was."

"She's a good person. She's the best person. I never deserved her, and I never should've pursued her because I *know* she's too good for me."

"So what do you deserve?"

I blinked at my aunt. She stared back at me, her back straight as a rod, her gaze steady. When she arched her brow to prod me to speak, I shrugged. "I don't know."

"Do you deserve to be unhappy and alone?"

Her words felt like a slap, but I relished the pain. "Probably, yeah."

"Why?"

"Because—" I gulped. "I just do."

"Explain it to me."

"I ruin everything. I can't get over these feelings inside me, and every year they rear up. Christmas brings out the worst in me. Just like my dad."

Margaret leaned back. "Ah."

Her quiet acceptance of my words stung, but how could she deny it? "He'd drink his way through the holidays and make our lives a living hell," I continued, throat tight. "He made us walk on eggshells. That's what I did to Melody. I didn't drink the way he did, but I drove her away. It's what I did to Aaron and his family. To Lizzie."

"So it was your fault that your wife was unfaithful?"

"Yes!" I exploded, then shoved my palm against my short hair. I gripped the strands as best I could and pulled, then let out a long breath. "If I'd been a better man, she wouldn't have had to go looking for affection somewhere else. The office holiday party would've been a chore instead of an opportunity to cheat."

Margaret traced the base of her mug with a finger and was silent for a long moment. Then she said, "What do you want for Mikey?"

Confused, I looked up at her. "What?"

"What kind of life do you want for your son?"

"I want him to have everything. I want the best for him. I want him to grow up surrounded by people he loves. I want him to meet someone and have a great life. I want him to be happy, to thrive."

"That's why you moved back to Heart's Cove."

"Of course."

"It's what drew you to Lizzie. She's warm and nurturing, all the things you wish you could give your son."

I frowned at her. "Well, yes. But she's a lot more than that. She's not... She's talented and funny and bright. She's really clever, and she can keep track of a million things at once. Margaret, everyone thinks she's just good at being a mom. They don't *see* her."

"But you do."

We stared at each other. My heart thumped uncomfortably, and I didn't know why. I couldn't understand what my aunt was getting at, or why she was asking me all these questions.

Margaret's face softened, and she reached across the table to lay her hand over mine. It was warm and soft and small, birdlike bones barely covering the back of my palm. But the touch sent warmth spiraling up my arm and made me want to cry.

"Sean, darling," Margaret said quietly, "it wasn't your fault your father drank. It wasn't your fault he left. It wasn't your fault your mother got sick and passed when you were too young to truly come to grips with it. And the fault for your wife's infidelity lies at her feet, not yours."

"No," I said, shaking my head. "I should have been a better husband."

"Yes. And she should have been a better wife."

Her simple words cracked something inside me. I stared at her age-spotted hand atop mine and felt the ground shift like quicksand beneath me. "He used to get mad when I made noise on Christmas morning and woke him up," I said, thinking about my father. About his red-faced rage when he opened his bedroom door, the scent of old booze reeking from every pore. The way he thundered down the stairs when I stood peeking at presents under the tree.

Margaret's fingers curled around mine as her thumb swept over my knuckles. "You were a child, and you deserved better."

A tear escaped my eyes, and I brushed it away. "I don't know what I'm supposed to do, Margaret."

She squeezed my palm. "You own the things you did wrong, Sean. And you let go of the things that weren't your fault."

I lifted my gaze to hers, and the quicksand under my feet settled. "Yeah," I said. "Okay."

"Sean, darling?"

"Yeah?"

"Do you deserve to be unhappy and alone?"

My throat constricted as I tried to gulp down the ball of emotion clogging it. "I—"

She squeezed my palm hard. "No," she told me firmly. "No, you don't."

It took me long, long moments to eke out the words and repeat, "No, I don't."

THIRTY-FIVE

LIZZIE

THE DAY after the most disastrous Christmas of my life, I spoke to the kids in the morning, then stood in my quiet, creaky house while I wondered what I was supposed to do with myself. Staring out the patio doors to the graying wood of the deck and the bare trees and bushes lining the backyard, I tried to remember what I did the other years that the kids had spent the holidays with Isaac.

Laundry, probably. Or I'd go over to my brother's house and babysit his kids while he and Emily had time to themselves. Or I went to help my parents clean up.

Gritting my teeth, I squared my shoulders.

Not today.

I wouldn't spend one single minute serving other people. Not when my brother had looked at me with such bare disgust on his face. Not when I'd been run out of my parents' house for daring to chase one bit of pleasure for myself.

My phone was plugged in to a charger on the edge of the kitchen counter. I marched over to it and turned it off. Inhaling deeply, I stared at the dark screen and felt a weight lift off my shoulders. I hadn't turned that device off for years. I'd always been ready for a call, for an interruption. Always been ready to be needed.

Well, today, *I* needed me. I marched upstairs and got dressed in warm clothes, then packed my camera up and made sure both batteries were charged. I found an extra, blank SD card in the front pocket of the camera case, so I popped it into the appropriate slot and slung the camera strap over a shoulder. Then I grabbed my wallet and keys, and I left.

I drove to the coast and parked at a trailhead in a local nature reserve. Inhaling the fresh, cold scent of winter, I glanced up at the overcast sky and wondered how long I'd have before it would begin to drizzle. Didn't matter. I was here, and that was enough.

Setting off down the path, I took photos of trees and moss and dead branches. I took pictures of the gray sky through scraggly trees. I fumbled with my camera settings and struggled to remember everything that had been instinctive all those years ago. I made it to the cliffs and shuffled my way to the edge, then took photos of sea birds crying out at the crashing waves below.

I thought about nothing except the camera in my hands and the world I wanted to capture. For the first time in years—at least since my kids were born—I didn't worry about what anyone else needed. I breathed in crisp, fresh air and I took photos. Most of them were bad, and it didn't matter.

When my stomach rumbled, I realized it had been hours

since I'd eaten. I made my way back to the car and drove down the coast until I found a town I'd never stopped in, and I chose a restaurant at random. I ate by myself at a table by the window, and I watched people walk and drive by. I drank a leisurely coffee and went through the photos I'd taken.

I thought of nothing and no one except myself. When I left the restaurant, I walked by a bakery that had gleaming, sugar-encrusted pastries. I bought three and ate them all while I sat in a small park by myself, listening to the movements of the town around me.

When the cold began to seep through my jacket, I stood. A snowflake landed on my outstretched hand, and I glanced up at the sky. Not a drizzle, after all.

I drove home and drew myself a bath, then filled it with dried rose petals and bath oil that had come in a gift set that I'd been saving for a special occasion. The water loosened my stiff muscles, and I leaned against the edge of the tub and closed my eyes.

This was a special occasion. It was the moment that I realized it was okay to take care of myself.

When I got out of the bath, I reached for my old pink robe, and hesitated. It was more gray than pink now, and it had turned so rough with hundreds of washes that I wondered why I even kept it around at all. Huffing, I stomped, stark naked, to the linen closet and grabbed myself one of the nice towels—the ones I'd always saved for guests. Why? Why did I give myself the worst of everything?

Wrapped up in soft, nearly new terrycloth, I marched back to the bathroom, grabbed the ratty old robe, and walked it down to the kitchen garbage so I could toss it out. The cabinet door slammed when I closed it, and I stood there, hair dripping wet, fluffy towel clasping me in its soft fabric, feeling three feet taller than usual.

And I smiled.

Glancing at the time, I figured it was about time I turned my phone back on so I could talk to the kids. Messages popped up on the screen—mostly from my mother, but there was one from Aaron and another from Laurel. I ignored them all and let my ex-husband know that I was available to talk to the kids if they wanted.

Then I went upstairs, opened my closet, and stared at all the old rags with which I'd dressed myself for years.

Not anymore.

I wasn't a martyr. I was a mother. They weren't the same thing.

With a kind of feverish intensity, I grabbed all the hangers from the rails and dumped the clothes on the bed. Every drawer got ripped open and dumped out. I stared at the mound of clothing and got to work.

All but four pairs of underwear were either stained, ripped, or so stretched out they sagged in the butt when I put them on. They had to go. Old T-shirts with baggy collars got tossed in the same pile. I found dresses that no longer fit—they went too. I was done feeling bad about myself every time I opened my closet. Done dressing myself in worn-out, ill-fitting clothing because I thought it was all I deserved.

The only items I kept were ones that actually fit me and ones that made me feel good. That pile was pathetically small.

Halfway through my manic Marie Kondo-ing, my phone rang. I picked it up and swiped when I saw Laurel's name on the screen.

"Merry Christmas," she said, sounding amused. "I heard rumors about the Butler Christmas dinner that I was hoping you'd confirm or deny."

My bedroom was a disaster, and I was still naked. I glanced around the room, then perched myself on the edge of my bed. "Shoot."

"You were caught kissing Sean Hardy."

"True."

Laurel gasped. "And your brother went bonkers."

"Pretty much."

"He attacked Sean."

I glanced down at my toes. It was time to book a pedicure. "Maybe. I left."

"You left?"

"Seemed like the right thing to do."

"And Sean?"

"What about him?"

"Are the two of you together, or what? What happened with the kiss?"

I shook my head, even though she couldn't see me. "We're done. It's fine. It was a bad idea to get involved to begin with. I'm not surprised it all blew up in my face."

"You sound different."

"I'm cleaning out my closet."

"Huh."

"I'm sick of wearing things I don't like. And I'm also not

saving the nice towels for guests. Those are mine now. And I don't have special-occasion candles and bath stuff anymore. I'm using everything on me. And I'm buying nice undies."

Laurel was quiet for a moment, then let out a soft breath. "Good, Lizzie. That's really good."

My throat got tight, and I wasn't quite sure why. "Yeah. It's good."

"You got plans for dinner?"

"I think I have a frozen pizza in the freezer," I told her.

She snorted. "You sound very calm for someone having a nervous breakdown."

"That's offensive."

Laurel laughed. "I had dinner at Audrey's last night, and she sent me home with way too many leftovers," she told me, naming one of her best friends that had recently married the town mechanic. "They're having a quiet family day today, so what do you say I come over and we make turkey and stuffing sandwiches? I can help you with the closet clean-out project, and then we can watch bad made-for-TV movies."

"And make sure my nervous breakdown doesn't escalate?"

"That too."

I laughed and was surprised to find it felt really, really good. "Sure," I said. "I'll see you soon."

When I hung up, I saw a message from Isaac. I called him, and he put the kids on for a quick conversation. They were thrilled with their days and admitted they'd eaten chocolate for breakfast. When I hung up, I was still smiling.

I'd taken the day for myself, done exactly what I wanted to do, and everything had worked out just fine. My kids were still happy, and I was no less of a mother for having used the nice towels and spent the day thinking of myself.

By the time Laurel came over, I'd finished sorting most of my clothes and found some sweatpants and a cozy sweatshirt to wear.

She gave me a tight hug, stared in my eyes, and nodded. "You decide if you want to tell me what happened between you and Mr. Hunky McHunkerson and The Butler Christmas Disaster."

Even an oblique reference to him sent a spear through my chest. I wasn't ready to face the storm of feelings lurking beneath the surface. "I think that might be the least interesting thing about the past couple of days, to be honest."

She grinned. "Sounds like it. Show me the damage you've done to your closet."

I made a detour to the kitchen, where I poured us both vats of wine, and then led Laurel up to the bedroom. She whistled at the sight of the piles on the floor. I kicked the first one and said, "Trash," then the second, "Donate," and then the third, "Keep until I can replace with things that fit properly." I pointed to the scant few items that had survived my purge. "Those are the clothes that actually fit that I still like."

"I'm going to call Audrey tomorrow and tell her about this. She's a closet organizer. She can change your life."

"I'm not sure I can afford her."

Laurel waved a hand. "Friends and family discount," she said. "Don't you want a gorgeous closet that makes you happy every time you open it?"

I opened my mouth, then closed it again. "Yes," I finally told her. "I do."

Laurel's eyes sparkled as she grinned, then she took a sip of wine. "I like this version of you, Lizzie."

The empty closet before me felt like it was full of possibilities. I took a deep breath and said, "I like this version of me too."

We didn't talk about Sean or the kiss or anything that had happened before or after, and I was grateful that Laurel didn't push it. We drank wine, ate leftovers, then watched enough TV that we got hungry again and made the frozen pizza too. I felt a little bit naughty, but mostly I felt great.

And I realized, when she finally left, that today hadn't taken anything away from my life as a whole. I hadn't suddenly become a bad mother or a terrible, irresponsible adult. I just felt more like me.

There was space in my life for more than just motherhood, more than just giving.

As I finally got into bed, I glanced at the pillow beside me and remembered the warmth of Sean's skin pressed against mine. It was like cracking the lid on a storm of emotions just enough to check that they were still there. I slammed the lid back down and turned my back to the empty space in my bed.

I wasn't going to chase after a man who called me a mistake. I wasn't going to mourn a relationship with someone who told me pretty lies and then failed to defend me when things got hard.

I'd been through that before, and I wasn't going back.

THIRTY-SIX

LIZZIE

MY MOTHER CALLED me the next day while I was lounging on the couch with a cup of coffee. I stared at my phone for a while and considered not answering, but the guilt got to me and I swiped. The new me needed more practice, apparently.

"Hi, Mom."

"Lizzie. I'm glad I caught you. How are you? How are the kids?"

I stared at the stockings hanging on the mantel and tried not to feel bitter about her questions. Would it have been impossible for her to simply ask how I was? She followed up so quickly with a question about the kids that it was obvious she didn't give a flying fig about me.

But maybe I was being harsh. "I'm okay. The kids are great. Isaac and June are taking them to visit his parents today."

"Oh, good for them."

"Hmm."

There was a silence. Then my mother inhaled. "Listen. I want to talk about what happened at Christmas."

"Mm-hmm."

"You and Sean..."

"We kissed."

"Right. I know that. See, Lizzie, the thing is, Aaron was really upset about it."

"Is there a reason you're telling me this instead of Aaron telling me himself?"

I could hear her shock in the gap of silence that followed my question. "Well. I just thought I'd reach out and see if you were ready to apologize."

I blinked. "What am I supposed to apologize for?"

"Lizzie!"

"It's an honest question."

"You're supposed to apologize for hurting your brother's feelings!"

"What does this have to do with Aaron? Am I supposed to ask permission every time I kiss a new man?"

"That's not the issue here, and you know it."

I pinched my lips. She wasn't wrong, exactly, but I still felt the burn of self-righteousness down the back of my gullet. Sean was Aaron's best and oldest friend. Me getting involved with him wasn't the same as getting involved with some other man. I knew that.

Still, it galled me that my mother was calling me to berate me, or to try to convince me to bend for the sake of family unity.

When she spoke again, her tone was softer. "I'd just like to get this resolved so we can have a nice New Year's together. Wouldn't that be good? And I also wanted to ask you what you need from me before the party."

"There won't be a party, Mom."

"What?"

"Well, not at my house."

"What do you mean?"

"I'm not hosting New Year's this year." And if I continued to feel the way I did, there wouldn't be any family parties at my house, ever. Nor would I be relegated to the kitchen while everyone else enjoyed themselves. Nor would I be the de facto babysitter for every gathering.

Something had snapped within me, and I wasn't sure it could ever be fixed. I wasn't sure it *needed* to be fixed. I felt freer and lighter than I had in a long, long time. Maybe ever.

"Lizzie," Mom chided.

"You know at Thanksgiving, I asked for one thing," I told her. "I asked you all to save me a portion of stuffing."

"Listen, there were lots of people there, and we were having a good time—"

"I cooked almost everything on that table, and then I spent the entire day taking care of everyone else's kids. I was a maid and a babysitter and a host, and it wasn't even my house. And I asked for one single thing, Mom. One little spoonful of stuffing."

Her silence echoed between us.

"I wasn't even worth that," I finally said, my throat growing tight. "So forgive me for not feeling like I want to put in hours and days of work to host a bunch of people who don't give a fuck about me."

"Lizzie, language!"

"Oh, give me a break, Mom," I said, even though that might have been the first time I'd sworn in front of her since a few memorable teenage storms. "When Isaac betrayed me and I finally worked up the courage to leave him, do you remember what you told me?"

I heard her breath, but she said nothing.

"Your exact words were, 'Are you sure about this, Lizzie? What did you do to make him look for comfort in another woman?'" I swallowed thickly. My arms and legs tingled like I needed to run around the block just to let off some steam. When I spoke, my voice was surprisingly steady. "You blamed me for his betrayal, Mom. You made me feel like I should have just accepted the scraps of his attention. And now I finally understand why. It's because that's what you, and Dad, and Aaron, and Kyle, and everyone else in the family think I deserve. Nothing but scraps. Not even one measly spoonful of stuffing."

I heard her sniffle, but my heart was made of stone. When she didn't speak, I pulled the phone away from my ear, waited a few seconds to see if she would say something, and then slowly hung up the call.

I felt like garbage. Tension stole through my entire body, and that need to run or box or scream still coursed through my veins. I felt like I'd just hurt my mom, which I hated, but the other, bigger part of me was so fucking angry that I'd let myself be treated this way for years.

I was done.

Done catering to everyone else's feelings. Done putting myself last. Done working myself to the bone with a smile on my face.

I took a deep breath, exhaled, and stood up. Then I got dressed and packed up my camera, and I headed out to search for peace in the crashing waves and bare trees, where no one demanded a thing from me.

THIRTY-SEVEN

SEAN

THE HOUSE WAS TOO empty without Mikey. Normally, I would've holed up until New Year's and thanked my lucky stars for my isolation.

Instead, I felt itchy and uncomfortable.

Margaret read me like a book, and I didn't know what to do about it. I'd ruined things with Lizzie. Ruined things with Aaron and the rest of his family. Was I in the process of ruining things with Mikey? Would I be so caught up in my own pain for the remainder of my life that I wouldn't see what was right in front of me? That I wouldn't see what my own son needed from me?

Lizzie wasn't home when I drove up to her house, and I stayed on the curb and watched the dark windows for long enough that I began to feel like some kind of creep. Then, with a deep breath, I put the truck in gear and headed to the one place I didn't want to go.

Aaron's Christmas tree was lit up and twinkling in the living room window. I cut the engine and slid out of my vehicle as my throat dried up and my heart began to thump. When I rang the doorbell, time slowed to an excruciating crawl.

Emily opened the door. Her eyes widened slightly. "Sean," she said.

"Is Aaron home? I should have called. I'm sorry."

"He's—yeah. Come in. I'll go get him."

"Thanks."

She led me to the den, where I sat down on the edge of one of the armchairs, lacing my fingers together as I waited. In the month and a half I'd been back in town, this room had become familiar. Now, it was uncomfortable. I was overstepping.

But that's what I'd been doing all along, and it was time for me to face my fears.

Aaron appeared in the mouth of the room. He hadn't shaved in a couple of days, his jaw showing more stubble than usual. He watched me with eyes of a lighter brown than Lizzie's, then dipped his head. "Sean."

I stood and wiped my hands on my pants. "Thanks for seeing me."

He nodded and took a seat across from me. Silence stretched; he wasn't going to make this easy on me. I didn't blame him.

I inhaled and started with the most obvious of my sins. "I should have told you I was interested in Lizzie."

Aaron blinked. Frowned. "You... This wasn't just... This has been going on for a while?"

I licked my lips. "Since I came back, yeah."

"She set you up on dates with other women."

"They were torture."

Aaron stared at me like he'd never seen me before. "I thought Christmas was the first time."

"I...no."

We were quiet for a while. I looked down at my hands and rubbed my knuckles, trying to think of what to say. I wanted to tell him what he meant to me—but I also wanted to tell him his sister was something else altogether. I wanted to rage at him for not appreciating her, but I wanted to ask him for forgiveness too.

I was a mess. I'd *made* a mess of this.

Thinking of the perfect way to fix this was impossible, so I settled for honesty instead. "We ran into each other the week before Thanksgiving, but it wasn't until Thanksgiving itself that I really noticed her."

"Noticed her," Aaron repeated, brows drawn.

I worked my jaw and stared at a spot on the floor before darting my gaze up to his then back down again. "Yeah. She was standing in the kitchen, staring out the window, and, I don't know... Just the way the light hit her, or the look on her face..." I trailed off and forced myself to look up again.

Aaron stared at me hard. I couldn't read the expression on his face. I had the sneaking suspicion I was making everything worse, but how much worse could it get? My best friend had caught me with his little sister on Christmas Day and punched me. Well. Grappled with me like we were teens again.

All I could do was keep going.

"We spent some time together while she was trying to set

me up on those dates, and she's just—great. She's funny and bright and she makes me feel like everything's going to be okay. It's like she has this light, you know? And I kept looking forward to our meetings, kept finding excuses to bring Mikey over to her house. She made me actually enjoy Christmas."

"She made *you* enjoy Christmas?"

I huffed a laugh and spread my palms. "I tried to stop thinking about her, because she's your sister and you're my best friend. The whole reason I moved here was to have a support system for Mikey, and the first thing I did was try to blow it all up. I tried, man. But she kept setting me up on these dates with other women and all I could do was compare them to her. There was no spark, or their laugh wasn't as bright as hers, or their eyes didn't pull me in the way hers do. I kept trying to make myself attracted to these women she set me up with, but none of them were right because none of them were her."

"Jesus," Aaron said in a hushed voice.

I swallowed thickly and put up my hands. "I'm not trying to antagonize you. I know I should have said something to you, but —but..." I exhaled. "It just caught me by surprise, Aaron. It was like a two by four to the side of the head."

Aaron gave me that same odd look, but the edge of it had softened. He gulped, then said, "You're in love with my sister."

"I..." I met his gaze as his words landed between us. All I could respond was, "Yeah."

"Holy fuck."

"Look, I don't want to fight with you. You're my best friend, and—"

"I'm not fighting. I'm just coming to terms... My *sister*? But

280

she's not... How could you... There are so many other women who are..."

"Who are what?"

"I don't know. She's my sister. I never thought of her like..." Aaron leaned back in his chair and scrubbed his face. "This is so weird, man. The kiss, I could kind of understand. Maybe. Sort of. I don't know. I thought you were drunk, or... I just thought you were an asshole. But this?"

"It's more shocking to you that I would actually care about her?" My words came out harsher than I'd meant them to, and Aaron pulled his hands away from his face to stare at me.

He shrugged. "I mean—yeah? Lizzie is just... She's just Lizzie."

"She's just Lizzie," I repeated.

"Yeah. She's always busy with her kids, and I just never thought..." He frowned at me. "Does she feel the same way?"

I scoffed. "I'm pretty sure she never wants to see me again."

"Oh." He seemed relieved, which annoyed me. "Mom just called and said she doesn't want to host New Year's."

"Makes sense."

Aaron reared back. "Why does that make sense?"

"Um, because we've all treated her like shit? Why would she want to see any of us?"

"Whoa, whoa! What's this got to do with me? If she's mad at you for coming onto her, that's not my problem."

"She's not mad at me for coming onto her, dickhead. She's mad at me for not defending her. She's mad at me for leaving her hanging when you confronted me."

"What?" Aaron looked utterly confused. Lost.

"I did to her what you and everyone else does, and now she doesn't want anything to do with me."

"What the fuck is that supposed to mean? What do I do to her?"

"You *use* her, Aaron!"

Aaron opened his mouth. Snapped it shut again. Drew his brows low over his eyes, then shook his head. "No, I don't."

"You call her to drop everything to come babysit without warning."

"She likes kids!"

"You host events at your house and make her do all the cooking."

"She likes cooking!"

"Not that much! Not so much that she wouldn't want some fucking help once in a while."

"So, what, the fact that she doesn't want to talk to you is my fault now?"

I opened my mouth and just about managed to hold back the harsh words that tried to fly out of it. Instead, I took a deep breath to calm myself, then said, "She steps up when she needs to, but she isn't appreciated for it, Aaron. And I added to that when I should have been the one person to stand up for her. I treated her exactly like her ex-husband did. I put my own pride, my own needs ahead of hers."

Aaron looked like he wanted to protest but was too baffled to do it. "Her ex?"

"She picked up his slack, just like she picks up everyone else's. She hasn't had someone in her corner in a long time. I saw it, and I still failed her. So no, she doesn't want to talk to me. And I don't blame her."

Aaron leaned his elbows on his knees and stared at the floor. "She bounced back so quickly after her divorce. I didn't realize..."

"She bounced back because she had no choice."

Rubbing the heels of his palms into his eye sockets, Aaron let out a long breath. "So, what now?"

"I don't know."

We sat there for a long while until Aaron finally said, "I think I owe her an apology."

I grunted in response.

Aaron stood and stretched, then angled his chin at me. "We good?"

A weight lifted off my shoulders as I got to my feet and nodded. "Yeah."

Aaron nodded. "Good."

When he turned to leave the room, I made a noise to stop him. Glancing over his shoulder with raised eyebrows, my best friend waited for me to speak. When I did, the words came out in a rush. "I'm still going to try to get her back."

He stared at me.

I squared my shoulders. "Is that a problem?"

"You going to hurt her?"

"No. Not if I can help it."

"Fine."

And that was it. Friendship mended and saved. Aaron walked me to the front door and gave me a back-slapping hug, and I wondered why I'd been so afraid to face him.

The whole point of having a support system was that they'd catch you when you fell. I'd learned at a young age to walk on eggshells around the people in my circle, knowing they'd leave or die or betray or abandon me when things got tough.

As I got in my truck, I glanced at the twinkling Christmas tree in the window again and let out a long breath.

Not Aaron. Our friendship had survived the turbulence of our teenage years. It had survived the ups and downs of life, of distance, of divorce, kids, changed circumstances...

It would survive this.

A piece of my heart knitted itself back together. For the first time in my life, I was sure of something—of someone. I knew that no matter what, my friendship with Aaron would endure. That support system I wanted to give to Mikey was something I should have craved for myself, but up until this moment, I hadn't thought I deserved it.

Security felt like a shelter in the storm, a harbor that I could return to when the seas got rough.

And as soon as I felt the wind die down around me, I knew that I couldn't give up on Lizzie. Not when she was still out at sea, alone in a leaky boat, being tossed around by waves that were taller than she was.

If she let me, I'd be her harbor, and never again would I let her down.

THIRTY-EIGHT

LIZZIE

THE KIDS WERE COMING BACK from their father's place tomorrow, and as much as I'd enjoyed my days of solitude, I was ready to have them home again. I couldn't wait to see Hazel's beaming smile and Zach's little side grin. I wanted to hear all about their weeks and give them tight hugs. I wanted the noise and chaos of having them in the house. I wouldn't even mind Zach's grumpy morning face if it meant I could hold him close.

My bath was halfway filled as I thought of my last phone call with them, when Hazel went into great detail to explain why her grandmother's apple pie was nowhere near as good as mine. It was petty for me to be delighted, but I never claimed to be perfect. Isaac's mother had never been a huge fan of me.

I trailed my fingers through the water to test the temperature, then went to the cabinet to check what bath oils I had. I'd opened so many old packages of "fancy" products lately that it felt like living in a Bath & Body Works every time I walked into my bathroom. I chose a lavender-scented oil and dropped a good glug of it into the bath.

And then the doorbell rang.

I closed my eyes, sighed, and turned off the tap. When I padded downstairs and peeked through the frosted side window, all I could see was a large shadow. My heart rattled, thinking I knew who was on the other side of the door.

But it wasn't Sean; it was my brother Aaron. I couldn't tell if I was disappointed or relieved, so I just stood in the doorway and blinked at him.

"Hey," Aaron said, rocking back onto his heels.

"Hi," I replied.

"You, uh, good?"

I arched a brow. "I'm fine. Just running a bath."

Aaron cleared his throat and rubbed the back of his neck. "You mind if I come in for a few minutes? I won't be long, I promise."

Last time I'd spoken to my brother, he'd yelled at me in front of our entire family. I would be well within my rights to slam the door in his face.

But as much as I missed my kids, I also missed my family. Usually, the days between Christmas and New Year's would be spent lounging at my parents' or brothers' houses. Or having them here to fill the house with noise and laughter. I'd needed the time to myself—and I'd enjoyed it—but I wasn't sure it was how I wanted to live. Not forever. There had to be a way to find a middle ground, if the rest of them were willing.

So, I opened the door wider and let him in.

Wrapped in my brand new, extra-fluffy bathrobe, I led

Aaron to the living room and took a seat on the couch. He grabbed the seat on the far end of the sofa and leaned his elbows on his knees. I glanced at his profile, noting the smudges under his eyes and the grim line of his jaw.

"Sean came to see me yesterday," he said.

"Ah."

"We talked."

"That's good."

Aaron looked over at me, then away. He gulped. "He, uh, mentioned you."

Curiosity prickled, and I batted it back. I'd been very clear with Sean about what I wanted from him, and it hadn't changed: nothing. I might want my kids at home and a mended relationship with my family, but I wasn't naive enough to think that I'd find the perfect man to cherish me as well.

I could find balance in my life without giving my freedom to yet another man who wouldn't have my back.

"I hadn't realized that the two of you were...together."

"We're not," I told him.

Aaron nodded. "Right. Right." He spun his wedding ring around his finger and cleared his throat. "We missed you this week," he blurted.

It was hard not to feel bitter. They missed me watching their kids while they enjoyed themselves, probably. They missed me doing all the dishes after dinner so they wouldn't have to.

When I said nothing, Aaron let out a long sigh. "Lizzie, I'm sorry."

Blinking, I turned to look at him. "For what?"

He spread his arms, looking helpless. "Where do I start? I haven't—" He exhaled loudly. "I haven't been a good brother to you. I've—I've walked all over you, and I didn't even realize I was doing it."

I sat there, stiff as a board, trying to understand what, exactly, my brother meant. Finally, I replied, "Yes. You have."

"And I'm not the only one."

"No," I agreed.

"I've relied on you for babysitting without even thinking about whether you'd want to do it. I thought—I *told myself* you loved kids and enjoyed it."

"My life has revolved around kids for a long time," I said. "I probably didn't help myself."

"But what option did you have?" Aaron looked at me, brows arched. "Sean told me we've been using you, and—God, it hurt when he said that. I didn't want it to be true. But then I thought about everything you do... And then Mom told me you weren't going to host New Year's this year, and..."

"And?"

"And I'm sorry, Lizzie."

It felt good to hear his apology, but a part of me still held back. It wasn't lost on me that he was apologizing to me after realizing that I wouldn't be taking on the hosting duties of yet another family party. Was he just apologizing so that things would go back to the way they were?

"I appreciate you saying that," I replied, hesitating.

Aaron nodded. "Good. Good. Mom's hosting New Year's. Will you come?"

I stared into his eyes and waited for the right answer to

present itself to me. The truth was, it would be easy to go to my mom's house and slip into exactly the same role I'd held for so long. I could tell myself I was doing it for my kids, that I wanted them to spend the holiday with their extended family.

But that would be a lie.

If I said yes now and wiped the slate clean for my brother and the rest of my family, I'd be setting myself up for taking on so much more emotional labor. I would have to navigate a familiar party with familiar dynamics and figure out exactly how I fit into it when I wasn't even sure what I wanted.

It was too soon.

"No," I finally answered. "We'll have a quiet New Year's here, just me and the kids."

Aaron's shoulders dropped. "Right. Yeah. That's fair."

My bath was singing a siren song, and exhaustion was hurtling toward me while it did. "Was there anything else?" I asked, making moves as if to stand up.

"Yes," Aaron blurted.

I froze.

He angled himself toward me, lacing his hands together as he leaned on his thighs. "I'm sorry for how I spoke to you, Lizzie. I shouldn't have blown up like that."

When my brother met my gaze, the exhaustion finally hit. I slumped against the sofa and nodded. I wanted to forgive him, to wave a hand and tell him everything was okay. The problem was, I wasn't sure it was true—and I was done protecting everyone else's feelings at the expense of my own.

"You humiliated me," I told him. "You blamed me for the kiss, even though Sean was just as much there as I was."

"You're my sister, Lizzie—"

"And?"

He snapped his mouth shut. Dipped his chin.

"Sean has been divorced half the length of time that I have, and you all jumped on him to start dating again. Why has no one ever asked me? Encouraged me? Why hasn't a single one of you wondered about *me*?"

Aaron looked torn. He shook his head. "I don't know, Lizzie."

"It's because you just see me as the kids' mom, Aaron. It's because I'm not really a person to you. I'm just a helpful side character."

He opened his mouth, but nothing came out.

I took a deep breath and let my anger dissipate. Aaron wasn't the only one to blame. He'd acted like an ass, yes. But I was the one who'd contorted myself to fit a box that was convenient for everyone else. I was the one who'd lost my spine, my confidence, my self. I was the one who accepted the roles that were thrust upon me.

Could I blame Aaron or the rest of my family when they accepted that at face value? When I never fought back?

"Thank you for apologizing," I told him. "I appreciate it. I just—I need some time."

Aaron nodded. "Sure. Yeah. You want me to take the kids one of these days? I probably owe you a year's worth of babysitting."

A knot untied itself in my heart, and I felt my lips curl into a smile. "A bit more than a year, I'd say."

Aaron huffed. "Probably, yeah."

"No more last-minute favors so you can go hang at the bar with your buddies."

He dropped his gaze. "No."

"No more making me cook everything for an event you're hosting."

His lips pinched. "We really did that, didn't we?"

"Yes. Over and over again. And if I ask you to save me some stuffing, you save me some damn stuffing. All right?"

My brother lifted his gaze to mine, and I saw real remorse in his gaze. He nodded. "All right," he agreed.

"And no more sending Mom my way to make me apologize to you."

Aaron's brows slammed together. "What?"

"She called me. Said I should just let it go and beg for your forgiveness, and did I need anything for the party on New Year's?"

My brother's gaze dropped. It looked like the same wave of exhaustion that had hit me was now landing on him. "I'll talk to her."

"Thank you. And in exchange, I promise to tell you when you're asking too much."

He sighed his relief. "That would be helpful."

"And if I want to start dating again, you don't get to say a single word about it except to tell me I look great and you'll be happy to watch my kids for the evening."

He was silent for a beat, eyes lifting to meet mine. "Do you? Want to start dating again?"

Not really, but I wasn't going to tell him that. This was the new me, stiff spine and all. So I just lifted my chin and gave him an arch look. "That's up to me to decide," I said, and Aaron's lips curled into a grin.

"Understood."

We got up and I walked him to the door. When my brother wrapped me in a tight hug, I hugged him back.

"Love ya," he said, squeezing my shoulders as he pulled away. "I know we don't say that to each other all that often, but I do."

My eyes prickled. "Love you too, Aaron."

"You sure you don't want to stop by for New Years? The countdown, at least?"

"I'm sure," I told him firmly.

He nodded. "If you change your mind, just show up. No need to give us advance warning. The door'll be unlocked."

When I thanked him, I did it through a tight throat. Locking the door behind my brother, I let out a long sigh, then climbed the stairs and started the bath again. A few minutes later, I slipped into the warm, lavender-scented water and felt every muscle in my body relax.

I could do this. I could rewrite my relationships with my family, no matter how difficult it would be. I could carve out some space and time for myself when I needed it. I could be more than Zach's and Hazel's mom. I *was* more than Zach's and Hazel's mom.

It made me feel strong and in control when the resolve snapped into place inside me, but there was a small corner of my heart where sadness still resided. That sadness curled around an old wound—the one that split open every time I realized I was on my own.

I'd love to have my own knight in shining armor. I'd love to feel protected and supported, to have someone at my back when things became difficult.

Rewriting my relationships with my family would be difficult. Taking time for myself would be difficult. Finding all the parts of myself that I'd let wither away would be a constant challenge. But I'd do it, and I'd do it on my own—because that's what needed to be done.

The old wound pulsed, and the sadness inside me contracted painfully. But what choice did I have?

It was either grow into a new version of myself, or accept the scraps of everyone's attention. There would be no knight riding to my rescue on a white horse. The past weeks had been a manic haze of giddiness, lust, and fantasy, and it was time for me to come back down to reality.

I would be my own knight in shining armor, because that's what I needed to be.

THIRTY-NINE

SEAN

MIKEY BLEW through the front door, red-faced with excitement as he carried an armload of Christmas presents. "Dad!" he screamed, beaming at me as I stood up from where I was sitting on the couch.

I hugged him, laughing. "Did you have a good time?"

"I went in the halfpipe!"

"Whoa." My brows shot up. "Wish I could have seen that."

"It was *awesome*."

I grinned and glanced up to see Melody carrying his bag through my front door. She placed it down next to our shoes and nodded at me.

"Say goodbye to your mom, buddy," I told him.

Mikey whirled around and hugged Melody. She smiled softly as she combed her fingers through his hair. When they parted, my ex-wife met my gaze. "Did you have a good holiday?"

"Not really," I answered.

Her smile was sad. "There's always next year."

We spoke for a few minutes, and then I watched her head back to the car and drive away. While I closed the door, I mulled over that sad smile. She hadn't looked surprised, nor did she seem annoyed or bitter.

It looked like pity. Like resignation.

"Todd said he could sign me up for ski lessons next year with someone who can teach me how to do tricks. Can I, Dad?"

I joined Mikey in the living room and slumped down on the couch. "That depends," I said. "Are Todd and your mom planning on renting another cabin at the ski resort?"

"I think so," he said, pulling a remote control car out of his box of gifts.

I smiled at my son. "You haven't mentioned those," I said, nodding to the wrapped boxes under the tree.

Mikey shot me a mischievous smile, then crawled toward the presents to read the name tags I'd stuck on them. "They have my name on them."

"Open 'em up."

I watched my son tear into his presents and couldn't help the smile from spreading over my mouth. He shouted in excitement at the new video game, holding it above his head as he howled. The robotics kit that was supposed to be for kids three years older than him earned me an awed, silent stare. I laughed, and a bit of the coldness that had spread through my chest over the past few days began to dissipate.

We spent the day together, and I almost felt like myself again. That evening, as I shut the lights off downstairs and made my way to my bedroom, I paused at Mikey's door and listened to his steady breathing. It was good to have him home, but I couldn't shake the feeling that I'd given up too much by letting Melody have every Christmas.

I owed it to Mikey—to myself—to fight to heal the old, crooked wounds inside me.

Going through the motions to get ready for bed, I stared at myself in the mirror as I brushed my teeth.

And I thought of Lizzie.

The warmth in my chest from a good day with my son was a poor substitute for the feeling of being next to her. She'd opened my eyes to new possibilities, and I'd responded by being too aggressive and then pushing her away when things got tough.

I'd done her wrong.

And I wanted to fix it—I just didn't know how.

NEW YEAR'S Eve had never been my favorite holiday. It had always felt like the first glimpse of the finish line at the end of a marathon. I'd never felt the hope and possibility of the turning of the calendar page; I'd only felt exhaustion and relief at having made it through another holiday season.

This year wasn't any different. I was wrung out and putting on a good face all through the day and into the evening, when I loaded Mikey up in the truck and drove to the Butlers' place. Mrs. B opened the door and greeted us with wide smiles and tight hugs, then ushered us inside where we were promptly presented with sparkly party hats and drinks. I got a glass of champagne, and Mikey got one of bubbly grape juice. He ran off to join the pack of kids roaming the halls, and I went with Mrs. B to the living room where the adults had gathered.

My eyes scanned the guests, even though I knew she wouldn't be here. I don't know how I knew, but from the moment I'd stepped inside the house, I was certain I wouldn't see Lizzie tonight. It was almost like I could sense her presence in the air; it was colder when she was away.

"Glad you decided to come," Aaron said, clapping me on the back. I lifted my glass and clinked it against his, and Aaron squeezed my shoulder. "You'll always be welcome here. You know that, right?"

My throat was tight, so all I did was nod.

"Let's enjoy tonight," he said.

"Yeah. Thanks, Aaron," I replied. And I meant it. I was grateful that he was still here, still welcoming, and still my friend. From the look in his eyes, I knew he understood what I meant.

Aaron dipped his chin in response, and then went to speak to one of his uncles. I took a seat beside Mr. Butler, who nodded at me.

When the silence stretched, I asked the question I already knew the answer to: "Is Lizzie coming?"

Mr. Butler gave me a long, steady look. Finally, when I was just about ready to squirm out of the interaction, he shook his head. "She's spending the evening with her kids," he told me.

I nodded.

"Her mother and I called her today to wish her a Happy New Year," Mr. Butler went on. "We had a long talk."

"Oh?" I asked, not sure where the older man was taking the conversation. The silence between us stretched.

"Felt like I finally got my little girl back," he finally replied. "The one who was stubborn and hard-headed while she smiled the whole time. Just waiting for the smile to come back."

My throat tightened. "She's one of a kind," I replied.

Mr. Butler gave me a long look and finally nodded. Then, as I breathed a sigh of relief, he shifted the conversation to my new job with Grant, and the topic of Lizzie—and her absence—was set aside.

It was an evening of good cheer and pleasant conversation, and it made me feel like dying. I hadn't realized how badly I'd hoped to see Lizzie here tonight. How much I wanted to pull her aside and find the right combination of words to fix the mess I'd made of our relationship.

How could a week without Lizzie feel like such an eternity?

The minutes bled into hours, and champagne and drinks flowed freely for everyone else while they tasted bitter on my tongue. The kids bounced off the walls, excited to be up hours past their bedtimes to ring in the New Year. I tried my best to ignore the itch under my skin, but as eleven o'clock became eleven thirty, my thoughts swirled and swirled around one person.

The woman I loved.

Lizzie.

It wasn't until the cold air slapped my face that I realized I was outside. And then I was in my truck, peeling off down the street toward the woman who'd made me remember that life wasn't just worth living; it was worth celebrating.

I couldn't keep hibernating during the holidays every year, and it wasn't just because I was letting Mikey down. I was living a smaller life than I should. I was keeping myself tied down to old hurts, just like Margaret had pointed out. I was letting my father's actions, my mother's passing, and Melody's betrayal get in the way of my happiness.

And right now, happiness had a face. It had deep brown eyes and a smile full of sunlight. Two cute dimples that only showed up when her grin was real. It had curves and soft lips, and it was the only woman I'd ever fallen head over heels in love with.

I'd tried to fight it. I'd tried to date women who were perfect and not-so-perfect for me on paper. I'd tried to pursue her while I ignored the gnawing ache in my chest.

But now I knew the truth.

The only way to get her back was to drop to my knees and beg her for forgiveness. I had to tell her what was in my heart. Prove to her that she'd changed my life—that she'd changed *me*.

I'd met my match, and I wasn't ready to let her go.

FORTY

LIZZIE

THE HOUSE WAS quiet except for the sound of the TV, where the big clock along the bottom of the screen announced how many minutes we had until this year rolled into the next. It was a matter of minutes.

The kids had dozed off around ten o'clock, snuggled under blankets on the couch. I sat beside them, sipping a mug of hot cocoa, wondering how my own new beginning would pan out.

I wasn't ready to turn my back on my family. Tonight—and the rest of the week since Christmas—had been a much-needed break from the chaos of family events, but it wasn't how I wanted to spend my years. I missed the laughter and too-loud conversation of our parties. I missed the little pastry-wrapped wieners my mom brought out around eleven o'clock every year. I missed the bad champagne and the ear-splitting noisemakers that would make all the kids laugh when the clock struck midnight.

But I didn't want to be the designated babysitter, cook, and maid. I wanted to be *me*—and it was my responsibility to make that happen.

So as the minutes quietly trickled by, I let myself absorb that reality. There would be work ahead of me. Work to rebuild and restructure my relationships. Work to carve time for myself, and to stop acting like a martyr because that's where I was most comfortable.

And I thought about Sean.

Things hadn't worked out between us, but I wouldn't begrudge him for it. I'd known from the beginning that it would never work between us. Still, he'd made me realize that I deserved more. He'd treated me like a queen—until he hadn't.

Maybe, with time, I would forget how his hands felt when they coasted over my skin, and I'd be able to smile and make pleasant conversation with him while he integrated into our family.

I'd find my own way to happiness.

It was a bittersweet kind of New Year's resolution for me. The past couple of months had felt like a rebirth: I'd realized I deserved more. But maybe I didn't deserve quite as much as I'd thought. I could have hobbies and a life and an identity beyond my children—but I couldn't have the impossibly attractive man and the nights of passion and sex.

From where I sat, in my comfortable home, next to my sleeping children, waiting for the next year to arrive, it felt like a fair trade.

And then I heard the engine.

Frowning when it cut off, I turned toward the sound of a car door slamming. By the time the knock on the door came, I was standing in the living room archway with my heart thumping hard.

I knew it was him before I opened the door. Don't ask me how; I just did.

He looked just as beautiful as he always had, with his short hair and turquoise eyes. The lips that had torn my body and soul to pieces parted, and he said my name on a breath: "Lizzie."

My heart rattled. "Sean."

He gulped. Tension stretched between us, and I didn't know how to break it. I didn't know if I should.

Finally, I cracked. "What are you doing here?"

Sean blinked at me and let out a huff of breath, as if he was asking himself that exact question. He closed his eyes for a beat, then lifted his gaze to mine. "I'm here to apologize."

"Oh," I managed through the vise clamped around my throat.

"I pursued you, and then I left you out in the cold when I should have defended you. I left you standing there on your own when the one thing you needed was to have someone at your back."

I breathed in then out again, motionless. He spoke the words plainly, like he was reading them from where they'd been carved into my heart.

"I hurt you," he said, his voice hoarse.

My eyes watered, and I nodded. "Yes."

"I'm sorry. You didn't deserve that. I'm so sorry, Lizzie."

I let out a noise that was half laugh, half sob. "I'm not sure what I deserve anymore."

He reached for me, then let his hand drop back to his side. When I lifted my eyes to meet his gaze, his face was drawn. He shook his head and whispered, "You deserve the world. You deserve everything good, Lizzie. More than I can give you."

I didn't think there was a part of my heart that hadn't been bruised until he said those words. It was the confirmation that he didn't want me, that we would never be together. I'd known it, of course. I'd told myself those very words over and over again throughout the past week. I *believed* them—or at least I thought I did.

But until Sean spoke them aloud, I hadn't realized that there was a part of me that hoped there'd be a way for us to come back to each other. That there was some sliver of connection worth fighting for.

But he couldn't give me what he thought I deserved. He didn't want to be that man for me.

Knowing this was my new reality, I straightened my spine as best I could and buried this final hurt deep in my heart. "Don't blame yourself too much, Sean," I told him, my voice surprisingly steady. "We got carried away. I know the holidays have always been tough for you. We all egged you on to find a New Year's kiss, and it's no surprise it blew up in everyone's faces. I got caught up in the attention you gave me, and—"

"Lizzie. Stop."

Blinking, I realized I'd been staring at his throat, so I dragged my gaze back up to his face. Sean's eyes were wild.

"What?" I said. "You don't have to—it's okay, Sean. I'm not going to stand in the way of your friendship with my brother. You taught me a lot about myself, and I'll always be thankful.

But you and me? We're good. We can just go back to the way things were. You said it yourself; it was a mistake to get involved—"

"It wasn't a mistake to get involved with you," he said, and this time he did reach for me. His hand wrapped around my wrist as he tugged me across the threshold into the cold winter night. "The only mistake I made was not standing by your side when I should have. Not shielding you from the shit your family flung at you." His free hand slid over my jaw, his thumb stroking my cheek.

Confusion swirled around me like stray snowflakes caught in a twist of wind. "What are you saying?"

His shoulders softened. "I'm saying I love you, Lizzie. I love you so much I can't stand the thought of spending another week without seeing you. You're my sun. Apart from my *son*, I mean," he added, which made me laugh. Sean let out a breath. "The two of you are all that's good in my life, Lizzie."

"But—" I blinked at him. My palm rested on his chest, and I could feel the pounding of his heart. "You said I deserve more than you can give me. You were letting me down gently."

Sean's strong arms tightened around me, and he let out a short breath. "You deserve more than I can give you, Lizzie, because you deserve the best of everything. Better than I am. But it doesn't mean I'm not going to try."

The snowstorm inside me settled in a dead wind. My hands slipped up to touch the stubble on his neck as my heart thumped so hard my vision went fuzzy. "You—"

"I love you. I love all the parts of you that make you a good mother, and all the parts of you that have been hidden away. I love your eye for detail and the way you see the world through your photos. I love your dimples and the darkness of your eyes. I love your body, and your laugh, and your light. I love you so much that I can't live without you, Lizzie. Please don't make me try."

His eyes were like chips of precious stones. Cold wrapped around us, but the heat of his body kept me warm. Behind me, the anchors on the television called out the countdown to ring in the New Year: "Five! Four!"

Sean tilted his head, listening.

"Three! Two!"

His lips curled into a dangerous smile. "You owe me a New Year's kiss, Lizzie," he murmured, tilting my chin with the tips of his fingers.

"One!"

Then Sean used his mouth to show me just how much he'd meant everything he said. It was a kiss made of fireworks and dynamite. It set me ablaze, destroying everything I thought I knew about him—and about me. It was a vow, and a promise, and everything I'd been trying to forget about the past week.

It was pure, blazing love, and I loved him right back.

When we pulled away, I was dizzy. His thumb stroked my cheek with gentle tenderness while the arm banded around my back tightened, as if he couldn't bear the thought of letting me go but wanted me to know I was safe and cherished in his arms.

And I knew. I *knew*. This was real.

"Sean?"

He leaned his forehead against mine. "Mm?"

"I love you," I whispered.

His exhaled breath was pure relief. "Thank God," he said, and I laughed as he kissed me again. I lost myself in his touch— or maybe I was finding parts of myself that I'd tried to pack away. All the pieces I'd thought were needy and dependent. All the weaknesses I'd tried to ignore while I kept my life together with spit and duct tape.

I didn't need to hide them anymore, because Sean was here to hold them for me.

"Mom?"

Jumping, I turned to see Hazel and Zach in the foyer, staring at us with wide eyes. Sean kept his arm around me, but I felt him straighten behind me.

"Hi," I replied.

"Were you just kissing Sean?" Zach asked, nose wrinkling.

"Um," I said. "Yeah."

"Are you in lo-ove?" Hazel asked, stretching the word into two syllables.

Sean's arm tightened around me, and I couldn't help the smile that stretched over my face. "Yes."

I waited, breath bated, for my kids' reaction. They blinked at the two of us, heads tilting in opposite directions as they processed the news.

Then Zach pointed toward the TV as his forehead wrinkled. "Did we miss the countdown?"

A LITTLE WHILE LATER, the four of us decided to head over to my parents' place to catch the tail end of the celebrations. It seemed right to me to start mending those relationships right away. The ground was steady beneath my feet, and besides, I wanted to see everyone. I wanted to blow a kazoo and have a glass of champagne with my mom. I didn't need to be stubborn or standoffish. My new beginning might as well start with the New Year.

The kids bounded down the pathway toward Sean's truck, chattering excitedly. They were wearing their pajamas, winter boots, and jackets, and didn't seem bothered about missing the countdown—although the novelty and naughtiness of being out and about way past their bedtimes probably buttered them up a bit.

I locked the front door and smiled at Sean. "Ready?"

He nodded but didn't move. Then he reached into his jacket's breast pocket and pulled out an envelope. "I never gave you this."

My brows furrowed as I watched him extend the envelope toward me. "What is it?"

"Your Christmas present."

I froze. "Oh. No, it's okay—"

"Take it, Lizzie. I got it for you before I messed everything up."

Biting my lower lip, I took the envelope and opened it. Inside was a thick, luxurious-feeling business card with the words Art's Cove embossed in gold lettering. On the back of the card, someone had scratched out a phone number.

Another peek inside the envelope told me that was it. I lifted the card. "What is this?"

"You know Georgia Neves who owns the art gallery on Cove Boulevard?"

I glanced down at the gold lettering. "I know of her."

"I talked to her. Showed her some of your photos."

My gaze snapped up to his. "What?"

A hint of guilt entered his expression. "Just the ones you sent me."

"You said those were for your phone background!"

His hands flew up, palms out in a placating gesture. "You're *good*, Lizzie. And Georgia agrees. She said she'd be happy to cover the costs of printing and framing if you wanted to show a few pieces in the gallery."

I turned into a fish for a few moments, my mouth opening and closing while nothing came out. Then I glanced at the card again. "What?"

Sean's low laugh wrapped around me like a warm hug. "I wanted to get one of them printed and framed to give to you with her card, but..."

"Things kind of fell apart."

He hummed. "Will you call her?"

I ran my finger along the thick edge of the card as the world went unsteady beneath me again. "I..."

"Say yes," he whispered.

The old me would never do it. It was scary and unfamiliar. It was out of my comfort zone. But I glanced up at his truck, where the kids were clipping themselves into the back seat, then up at Sean's expectant face.

We were minutes into the New Year, and I felt the significance of the moment in every nerve in my body. It was a new beginning with Sean, with my family, with myself. A doorway leading into the unknown.

Didn't I owe it to myself to take a step through it?

"I'll call her," I promised.

Sean's smile warmed me down to my toes. He threaded his fingers through mine and tugged me to his truck. We drove to my parents' house and stepped through the door into a house full of light, laughter, cheers, and the usual, familiar chaos.

My mother was the first to spot us. She let out a cry, then hugged me so tightly my spine cracked. Pulling away with tears in her eyes, all she said was, "You're here."

"I'm here."

"You're banned from the kitchen," she told me. "If you pick up a dirty dish at any point tonight, you have to leave immediately."

Laughing, I nodded. "Deal."

Her hand coasted over my cheek in a soft, motherly caress. When she did the same to Sean, I knew we were at the start of something wonderful.

EPILOGUE

LIZZIE

Ten and a half months later...

THE BEST TWENTY dollars I'd ever spent was the packing tape dispenser I bought on a whim when I went to pick up a bunch of Sharpies from the local office supply store. As I taped up the final box in my kitchen with one satisfying swipe across the top of it, I straightened up and let out a happy huff. Zach used his trusty Sharpie to write the word KITCHEN on top of the box, then capped the marker and grinned at me.

"Last one," he said.

"Last one," I confirmed.

The stomp of heavy footsteps made us both turn toward the hallway, where Sean appeared in a tan Carhartt jacket, black beanie, and faded jeans. He arched his brows. "Ready?"

"Ready!" Zach said.

"Let's head on over with the first load, then," Sean said, ruffling my son's hair.

Zach took off at a dead sprint as Sean and I watched him go. Then Sean closed the distance between us and slid his hands over my hips.

"How are you feeling?" he asked.

"Nervous. Excited."

"Sad to be leaving this place?"

I glanced around the room at the old, orange-tinged cabinets and off-white tiles, at the stone hearth and old carpet. "A little," I admitted, "but mostly it feels good."

As his arms went around me, Sean bent down to press a kiss to my forehead. "I love you, Lizzie."

He hadn't stopped telling me exactly that in the past ten-plus months, and every time, my chest buzzed with happiness. "I love you too," I replied as I tilted my face up to accept his kiss.

"Gross!" Zach called out from the mouth of the hallway, now dressed in his jacket and shoes. "Mom, ew!"

I pulled away from Sean and stuck my tongue out at my son, who stuck his tongue out right back. Then the three of us cackled, and Sean threaded his fingers through mine to tug me toward the front door.

He'd already loaded a few boxes into the bed of his truck, and the plan was for me to join Hazel, Mikey, and my mother at our new home to clean and unpack while Sean and my brothers did the bulk of the moving. I closed the door behind me and walked to the truck, then turned and took another glance at the house where I'd lived for the better part of two decades.

Sean's arm went around my shoulders, and I leaned my head against his chest.

"Isaac and I bought this house together not long after we got married," I told him. "It's the only home the kids have ever known."

"Full of memories," Sean replied.

I nodded, then looked into his blue-green eyes and smiled tentatively. "But it's too small to fit all of us."

The soft, relieved sigh that left his lips told me that I'd just said exactly what he needed to hear. That I was ready to move on and excited to take this next step together. I got up on my tiptoes and pressed another kiss to his lips, then pulled away, took one more long look at my house, and then got in the passenger seat of the truck.

We were halfway to the new place when Zach asked, "Mom, can me and Mikey share a room?"

I glanced over my shoulder. "I thought you'd already picked out your rooms."

"We want to get bunk beds in one room and then use the other one for computers and robots."

"I see," I said, glancing at Sean.

Sean had a half-smile on his lips when he met my gaze. "Sounds pretty cool to me."

"It's going to be *awesome*," Zach said. "So, can we, Mom?"

"I don't see why not," I said, glancing into the back seat of the cab where Zach flashed me a euphoric smile. Grinning back at him, I settled into my seat and watched the houses go by. We were moving to a neighborhood a little farther from the town center in exchange for more space. It was about the same distance to school, though a bit farther from my work and a few minutes' extra drive to my parents' and brothers' places.

But in the past year, I'd only been called for emergency babysitting one single time—and it had been a true emergency, when Levi had fallen ill, Aaron had been away for work, and my parents were unavailable. I'd been happy to step in and watch Jacob while Emily took Levi to the hospital. And I'd gotten a sincere thank you afterward, which had meant more than I could put into words.

We still had lots of family events for holidays, birthdays, anniversaries, and random summer barbecues, and I'd had to set a few boundaries in terms of what I was bringing and how many times I was hosting. There'd been some grumbling, but Sean had backed me up every time and I'd been able to actually spend time with my family and friends instead of being relegated to kitchen duty for hours on end.

Laurel and I had grown closer, which turned out to be a breath of fresh air in my life. We had girls' nights about once a month, and she dragged me out shopping to replace all the clothing I'd gotten rid of in my haste to remake myself into a new woman. She introduced me to Audrey, who helped me design an amazing closet system that I hadn't been able to afford after my excessive shopping spree with Laurel, even with the friends and family discount Audrey offered—but I'd saved up a special pot of money to get the closet of my dreams in my new home.

The kids were still made of boundless energy, and I still found myself spinning a million plates while I managed work, school, relationships, chores, and all the other commitments that came with being a busy mom. The difference was, I wasn't alone. Multiple times a week, I'd come home to dinner already prepped and cooking on the stove. We hadn't officially moved in together yet, but Sean still picked up my slack and acted like an amazing role model to our kids. I couldn't wait to spend every night with him.

Life was still made of chaos. There were ups and downs.

But I had *balance.* I spun plates from a stable base. And if I dropped one, there were a dozen people there to help me sweep up the shards so no one got hurt.

As we pulled up to our new home, I let out a deep, satisfied sigh. Then the front door flew open, and Hazel ran out.

"Mom!" she screamed before Sean had even cut the engine. She hopped from one foot to the other. "Mom!"

I unclipped my belt and opened the door. "What's up?"

"Can I get bunk beds too? But I don't want the bottom bed, just the top one. With a ladder. And can I paint my room purple?" She hopped her way over to me and gave me a face-splitting smile. "Please?"

I laughed and pressed a kiss to the top of her head. "Of course."

"Yes!" She fist pumped, then ran over to Zach to tell him the good news.

Over the hood of his truck, Sean gave me a wry grin. We all headed for the front door, kids in front, Sean at my side. I could hear Mikey's voice inside and, oddly, what sounded like shushing. Sean motioned for me to head inside ahead of him, so I stepped across the threshold—and froze.

My parents and brothers were in the living room, along with

Dorothy, Margaret, Laurel, and a few other friends and family. They stood under a banner that read, "CONGRATULA-TIONS," and all shouted, "Surprise!"

"What's going on?" I asked, stunned.

My mother had tears in her eyes as she clasped her hands at her breast. She nodded, then her gaze shifted behind me.

I turned to see Sean on bended knee, holding a black velvet box in his hand. His eyes were bright, bright turquoise and full of love.

"Lizzie," he rasped, and tears flooded my eyes.

I wiped them away and took a step toward him. "What's going on?"

"Lizzie," he repeated, his own eyes wet with unshed tears. "You're the love of my life. You've shown me what it means to be happy. You've made me feel whole. Please, I'm begging you, baby, please make me the luckiest man in the world and tell me you'll be my wife."

"Oh, Sean," I said—and he flipped open the top of the box. A glittering diamond ring—solitaire, with a buttery gold band—twinkled back at me. I clasped my hands at my chest. "Sean—yes. Yes, I'll marry you."

His smile was unlike anything I'd seen before. So bright and happy, I could hardly believe that I'd put it on his face by agreeing to marry him. With trembling fingers, he took the ring out of its velvet slot and slid it onto my outstretched finger. It fit perfectly.

I stared at the thousand colors reflecting off the stone, then lifted my chin to meet Sean's gaze as he got to his feet before me. Then his arms were around my waist, and he was kissing me right there in front of all our friends and family.

This time, it didn't end up with a punching match. When I pulled away, my cheeks were wet with tears. I turned around in time to be swarmed by all the people I loved, laughing and crying as I accepted their congratulations.

I found Sean in the hubbub and nuzzled against his chest. I pointed to the wall in the living room. "The banner was a little presumptuous, don't you think? What if I said no?"

His smile was soft and sure. "We're made for each other, Lizzie. How could you say no?"

I couldn't even pretend to disagree. When Hazel bounded over to us and asked to see the ring, my heart overflowed with happiness. She gave Sean a tight hug around the waist and asked, "When are you getting married? Can I be a flower girl?"

"Of course, honey," I told her.

"I was thinking Christmas," Sean replied, answering her first question.

Still leaning against his chest, I froze, then pulled away and gaped at him. "Christmas? This year? You want to get married in six weeks?"

"I want to get married in six minutes, Lizzie. Six weeks is my absolute maximum."

"We can't pull off a whole entire wedding in six weeks!"

"No?"

I bit my lip, then glanced down at Hazel. Zach and Mikey had crept closer, watching me with hesitant smiles on their faces. "What do you think?"

"I like Christmas," Hazel declared.

"Me too," Mikey agreed.

"Me three," Zach said.

Sean tightened his hold on me. "Me four," he told me quietly, and when I turned to look in his eyes, I knew it was the truth. And I could see his desire to rewrite all the bad memories that he'd associated with the holiday with new ones.

What better place to start than a wedding?

"I guess we're getting married on Christmas Day, then," I said, and then laughed when Sean dipped me and pressed another kiss to my lips as if he needed to seal my promise with his lips.

My year of new beginnings wasn't quite over yet...and I couldn't wait to see what would come next.

———

BONUS EPILOGUE

LIZZIE

SIX WEEKS WAS NOT a long time to plan a wedding, but as it turned out, it was long enough. By the time Christmas Day rolled around, I was ready to be married already.

Sean had been right. Six minutes would've been the ideal length of time to wait. Six weeks had nearly been torture.

The hardest part was finding a dress. In the end, I found a V-neck dress that nipped at the waist and fell in a graceful A-line to my feet. My mother brought out the pearl-studded shawl she'd worn at her wedding and gave it to me with tears in her eyes. It suited the simple lines of my gown to perfection, and it matched the hair accessories I planned to wear.

We had the wedding at the Heart's Cove Hotel, with space generously donated by Dorothy and Margaret. They threw themselves into wedding planning with the kind of fervor that I'd hardly seen before. When I finally got to see the space, draped with garlands of evergreen, swags of fabric, and tons of twinkling gold and silver accessories, it felt like I'd stepped into a winter wonderland.

So, in my perfect dress, with my mother's stole around my shoulders and my father extending his arm toward me, I stepped onto the petal-strewn aisle and lifted my gaze to where my soon-to-be husband stood.

I barely registered the music, or the turning heads, or the decorations. All I saw was Sean.

He stood at the other end of the aisle in a well-tailored tux. His bowtie was black velvet. When he saw me, his lips parted, and I'd never felt more beautiful in all of my life.

My father patted the hand I'd hooked into his elbow. We floated down the aisle, and I finally tore my gaze away from Sean to smile at my children, who were standing on either side of him with the bridesmaids and groomsmen. When we got to the altar, my father took my hands.

"Love you, Lizzie," he told me quietly before pressing a kiss to my cheek. "My girl."

"I love you too, Dad."

His eyes were wet as he turned and placed my hand in Sean's. "Take good care of her."

Sean's gaze was steady and solemn as he held mine. "Always," he vowed.

The ceremony was short, but by the end of it, there wasn't a dry eye in the place. When Sean was finally instructed to kiss me, the applause was deafening. We kissed as a married couple for the first time, and when Sean pulled away from me, his eyes were full of mirth.

"What?" I asked, slightly breathless.

Sean flicked his gaze upward, and I followed it. A bundle of mistletoe hung above us, perfectly positioned between our heads. Laughing, I pulled him in for another kiss.

We were rewriting all kinds of memories with this wedding —why not that one too?

Then, finally, we turned to face all our loved ones. Sean brought my hand to his lips, then guided me down the aisle and around the corner to the room that had been prepared for our reception. A gigantic Christmas tree shone in the corner, with more bundles of evergreen, and beautiful winter-themed center- pieces on every table.

We ate, drank, and danced into the night.

When the kids had been carted off by grandparents and the party became rowdier, Sean leaned over and brushed his lips against my neck. "I want to take you home," he said.

I turned to meet his gaze, unable to keep the smile from my lips. "I'd like that," I said.

It took another hour to say our goodbyes and make our exit. A taxi took us to our new home, which was lit up with all the decorations that Sean, the kids, and I had put up together. With my heart light, I followed my husband into the house and was surprised when he towed me to the living room and pulled out a small box from behind a book on the bookshelf.

We'd already done presents this morning, so I tilted my head. "What's this?"

"Open it," was the only answer he gave, and then he wrapped his arms around my stomach and pulled my back to his front.

I tugged on the velvet ribbon, then carefully ripped open

the green and gold paper. Inside, I found a beautiful, delicate Christmas ornament. It was shaped like a three-tiered cake, with a tiny cake topper on the smallest tier. The icing was piped with the most delicate silver work, and the bottom of the ornament had the date and year etched into the material.

"Oh, Sean," I whispered, opening the box so I could pull the ornament out and admire it properly.

"I figured it's about time I started collecting them with you," he said.

My throat was tight as I held the ornament, admiring all the tiny details. It was such a small, simple gift, but it meant more than anything he could have given me. I spun in his arms and lifted my gaze to his. "It's perfect."

His smile was full of tenderness. "Hang it on the tree. Make it official."

I hooked the silver ribbon over my finger and turned to admire our tree. It was a real one this year—Sean had insisted. Wrangling kids and a tree was a lot easier with Sean around, and the scent of the evergreen needles filled the room.

I found the perfect gap in the decorations for our new ornament and hooked it onto the end of the branch before watching it dangle and sway against the dark-green needles.

"I feel like my heart is about to explode," I said. "I'm so happy."

Sean's hands slid over my shoulders, and he pressed a kiss to the side of my neck. "You think your heart can handle a little more excitement?"

Smile teasing the corner of my lips, I turned my head to catch his gaze. "I'm willing to find out."

We didn't tear each other's clothes off. We didn't rip and shred and bite. Sean just let out a soft breath, then let his thumbs coast up the back of my neck and back down again, tracing the edge of my dress until he found the row of tiny buttons running down my spine.

One by one, the buttons popped open at his touch. I held my dress to my chest as he loosened it, focusing on the feel of his knuckles against my skin and the sound of his breath behind me. When the final button gave way, I teased the straps off my shoulders and stepped out of the dress before laying it over the edge of the sofa.

"Oh, Lizzie," Sean said, voice rough.

I glanced over my shoulder to confirm what I already knew—his eyes were glued to the *very* expensive lingerie I'd bought for this exact moment. The top was shapewear that was boned and clipped to the garter holding up my thigh-high stockings.

Sean traced the little strap running up the back of my thighs with the tips of his fingers, letting out a rough groan as he did. "You've been wearing this all day?"

I smiled at the strangled quality of his voice, then turned to face him so I could drape my hands over his shoulders. "You never fail to make me feel like the most beautiful woman in the world. You know that?"

"Not hard to do, when you look like this, Lizzie," he admitted. His hands roamed over my body, tracing the edge of my underwear, squeezing my curves. Our lips found each other, and then all bets were off.

We didn't make it to the bedroom.

It was almost like the first time, all frantic lust and clawing need. Almost—but not quite.

Because when Sean slipped my white satin panties to the side and brought his mouth to my sex, I felt the depth of his love for me in every touch of his tongue. When he tugged me to the edge of the sofa and aligned himself at my opening, a smile bloomed over my lips at his desperation.

And when he drove himself inside me, I felt the same spinning, weightless sensation I'd felt that day in my foyer—but I also felt the endless, enduring love that existed between us. He brought me to orgasm with my legs spread and my ass hanging off the edge of the sofa, and then I pushed him to the floor and had my way with him under the twinkling lights of our tree.

When he told me I was beautiful and perfect and his, I knew he was speaking the truth. And as I rode him to orgasm and panted out how much I loved him, the look in his eyes told me he felt the same.

We took our pleasure and then collapsed on the floor, drowsy and sated. Sean ran his fingers over my arm and kissed my sweat-damp brow, then let out a long, satisfied sigh.

"Best day ever," he said.

I smiled. "Yeah," I agreed, then looked up at him. "Merry Christmas, Sean."

His arms came around me, and then I was turned onto my back while he draped himself over me. "Merry Christmas, Lizzie."

Eventually, we made it up to the bedroom. And a long while after that, we fell asleep in each other's arms. Exactly where we were supposed to be.

WANT MORE?

Keep reading for a preview of Fiona and Grant's story, *Dirty Little Midlife Crisis*!

ONE

FIONA

A TIRED GROAN shudders out of my best friend's rusty old Toyota. That...doesn't sound good.

On the bright side, Simone's hooptie has successfully gotten us three hundred miles north of Los Angeles and into our destination vacation town. Unfortunately, it doesn't look like it's going to make it much farther.

I grip the worn plastic door handle as if it'll help keep the car together. If Simone's worried about her car breaking down, she doesn't show it. With wild red hair tied back in a messy bun on top of her head and thick, black-rimmed glasses framing her pale blue eyes, Simone looks far younger than her forty-four years—a fact that has often needled at my own insecurities. Time hasn't been so kind to me.

Another screechy noise escapes the hood of the car as we turn onto the main drag of Heart's Cove, and I start hunting the signs on the street for a mechanic. Even if Simone isn't worried about this hunk of junk, I need a way to get out of here at the end of our two-week stay.

We make it about fifty more feet before the engine sputters, the car rattles, and the whole things dies right there on the street. Simone expertly navigates the coasting car to the curb as smoke curls out of the hood in thick black puffs. Parked in a semi-appropriate spot and acting like nothing at all is the matter, she pulls the handbrake and tucks a strand of flame-red hair behind her ear.

I throw my best friend a glance. "We should have taken my car."

"We couldn't take your car. It reminds you of Voldemort."

"Voldemort?"

"He Who Shall Not Be Named. That shiny white Mercedes is the only thing that asshole left you in the divorce and looking at it reminds you of his cheating ass. I see it in your eyes every time you turn the key in the ignition. There was *no way* we were taking your car. Big Bertha did just fine." She taps the dashboard fondly, as if there isn't a plume of dark smoke coming from Bertha's hood. My best friend gives me a mean-ingful stare. "This vacation is about us, about pampering, about being the women we were always meant to be. Besides, we made it, didn't we?"

"Barely," I grumble, fighting the grin trying to curl my lips.

"I'll find a mechanic this afternoon. We won't need the car for the next two weeks, anyway—everything in Heart's Cove is within walking distance from the Heart's Cove Hotel. It's in the brochure."

Through the windshield, past the smoke, I spy a faded

green-and-white awning above the hotel door. A screen door hangs slightly crooked and lace curtains frame the interior of every window. Paint is peeling on the old siding, but neatly trimmed grass lines the front of the hotel and baskets bursting with colorful flowers hang from every post. A low hedge lines the sidewalk leading to a small parking lot, the other side of which is a well-maintained path to the front door.

This accommodation is quaint, though a bit worse for wear. It isn't exactly what I'd put as my first pick.

Or maybe it's not what John, my ex-husband, would have liked. Do I *actually* mind this place? It's kind of cute, in a lost-kitten-with-patchy-fur-and-three-legs kind of way. If Simone's to be believed, it's got great reviews and a killer continental breakfast.

John would've taken one look at this place and complained nonstop until we found someplace else, maybe even canned the whole vacation—but he's not here. He's in his swanky office in L.A. with whatever hot, young assistant he's decided to stick his junk into. Or maybe a paralegal. Or a junior partner. Or an intern. Or all of the above.

Deep breaths.

Simone must see my pursed lips, because she punches me in the arm. "Quit sucking lemons, Fi. Come on. We have art to create."

"How many times do I have to tell you I'm not an artist? Why did you have to choose an art retreat for our big self-actualization getaway? I'm a precision gal. Organizing. Planning. Why can't we have a vacation job hunting or something? At least it would be useful."

Simone lets out a snort and exits the car, casting a quick glance at the smoke still escaping her hood. She kicks a tire for good measure, then slings her purse over her shoulder and waves me forward. "Come on! The sign on the door says to check in inside."

Pushing thoughts of my ex aside, I follow Simone out of the car. The air tastes fresh here, if you can ignore the smell of Bertha's dying engine. Full of floral scents and a hint of salt from the sea, the smell unwinds a knot of tension between my shoulders. Simone's right. I need a vacation—and why not do something that I never would have done before? Why not try something new?

It's not like there's anything for me back in Los Angeles. Now that the fancy penthouse was transferred to John's name last week and my half of its worth has finally hit my bank account, I'm officially homeless. The divorce is settled, so I'm officially single, too. My dream of moving to the hills and getting my picket fence and perfect little family are gone with the penthouse, but I'm trying not to think about it too hard. Starting over at forty-five isn't something I'd planned on.

Simone decided I needed some time to figure myself out, so I'm here. About to do two weeks of art, yoga, and meditation classes in the hope of *finding myself*, even though I'm terrified of what I might discover. I find myself in the mirror every morning, and I'm not sure I like what I see. I'm on the other side of forty-five, with new wrinkles appearing every day. Things are sagging where they never used to, and soft where they were once taut.

Compared to John's younger, prettier, more docile playthings, I feel positively dumpy. I'm not sure a week of painting and *ohm*-ing will help any of that.

Simone's already halfway to the door by the time I take a step. She turns around and plants her fists on her hips, arching her brows at me. "Um, earth to Fiona! Get a wriggle on, girl. Our first class starts in half an hour."

I pause, tilting my head. "I thought you said tomorrow was day one."

"I lied. Deal with it." She pushes a stray piece of red hair off her forehead, looking zero percent remorseful. Her eyes sweep down the street then back to me, shoulders dropping slightly. Speaking more gently, she says, "I knew you'd never get in the car if you knew you had to try drawing something today. Your comfort zone is doing its best to keep you hostage, so you know, desperate times and all that."

"Who are you calling desperate?" I pop a brow.

Simone grins, but before she can open her mouth to answer, a rumble sounds from the asphalt separating us. My best friend's eyes widen as she looks at the ground where a crack is splitting the pavement apart. I take a step back, a hand on my chest.

Then the parking lot of the Heart's Cove Hotel explodes.

No, really. It explodes.

Asphalt everywhere. A geyser of water shooting fifty feet into the air, cascading down on top of us. I scream, putting my purse over my head while I crouch down. Rocks and bits of asphalt rain down around me, biting my skin as they land. I put a hand on the back of my neck, pull it back, and see blood.

What the...?

Water's still raining down on me as shouts erupt. Doors open, and a siren sounds in the distance. I'm still crouched on the sidewalk, staring at the blood on my fingers.

What in the name of self-actualization is wrong with this town? Where the heck did Simone bring me? Maybe I should hightail it out of here, but how would I even do that? Our car is out of commission.

I'm stuck, stuck, stuck. Just like I was stuck in my marriage. Stuck in a penthouse I didn't like. Stuck in a city I never wanted to be in. Stuck around sycophants and snobby housewives preening and gossiping while I felt like I was dying a slow and painful death as life passed me by.

Water seeps into my dress, soaking my back. I curl myself into a ball, worried another stray chunk of asphalt is coming for my skull. My thoughts rush around me, and my comfort zone constricts inside my head.

I should have stayed at home. What if John needs me for something? I should be apartment hunting and trying to find a job. A vacation is the last thing I need. Why would I even deserve a vacation? I need to get my butt in gear and start figuring out how to start my life over.

Emotion chokes my throat, and I feel silly. I'm not the kind of person who falls apart. I'm the rock. I'm the one who keeps the family together.

That didn't go so well, did it?

Tears threaten to spill onto my cheeks and I fight my rioting emotions to hold myself together. It's just a burst water main. I have a shallow cut on the back of my neck, but I'm fine. Just wet and weirdly emotional.

Then, a shadow. The water stops, and I hear the pitter-patter of a geyser hitting an open umbrella. The lack of water raining down on me allows me to take a full breath. I lift my head to see the owner of the umbrella currently helping me maintain a shaky hold on my own sanity.

Holy *ohm*.

Heart's Cove might not be so bad, judging by this vision in a wet t-shirt.

Tall, dark, and handsome doesn't even cover it. This guy looks like he belongs in every forty-something woman's wet dream, not in a sleepy town called Heart's Cove. He's broad, and by the way his wet shirt clings to his chest, I can tell he's packing serious muscle. My eyes sweep over the curves of his pecs and shoulders, down his arms and over his trim waist. Snapping my eyes back up before they reach dangerous territory, I see a hint of a smile on his full lips.

"Um, hi," I stammer, standing up as I brush my hands down my navy wrap dress. The back of it is soaked. My dress clings to me as much as his shirt hugs him, and I catch my mystery man's eyes heating as they take me in. A strange kind of warmth knots in the pit of my stomach as I tuck a strand of black-brown hair behind my ear. I gulp, still staring at my savior.

He has dark hair and rich, tan skin with two patches of grey hair above his temples. The rest of his hair is piled to one side in short, loose curls, one of which slides down across his forehead.

I watch in fascination as he lifts a broad hand to sweep the stray piece of hair back, his grey-blue eyes still studying me. Is he even real? I'm not sure people this good-looking exist in real life. Maybe I finally snapped after the last horrendous fifteen months. The geyser was the last straw. Something in Bertha's engine fumes has turned my brain to mush. I've finally lost my marbles.

"I'm Grant." His rich, deep voice sends a tremor shivering down my spine. It sounds real enough.

I barely manage to croak out a response. "Fiona."

His lips curl into a smile, as if the sound of my name pleases him. A curl of heat beads in the pit of my stomach and I place a hand over the offending spot. I feel... I'm not...

I haven't felt this in a *long* time.

Grant lifts a hand toward me, and I suck a breath through my teeth as he reaches around the back of my neck. As I close my eyes, I imagine him pulling me close, crushing me against that glorious chest of his, and taking my lips in his.

A man like him would take control. I can sense it in the electricity zinging between us. He'd pin me to a wall and show me what I've been missing for the past twenty years. He'd light up every nerve ending in my body and be as rough, as commanding, as demanding as he'd need to be.

And I would melt like freaking butter on his tongue. God, his tongue—I wish I could melt on it. Preferably when his hands grip me tight and I feel the raw power coiling in his huge body. *Wet and weirdly emotional*, huh. Yup, still accurate.

But Grant's touch is feather-light when the pads of his fingers brush across the back of my neck. They're calloused, rough. Not at all like John's doughy, soft hands were when he palmed my skin back in the days when we actually touched each other.

Grant's skin may be rough, but his touch is soft. A silent

gasp escapes my lips before I can stop myself, heat flooding between my legs, spreading through my core, and all the way up to the tips of my ears.

This is... Oh, no. Is this menopause? Did I just have my first hot flash under a geyser in the middle of a parking lot?

But when I open my eyes, Grant's expression is soft. "You're bleeding," he says, almost to himself. Before I can stop him, he hands me the umbrella, then grabs the edge of his shirt and rips off a strip.

The man *rips his freaking shirt apart* and uses it to dab at my admittedly very minor wound.

I might faint.

This is a fever dream. This isn't real life. It can't be.

I stare at the strip of skin now exposed by the rip, just above the waistband of Grant's pants. His stomach is hard, and the unholy desire to run my tongue over that bit of flesh bubbles through me without warning.

"Fiona!" Simone's voice cuts through the lust fogging my mind. My best friend runs over, shielding her face with her hands as she laughs. "Can you believe it? I think it's a sign."

"Of what? Poor municipal plumbing?"

Grant lets out a chuckle at my words, and the desire to make him laugh again overwhelms me. I steal a glance at him as Simone walks up to me, her eyes widening as she takes in the specimen standing next to me.

"Well, hello there, handsome. I'm Simone." She wiggles her eyebrows at me, then drops into a curtsy in front of Grant.

A freaking curtsy, as if the man is the King of England.

My best friend is a maniac.

"Grant," he replies with a smile, not at all bothered by the fact that Simone is insane. "I'd better go check on the twins. They've been having trouble with the hotel maintenance lately, and I'm sure they could use a hand." I make to give him the umbrella, but he shakes his head. "Keep it. I don't mind getting wet." A flash crosses his eyes as his gaze drops to my lips then away, so quickly I wonder if I imagined it.

Call me the Wicked Witch of the West, because I'm about to melt right where I stand.

Simone squeals as she hooks her arm through mine, and we watch Grant stride around the geyser, his white shirt soaking through and clinging to every muscle in his back. "He is *delicious*. It's definitely a sign."

"A sign of what?"

"That this vacation is *exactly* what you needed."

"He's just a friendly local."

"I *hope* he's friendly," Simone answers, the word sounding *very* different when she says it.

I shake my head, laughing, and nod to the hotel. "Should we go find out what's going on?"

"Yeah, but first let me grab some tissues. I don't want to drool all over the hotel floor if I'm going to be in the same room as that *friendly local*."

Rolling my eyes, I fight the smile off my face and jerk my head toward the green-and-white awning, setting off in the same direction as Grant went as if there's a tether pulling me toward him.

Maybe Simone's right. Maybe this vacation was a good idea, after all...

Fiona is only in town for a vacation, until a flooded hotel room sends her to look for alternative housing arrangements...with the town's hunky handyman.

Get DIRTY LITTLE MIDLIFE CRISIS!
https://geni.us/KtwYr

ABOUT THE AUTHOR

Lilian Monroe adores writing swoonworthy heroes and the women who bring them to their knees. She loves making people laugh and is eternally grateful to have found people who share her sense of humor.

When she's not writing, she's reading (or rereading) a book, walking, lifting weights, or attempting to play the guitar with very limited success.

She grew up in Canada but now lives in Australia with her Irish husband. He frequently asks to be used as a cover model for her books, and she's not quite sure whether or not he's joking.

ALSO BY LILIAN MONROE

For all books, visit:

www.lilianmonroe.com

The Four Groomsmen of the Wedpocalypse

Conquest

Craving

Combat

Calamity

Manhattan Billionaires

Big Bossy Mistake

Big Bossy Trouble

Big Bossy Problem

Big Bossy Surprise

Forbidden Boss

Later in Life Romance

Dirty Little Midlife Crisis

Dirty Little Midlife Mess

Dirty Little Midlife Mistake

Dirty Little Midlife Disaster

Dirty Little Midlife Debacle

Dirty Little Midlife Secret

Dirty Little Midlife Dilemma

Dirty Little Midlife Drama

Dirty Little Midlife (fake) Date

Filthy Little Midlife Fling

Merry Little Midlife Matchmaker

Brother's Best Friend Romance

Shouldn't Want You

Can't Have You

Don't Need You

Won't Miss You

Protector Romance

His Vow

His Oath

His Word

Enemies to Lovers/Workplace Romance

Hate at First Sight

Loathe at First Sight

Despise at First Sight

Secret Baby/Accidental Pregnancy Romance

Knocked Up by the CEO

Knocked Up by the Single Dad

Knocked Up...Again!

Knocked Up by the Billionaire's Son

Yours for Christmas

Bad Prince

Heartless Prince

Cruel Prince

Broken Prince

Wicked Prince

Wrong Prince

Lone Prince

Ice Queen

Rogue Prince

Fake Engagement Romance

Engaged to Mr. Right

Engaged to Mr. Wrong

Engaged to Mr. Perfect

Mountain Man Romance

Lie to Me

Swear to Me

Run to Me

Doctor's Orders

Doctor O

Doctor D ,

Doctor L